CYN & THE PEANUT BUTTER CUP

CYN & THE PEANUT BUTTER CUP

PRU WARREN

QUI
LEGIT
REGIT
PRESS
She who reads, rules

Cover design by the Killion Group

Published by Qui Legit Regit Press
Alexandria, VA

ISBN 978-1-7359919-1-7

Discover other titles by Pru Warren at pruwarren.com

110422wch

To Barbara, who found me Gwynn,
and to Gwynn, who found me Mindy,
and to Mindy, who taught me everything

And to the Bunnyhead—my sister Lexie.
Best cheerleader ever!

PROLOGUE: MADDY

The woman in front of me is so adorably cute that I want to pick her up and put her in my pocket.

She's just a bitty mite of a thing—no taller than me—like a dark-haired pixie. She could wear a bluebell hat and sip dew from rose petals.

And she has the light of challenge in her eye. Like me.

"Now, Maddy," she says. How does she know my name? I'm delighted. "You're not getting in this shopping cart."

"Oh, yes, I am!" I crow. "I want a ride, and I'm going to have one!" I eye my prize: the shiny cart in front of the dairy case.

"No, you're not." She's a tiny linebacker braced between me and my goal. "Do you remember what happened the last time? We needed the assistant manager to help me get you out. We had to tip the entire cart over and pour you out. And you laughed at him the entire time."

"I never did!" Just the idea is making me giggle. "I can get out of that cart as easily as I get in. Watch me."

She raises a graceful, mink-colored eyebrow at me. "I don't think so. You're ninety-three years old, Maddy."

"Oh, tosh! Ninety-three!" I can't help but go off in peals of laughter at the thought. Me—an old lady!

"Do you remember me?" she asks.

"No. Should I? You're cute as a button. I'm sure I'd remember you if I'd ever met you before."

"I'm Cyn. Short for Cynthia. I'm your caregiver while your daughter is in Switzerland."

"My daughter? Don't be silly. She's in kindergarten."

"You have just a little dementia, Maddy, and you're not getting a ride in this shopping cart." Her words surprise me. What an excellent joke she's playing! "Now please stand there and let me get your yogurt."

I see my opportunity. She's bent entirely over the shopping cart to block me, reaching her arm past the now-open door to snag a few containers. It couldn't be a more awkward pose. So that's when I strike . . .

. . . climbing quickly into the shopping cart of the blond guy coming down the aisle.

"Ha-ha!" I scream in victory, folding myself up and plopping down on his groceries. "I win!" Madcap Maddy strikes again!

The pixie gasps as she spins. The man pushing the cart utters a naughty word and then starts to laugh. "Hello?" he says. "You've crushed a dozen eggs."

I grin up at him. "That makes me the prize layer at the fair! I'll get the blue ribbon for sure. Best Hen in the County!"

He and I exchange chuckles as the pixie rushes up. "Maddy! What have you done?" She turns to him. "I'm so sorry!"

She looks at the guy and her words dry up. She's not very smooth in the presence of a handsome man. Fortunately, I'm a charmer. "You look like a surfer in a nice pinstripe suit," I tell him. "I'm Maddy. This is Cyn. Not sin like 'the sins of the fathers.' Cyn is short for—what was it again?"

"Cynthia." She gulps, red in the face. The pixie is embarrassed for some reason. She's so cute I could hug her.

"And what is your name?" I ask him.

"Rhys," he says. "Like the peanut butter cup, but with the Welsh spelling."

"Peanut butter cup!" I crow. His name sends happy shivers all through me. "I do love a peanut butter cup!"

"Well, who doesn't?" He's charming right back. I'm in love. He has beautiful brown eyes that hold on to his laughter, and a broad, white-toothed smile in a square jaw. A classic good-looking guy. Cyn is fluttering in agitation, and he turns to soothe her. "It's okay. I can get more eggs."

This gives me time to satisfy my curiosity. What are all these boxes and bags piled around me? It's Christmas, but without the wrapping paper, and I'm always interested in exploring. "Would you look at that?" My voice carries beautifully. I know how to make myself heard. "This guy has three huge boxes of condoms in his cart!" I gather them up to wave in proof.

Now he's the one who is red in the face. "Um, they're not all for me . . ."

"Look at you, you delicious peanut butter cup!" I cry. "Is this a week's supply for you?" I'm questioning him on his plans for a hot Friday night when the happiness drains out of me.

Because I see *him*.

The other man. The evil nightmare. Creeping behind my large, blond surfer, scuttling past the breakfast cereal like a rat. Thinking I wouldn't see.

"Pick me up!" I demand to the Peanut Butter Cup. I've seen what this handsome man has secured under his charcoal pinstripe coat. "Pick me up right now!" I hold my hands up and, obediently, he reaches for me.

I pretend to lose my balance and fall against him, my quick hands reaching inside his jacket. Before he realizes it, I'm standing on the ground holding his pistol firmly in my two fists. He rears back in astonishment, and I spin away from him in a half-circle, locking my fury onto the Oatmeal Man. "You! You're not going to follow me this time!"

I flip the safety and squeeze off a shot, like Hector taught me. My aim is poor. The bullet passes between the Oatmeal Man's arm and his body, leaving a tidy hole in his leather jacket. *Take that, you nasty thing!* His mouth drops open in horror. He's a cartoon of astonishment, and it makes me scream in victory. "Didn't think I could take you, did you, Oatmeal Man? Well, this is it for you!"

I shoot again, but the Peanut Butter Cup is quicker than I expected. From behind me, a large hand appears and pulls my wrist up. My bullet shatters a fluorescent light in the ceiling with a startling spray of sparks. Fireworks! Suddenly I'm not holding the gun anymore. "Hey!" I cry, "Give that back to me!"

People are screaming, and the pixie is in tears. "Maddy! What are you doing?"

She's upset, and I want to pull her into a hug. "What's the matter, darling? Does something hurt? Come here and tell me about it."

She lets me wrap myself around her, and a strong arm is withdrawn from around my waist. There's a handsome blond man behind me in a charcoal pinstripe suit, holding a pistol. He's upset. "What's going on? Who are you?"

But he doesn't answer me. So I smile at him. It's a lovely day, and all the colors are so bright and cheery here. "Why is everyone making such a fuss?"

ONE

CYN

I'D NEVER BEEN ARRESTED BEFORE.

Well, not arrested. But I was the caregiver of the arrestee, and I figured that was as shameful. If you were responsible for a sweet old lady and she managed to filch a pistol off a passing hunk and start shooting, who *really* deserved to be put behind bars? Really?

"Damn it. I hate this thing. Hang on."

The policeman at the desk in front of me was doing nothing to distract me from my tangle of remorse. His computer had locked up on him, and finally he gave up and rebooted it. More time to sit waiting, feeling awkwardly idle and of little value. My nerves were stretched tight waiting for him to get on with it. Slap on the handcuffs and throw me in the pokey. The hoosegow. The Big House.

Maddy was laughing in a glass-fronted office across the large room. She was chatting with the doctor they'd brought in to assess her. For now, it was enough to know she was safe.

The room was clean, bright, and pleasant. Based on the cop shows I'd watched all my life, I decided that the Arlington Police Department was a terrible disappointment.

There were no thugs handcuffed to sturdy, 1930s oak office chairs. There were no cigar-chomping sergeants making ironic

1

comments. No half-wall between the filing and coffee area and the "bullpen." This place was surprisingly ordinary. More proof that I'd spent most of my twenty-six years watching life through a TV or computer screen.

My brother—he'd know what a police station was like. He had a misspent youth to look back on. Even my pillar-of-society sister had run afoul of the law in high school when she and her giggling friends had been caught in the school's swimming pool at midnight.

Not me. I'd been studying. Or reading. Or watching TV. My friends were all books. Not too many kids wanted to hang out with the too-young girl who kept skipping grades.

Still, all those degrees I'd earned gave me the undeniable right to judge the architecture of this police station in Arlington Court-house, which I then proceeded to regard very sternly. On reflection, I found it to be pleasingly designed on a human scale.

"Hang on," said Officer Talbot. "Sorry this is taking so long."

He startled me out of my reverie. I snapped back to my unhappiness and made a noncommittal noise designed to keep me as invisible as possible. As small as I am, I wished I were smaller.

He turned to me. "Okay. I'm back." Officer Talbot had a basset hound's long-suffering face. Clearly, to this guy, a crazy old lady shooting up the Harris Teeter was interesting, sure. But it was nothing to get worked up about. "All right. Help me understand."

If only I could. "Maddy has dementia. She's the sweetest thing, really."

"Uh-huh." He was clearly unconvinced. "Dementia makes people fearful and mean. That old lady doesn't act like someone with Alzheimer's."

I held my hands out imploringly—uselessly. "Not everyone with dementia has Alzheimer's, and not everyone with dementia presents the same way. Most people, yes. You're right. It's like sense, compassion, and humor get slowly switched off. Only fear and anger are left. But not everyone."

In the glass-fronted room, the happiest old lady on the planet was charming the people who spoke with her. How could I make Officer Talbot see? "Some people, like Maddy," I tried, "it's the fear and anger that get turned off. She has no short-term memory. Really. None. But"—and my voice broke as I said it—"she's a darling. She's never done anything like this before, I swear. She's . . . I don't know. Playful. Her nickname has always been Madcap Maddy. But she's really harmless." I could hear the pleading in my voice and knew I didn't sound convincing.

"Yeah," Talbot replied darkly. "She's harmless."

Across the room, the sound muffled by the glass walls, Maddy burst into delighted laughter. The doctor was grinning. Maddy had, typical for her disease, forgotten that she'd tried to kill a stranger at the grocery store two hours before.

Being with Maddy always made me feel good. She lived entirely in the present and never forced me to examine the mistakes I've made in my life. Her condition, I'd decided, was a huge gift. To have no short-term memory and to see the world as a source of joy? I envied her. Her laughter brought on my laughter.

But this time—for the first time—her joy made me fearful.

Her happy smile in the aftermath of such violence filled me with despair. Would Maddy be arrested? Institutionalized?

What the hell had gone wrong? How had it escalated so quickly?

Just how badly had I screwed up?

"So you're not family." Unlike me, the officer wasn't going through a mental crisis. This was another day at work for him, and he was doing his best to wrestle the situation into a manageable box.

"I'm her caregiver. I was hired by Maddy's daughter, Dr. Belinda Root. She's with the World Health Organization. She travels a lot, so I live with her and Maddy."

"Is the daughter coming in?"

"She's overseas. I tried calling her, but I had to leave a message."

"Uh-huh." Talbot made a note, and I felt another burst of guilt for no reason. "And how long have you had this job?"

I didn't have to count. "Seven months now." Seven months since my divorce was final. Seven months since Don had turned his back on me.

"And there's been no evidence of violence in that time? Most people with dementia act out."

"Not Maddy. She's peaceful and kind. She'd never try to hurt anyone." Again, I checked on Maddy. I did it compulsively. She was so quick to forget what she was doing that I needed to keep an eye on her. She and the doctor were smiling as they carried on a friendly chat. She was clearly charming him. She charmed everyone. Maddy leaked happiness on everyone around her.

Until, that is, she'd started shooting.

My mind kept tripping across that part. I was perpetually surprised by the realization that things had gone very severely wrong at the grocery store.

"Peaceful, you say. Uh-huh. I'm sure. So she hops into the cart of a passing FBI agent."

"He's FBI? Oh. That's why he had a gun." Maddy and I weren't the only ones who had been escorted to the police station. I could see through a window into an office where beautiful Rhys, the Peanut Butter Cup, had his golden head bent over the desk, with the police captain and a stern-looking blade of a man who had arrived at the station not long after us.

"Yep." Talbot's tone unexpectedly warmed. "Your old lady fired the shots, but I'm betting it's that guy in there who's going to pay the price." He, too, looked at the huddle in the office and shivered in sympathy. "Lost control of his weapon. Poor bastard."

This further wrinkled my brow. When it came to guilt, I was pretty sure I was the one who deserved sentencing, not the charming cute guy.

The basset hound faced me again. "So Old Lady Dementia gets the Feeb's gun and starts shooting."

"That's right." There it was again. The realization that Maddy —*my* Maddy, whom I was responsible for—had almost killed someone. "I have no idea why she did it."

"And she's shooting at someone she called"—he consulted his notes—"the Oatmeal Man."

"That's what she said."

"Who turns out to be a guy from Winchester named Barry who's never seen any of you before."

"I can't think of how to apologize to him." I wrung my hands. "It's not like Hallmark makes a card. *Sorry I Shot at You.*"

The policeman found that amusing. His droopy face broke into an unexpected snigger. I wished I'd meant to be funny. He focused again. "Any idea why she was shooting?"

"She said something about him not following her anymore."

"Ever seen him following her?" He watched my sad headshake. "Ever seen anyone following her?"

"No one. She's never done anything like this. I'm so worried about her." Had she been having delusions before this and I didn't even notice? Just how clueless was I? "What's going to happen?"

"Good question. We'll wait to hear what the doc says, and we'll call her—what did you call him? Neurologist. Uh, Krishnamurthi. We'll talk to him and see what he says. Then we'll figure it out. Okay. You can go wait with her now. I'll let you know when we hear something."

———

Maddy and I were moved to a seating area. It had a firm, modular sofa and several matching armchairs. It wasn't at all the stern "holding area" I'd been expecting. Magazines were fanned attractively on the low table, and there was a coffee maker against the wall. The whole setup increased my sense of guilt. I didn't deserve this anonymous, pleasant place to wait out my sentencing.

We sat, the two of us, and watched the world move around us. The officers and patrolmen all had places to go and things to do. It made my idleness all the more frustrating.

"What's this?" Maddy had fished her cell phone out of her pocket and was regarding it as if she'd found a priceless treasure.

"Deck of cards," I said automatically. Having had this conversation quite literally dozens of times with her, I no longer tried to explain. Sometimes she understood the phone completely; sometimes she laughed when I tried to explain she could make a call on it if she needed to. That was just part of being with Maddy.

"A deck of cards! We could get up a rubber of bridge! Let's see if any of these policemen would want to play. You could meet a nice young man."

"Let's give them a few minutes. Put it back in your pocket and we'll ask them in a bit."

"All right."

The phone went back in her pocket, and she and I settled down to wait. I realized that I was no longer exactly sure what we were waiting for.

Nothing very exciting happened.

Maddy, not burdened by self-questioning, guilt, confusion, or any of the things that were making my brow wrinkle, soon curled up on the sofa and began softly snoring. Her faith in the world, her belief that she was safe and all was well, spurred a wistful smile in me. I wanted so badly for that to be true.

And there I was, with plenty of time for bleak self-reflection.

Of all the bad feelings roving the world in search of weak characters or weak moments, the one I hated the most was guilt. Knowing that I was the one who was at fault was tightening my stomach and wrinkling my forehead. The phrase "dereliction of duty" kept echoing through my head, and I was having a hard time silencing it.

Clearly my attempt to hide from reality for a few years wasn't working out so well. And I was chewing my lip again. Take a deep breath, Cyn. I recited my new Maddy mantra to myself. *Be in the now—be like Maddy.* Stop thinking so much. Don't invite trouble.

Like all mantras, it was hard to focus on this for very long. I opened my eyes again on my crowded-and-yet-still-painfully-isolated reality.

I knew it was wrong to think of myself as alone. I had a family in Tallahassee who would take me in if I crawled home in defeat. They didn't understand how an instinctive "book learner" had been born into their "guess I'll wait for the movie" family, but they loved me all the same. And I loved them. Even if we'd been practically speaking in different languages since I began leapfrogging grades in school. Nevertheless, I *felt* alone. My parents had never understood my desire to keep learning.

The person I'd connected with most easily in my adult life was my husband, who was now my ex-husband. Our divorce had come as a surprise to me, which of course made the sting that much sharper. I'd been a trusting fool. His betrayal of the life I thought I'd been living still smarted. Somehow Don had gotten my identity in the divorce. And now I didn't know who I was or what I wanted to make of myself.

But recently, a flicker of anger had begun to burn amid all the loathsome self-pity. Was I a trusting fool? Or had Don been playing me? I questioned whether I'd done anything to deserve the confusion and despair that was clogging my spirit. I was hoping that tiny bloom of anger was a positive step forward. With this dawning anger, I couldn't decide. If offered the chance to return to my well-defined place in Don's life, would I take it?

I didn't know. Certainly, giving in and returning to that life would be easier than discovering who I'd become.

In an effort to distract myself, I flipped through magazines, but I couldn't concentrate. I checked my phone to see if Belinda had tried to call back. Nothing. Inevitably, my thoughts returned to the subject of Don, the way a tongue will return to the place where a tooth used to be, to probe the tender flesh revealed when something important has been torn out.

I was once again imagining ways my ex-husband could be made to suffer and then be rescued by me, so he'd profess endless love and beg for me to come back. Enough time had passed from the shock of the divorce that I'd begun to wonder if I'd loved him or if I'd loved being part of a pair. Was Don important to me? Or was simply being married the part that I valued? Having that identity? Being someone other than the shy, bookish girl who never had friends, who was always forced to hide that, quite often, she knew more than her teachers?

No satisfying revenge scenario had occurred to me by the time the door to the captain's office opened. I wanted the captain to be a stocky man in shirtsleeves who defended and berated his brilliant rebel detectives. But this man was slim and dressed in a normal suit. He beckoned me to join them but almost immediately realized that Maddy was asleep on the sofa.

He shot me a smile I felt undeserving of and patted the air, telling me to stay put. All three men—the captain, the new guy, and the luscious Peanut Butter Cup—crowded into the seating area with me.

"She's out, huh?" the captain said unnecessarily, nodding at the sleeping marksman. Markswoman.

"Well, even for her, this has been a big day." I tried a timid smile. I felt like a dog groveling for table scraps. *Please don't be mean.*

"We won't wake her?"

"She sleeps like a baby. Well, like a baby is supposed to sleep. We can talk." My anxiety overwhelmed me. "What's going to happen to her?"

"Don't worry. Let me introduce these gentlemen. I think you already know Special Agent Rhys Jones of the FBI."

It was hard to look at the beautiful man before me, not just because he was too handsome, making me feel plain and boring.

No, I was also embarrassed. Once the police had arrived at the grocery store, once Maddy was being walked to the squad car between two cops (her arms linked elegantly through theirs, as if they were all going to a cotillion), I'd gotten the shakes and started crying again, and it was Rhys's soft jacket that had absorbed my tears.

He'd held me. In fact, he'd held me up, strong hands under my elbows. He'd folded me into him as if it was the most natural thing in the world. I'd stood there, my muscles suddenly tight enough to break, and cried on that man's breast pocket. He'd crooned at me and given me the warmth of his body while mine shivered in sudden cold. He smelled of clean male and now-damp wool, and I tried not to sniff him too obviously. It had been a moment of calm in the middle of a morning-turned-nightmare, and it had ended all too soon.

I ducked my head, blushing at the memory of my weakness and his kindness. "Agent," I murmured in acknowledgment.

"And this is his partner, Special Agent Dash Ashwood."

The movie star name startled me. Horrified, I realized I'd almost giggled. "Dash Ashwood," I repeated stupidly.

He was a hawk of a man. Older than the Peanut Butter Cup, crisply drawn, with a lean face and deep-set eyes. He looked both wise and capable. "Ms. Quimby," he said, effortlessly taking control from the captain, "the Bureau wants to extend its formal apologies to you and to your charge. Don't we, Agent Jones?"

He glared at his younger partner, who straightened his shoulders and spoke in a rumbling baritone.

"I apologize wholeheartedly. I'm very, very sorry."

I gulped. "You're . . . you're apologizing? To me?" Officer Talbot had been right. Peanut Butter Cup was in trouble. Perhaps we could share a prison cell. "But it was Maddy who stole your gun. And I'm the one who was supposed to be watching her. Why would you apologize?"

Agent Ashwood stepped in again. "Jones should never have lost control of his weapon. The fact that it was taken—and fired—by a senior with dementia . . . a very *small* senior . . . is absolutely unacceptable. If you intend to sue Agent Jones or the Bureau, rest assured that we shall cooperate fully."

"Sue you?" I was adrift in a sea of confusion. I risked a glance at Agent Jones and found the blond hanging his handsome head . . . in shame? It was an emotion I could relate to. "Well, I'll have to talk to Belinda. That's Maddy's daughter," I clarified.

"Here's my card," Agent Ashwood said. "Agent Jones, give her your card."

"I want one too." Maddy was awake, her eyes bright and alert. Gravely, Rhys handed both of us his card. Maddy regarded it with the delight of a child on Christmas morning. "Thank you! I'm going to put this in my phone!"

Agent Ashwood regarded Maddy blankly.

"Huh," he said. He favored her with a suddenly radiant smile, and then he turned back to me. "Mr. Barry Gambert—the man Miss Maddy shot at—understands that she suffers from . . . well, he's agreed not to press charges."

Relief flooded through me. I crumpled in my chair and hoped I could hold back the sudden rush of tears.

"And the store manager asks only for payment so the lighting fixture can be repaired."

"Of course," I said willingly, but he cut me off.

"Agent Jones will be paying for that."

Peanut Butter Cup was nodding. "Absolutely. It is truly the least I can do."

"Yes, it is," Agent Ashwood said severely. "Both the police physician and Dr. Krishnamurthi, Miss Maddy's neurologist, confirm the diagnosis, and the neurologist agrees with your assessment that she hasn't acted violently or dangerously before. On the promise that you will enhance your supervision of her, you're free to go."

The police captain, possibly annoyed that his thunder had been thoroughly stolen by the FBI, hastened to add, "We'll give you a ride back to the grocery store, or to your home, if you like."

"That's not necessary," Agent Ashwood interjected. He was an interrupting kind of person. "I'll take them wherever they want to go. Ms. Quimby?"

I goggled, unable to think clearly. It was over? Maddy was forgiven? I was forgiven? "Thank you. Well, the car is at the grocery store. And I still need to buy yogurt."

"Oh, good," said Maddy. "I want a ride in one of those shopping carts."

TWO
RHYS

I could feel my Glock lying against my ribs.

Dash was driving us back to headquarters with his customary confidence, and I couldn't get over the feel of my pistol in its holster.

I was nine the first time my father put an air rifle in my hands and discovered I was a "deadeye." I was thirteen when I won my first junior competition, and seventeen when I got a partial scholarship to the University of Michigan to be on their rifle team. I might have qualified for the Olympics if I hadn't set my heart on a career in the FBI.

I've cursed pistols. I've coveted pistols. God knows I've cleaned pistols.

But I've never lost a pistol before. I've never lost any gun before.

Yes, I felt ashamed. Yes, I felt humiliated. But below all that?

I felt betrayed.

How could my Glock have done that to me?

I've been a slave to the gun since that first air rifle nineteen years ago. I went to the range throughout my adolescence and beyond, when there were plenty of things I really would rather have been doing. Three times I've contributed to the saving of lives because of my ability to shoot.

And after all we'd been through together, that gun, lying like a rock along my ribs, had allowed itself to be neatly filched right out of my holster by a ninety-three-year-old woman with dementia.

I dropped my heavy head into my hands and groaned.

Dash reached over and slapped my shoulder in friendly fashion, the mild sting doing nothing to distract me. "Chin up, little buckaroo."

He'd dropped the frowning, formal attitude he'd worn for the police chief and was back to the big brother vibe that had made me like him since I arrived at FBI headquarters six weeks earlier. Dash had become more than a partner; he'd become my friend.

"You fucked up," he said unnecessarily. "It happens. Of course, I don't want you to take this incident lightly. Someone could easily have been killed."

"Christ." My head got even heavier. The smell of cordite clung to me from the two shots fired, and my ears were still ringing from the sound. People can spend hours (and hours and hours) at the range with proper ear protection and still forget what an assault of sound comes out of a nine-millimeter. I was haunted by the terror of the poor schlub who nearly lost his life because he was out of cornflakes.

That thin, scarlet ribbon of panic had barely faded from the moment the world descended to horrible slow motion and that tiny, frail hand swung past me to target an innocent. With *my* gun.

Someone could have been killed. Oh, yeah. I definitely knew that.

Dash went on.

"But there's really no reason why you should have expected her to go for your weapon. This wasn't one you could have anticipated."

"I don't know," I said ruefully. "If an ancient old lady clambered into your shopping cart, it wouldn't be wrong to assume she was compromised mentally in some way."

Dash had the kindness to not laugh. He piloted us into DC across Arlington Bridge with the effortless skill that characterized everything he did. In the short time I'd known him, it had become impossible to ever imagine him cringing in embarrassment. The man didn't make mistakes. He was the perfect agent. "Incapacitated, definitely. And you were handling that. But violent? Putting you or others at risk? No. You were taken by surprise and you recovered quickly. And you were lucky nothing worse happened."

"Lucky as hell." I raised my head and checked. My hands had stopped shaking. Good. But all my muscles were still jumpy. I was off-balance. Wrong. Twitchy. This was, I know, the aftermath of an adrenaline dump. I needed to go for a long run or put in an hour or so at the pool. Neither one was likely this afternoon. I anticipated a series of painful discussions in progressively larger offices.

"So we'll file the report, you'll take your lumps, and we'll hope like hell the old lady's family doesn't want to litigate." Dash turned onto Constitution Avenue. "The good news is, if they don't sue, you can ask her out." He watched me with a half-smile.

"Who?" I asked, taken by surprise.

"Who." He scoffed. "The old lady. Obviously I mean the cutie. I saw you looking at her."

Dash was observant; nothing escaped him. That was part of what made him a great agent.

I'd idly checked her out when I turned into the dairy aisle at my local grocery store. She was slight. Willowy. The hint of curves in all the right places. Who wouldn't look?

And then crazy Maddy had climbed into my cart and Cynthia had rushed up, and I saw her gorgeous eyes for the first time.

Later, during the painful discussions between Dash and the chief at the police station, I'd allowed myself a few glances through the glass walls to where Cyn was being interviewed by an officer.

She watched the policeman and she watched Maddy. And, a few times, she'd nervously watched me.

Those were the best times—when I could see her eyes.

And it was her eyes that brought on the craving to paint. I knew exactly how I'd capture the color—which six or seven shades in blue and ultramarine and green I'd use to capture the unusual spectrum (the phthalo turquoise, of course, and the cobalt teal, and then the tenderest strokes of indanthrene blue—not usually a color associated with tenderness), plus warm gray for the highlights because it'd pick up the faint, clear, rosy blush high over her cheekbones.

The question was: Could I capture the tension in her expression? The liquid wash of her tears? The bright electricity of her smile?

Would she be better served by pastels?

Or the stark, mutable chiaroscuro of charcoal?

No. I shook myself mentally. I'd left all that behind in Minneapolis. All of my supplies, neatly and (as far as I was concerned) permanently boxed up and locked away in a storage facility outside Wayzata.

I'd been given a second chance by being posted to DC—all right, a *third* chance—and I wasn't going to blow it this time.

Dash was still watching me with a ghost of a smile. He wanted to tease me. Suddenly I could see him as a bright-eyed eight-year-old, sing-songing on the playground, "Rhys likes Cyn! Rhys likes Cyn!"

I tried to deflect his interest. "Oh, right. Asking her out after I nearly got her killed. I'm sure that would work out beautifully."

"I admit it. It'd be the strangest 'boy meets girl' in modern history. But what the hell. She's hot. You're new in town. Looking for some entanglements. Why not?"

Surprised, it occurred to me that the teasing had been in my head. Here was my new partner looking out for me—trying to encourage me to date, to feel at home, to get settled in my new position.

Again, I was off-balance. But . . .

"It wouldn't be considered a conflict of interest?" I asked.

"What interest? She's not a suspect, and you're not protecting her. She's no part of a case you're working. You'd be in the clear."

"Assuming I'm still employed by the end of the day."

"This isn't going to be the kill shot. You're not getting fired, Rhys. Relax."

"Relax." I could as easily fly to the moon. "This isn't going to look good, Dash. Not with my record."

"Don't kid yourself, buddy. It wouldn't look good with anyone's record." He blithely ignored my wince. "Don't worry about it. You know you've got a couple of guys pulling for you in the department."

His easy grin reignited my gratitude, but I didn't share his confidence about a cheerleading squad. One of the guys he clearly thought was "pulling for me" was my father, riding a desk because of the artificial leg that kept him out of the field. The FBI had rightly promoted him to a senior position. I wasn't so sure the legendary Owen Jones would agree that I'd honored his tradition of service and covered myself in glory. Still, my new partner's thought was well-intentioned. "Thanks, Dash. I really appreciate your support. How you're handling this."

"We're partners. You've been a real help with Hartwell Securities."

Our primary case. A wealthy stockbroker thought he was successfully hiding embezzled assets in the Caymans. Dash and I were slowly building the case that was going to prove he wasn't as smart as he thought he was.

"I'm just following your lead." I couldn't have a better person to trail behind, either. Dash Ashwood had been a decorated agent for seventeen years. He knew the ropes and never fucked up. It was no accident that I'd been partnered with him. I knew why I'd scored Dash for my partner. I was supposed to learn from his careful attention to detail and meticulous professionalism.

Losing my weapon to a crazy old bat was proof that Dash hadn't upgraded my game quite yet.

No—not a crazy old bat. That was a disrespectful and inappropriate way to think of her. She was a senior citizen with impaired capacities. It's not enough to speak the company line, I lectured myself sternly. You have to think it too. You have to believe it.

My good intentions were ruined as I remembered the old lady laughing up at me, cackling over her blue ribbon for egg-laying at the county fair.

I turned my face to the window to hide the unwilling smile that crept up on me. That Maddy was a little-old-lady terror and I liked her instinctively, but this wasn't a time to smile. Instead, I watched the city roll past. It was a beautiful day. The autumn light had a luminous quality that made ordinary street scenes glow, like a Canaletto painting of Venice.

Nope. That was definitely not what I meant. I shoved art history into the background again. I meant the day was in the high forties, cool and clear. The streets were moderately crowded with office workers enjoying the sunny fall afternoon. The situation was calm, and there were multiple avenues of ingress and egress.

Dash pulled into his space under the FBI Headquarters building, and I envied him again. As a junior agent, I was left to scrounge for parking. Fortunately, Washington, DC, has a good subway system that runs smoothly under jaw-dropping traffic jams throughout the region. On most days, it was faster for me to ride the Metro from my still-chaotic apartment in Ballston than it would've been to drive across the river in the rush-hour logjam.

We passed through security and walked to the elevators. "I feel like I'm going to my execution," I admitted.

Dash laughed and chucked me on the arm. "And you were going to have such a quiet, long lunch too!"

"Scrambled eggs," I said mournfully. "Scrambled eggs and an

afternoon off to finally get some boxes unpacked. And now, this. Damn, life changes fast."

"Got to hold on tight," he agreed, selecting the elevator button that might as well have been labeled "Important People Work on This Floor." I winced. "Take my advice," he said. "Own it. Own everything. Make no excuses and accept whatever happens without saying a word."

"That's a good plan. Thanks. That's exactly what I'll do."

We rode upward and he continued, "You're not the first agent to lose control of his weapon. You won't be the last."

"How many of the others have lost a weapon to a ninety-three-year-old female with dementia?"

He considered and finally admitted defeat. "You may be unique there."

"Instead, can we say that there were six gang members who beat me with tire irons, and the one who finally pried my bloody, broken fingers from my Glock was a bruiser named El Diablo Gigante?"

"Watch that stereotyping," he said automatically. "And that imagination."

"Just the facts, ma'am."

"Now you're talking." The doors slid open onto slate-gray industrial carpeting and the icy stench of power. "Better yet, don't talk at all. Let's go."

THREE
CYN

I WANTED TO BE DR. BELINDA ROOT WHEN I GREW UP.

Maddy's daughter had it all going on in a way that filled me with awed respect. This, I thought, is what a woman ought to be. Career? Check. Unlike me, nothing had derailed Belinda in her plans (nothing would have dared). She was an epidemiologist—a specialist in communicable diseases, already skilled and experienced at a time when the whole world was vulnerable to pandemics. Big office and large staff at the World Health Organization. Natural confidence because she knew what she was talking about, down to the cellular level.

Beauty? No question. She was sixty-four years old and had that *Downton Abbey* patrician elegance. Upright and tall, naturally graceful, a blue blood with great cheekbones. She didn't bother chasing her youth; she wouldn't stoop so low. Her dark hair was silvering naturally in lovely highlights, and she never tried to hide a wrinkle. I felt like a lesser species when I stood at her elbow, my head barely clearing her shoulder.

Men? Oh, I suppose. Belinda had never been married. She didn't need to be. Her opinion of herself was perfectly healthy without it. She dated a carefully curated selection of handsome older men, every single one of whom was interesting and could make a little nothing of a caregiver like me feel important. For a while, at least.

Kind? Endlessly. Belinda had no children, but she had a strong maternal streak in her. And she'd taken me on as someone who needed help. I tried to hide my gratitude because it made me feel pathetic in the brilliant light of her calm self-reliance.

In fact, the only gray cloud in Belinda's life was that her vivacious, funny mother had somehow slipped, while no one was really paying attention, into dementia. So she sold her place in the city, and Maddy's home in North Arlington, and had moved them both into a sun-filled condo in the new Courthouse area, with an extra bedroom for a live-in.

And then she gave me a key and told me to make myself at home. "Take care of my mother when I'm at work. Keep her clean and happy. When I'm not traveling, you can have weekends and evenings off. When I am traveling, there's an agency we can call to relieve you, but I'd like you to stick around if you can."

She gave me three weeks of vacation, a reasonable salary, room and board, and a place to hide after the divorce.

Sometimes I felt like a part of her family—that Maddy was as beloved to me as my own grandmother, and Belinda a wise aunt. Sometimes I confronted the reality that perhaps I was a bit too deeply in hiding amid the acres of soft vanilla carpeting and suites of handsome furniture and once-weekly cleaning service. Belinda's condo had become my sanctuary.

And sometimes I knew that seven months was a reasonable length of time to "get over" the shock of losing my husband and maybe just a few more weeks would be acceptable too, before deciding whether or not to finish up my degree or become a burlesque dancer or set a new world's record by jumping a pogo stick to Antarctica.

Surely something would occur to me?

"Of course I don't blame you, Cyn." Belinda was sitting next to me on the sofa, surrounded by the piles of mail that had awaited her return from Switzerland. "She's climbed into shopping carts on me too."

We looked at Maddy, seated in the chair across from us. Unlike her daughter, Maddy was small-boned and little like me, but her larger-than-life personality took up more space. I could tell that the old darling had been distracted. She was smiling at a beam of sunlight that had broken through the gray wool clouds outside.

"It's a celestial searchlight! Will you look at that! What's it shining on?"

Spry as ever, Maddy rose and went to the window. Placing her hands flat on the glass, she peered down at the street five floors below.

She laughed. "It's a truck! A ratty, old red truck that quite badly needs a bath!" She turned back to us, a wrinkled, wizened, delighted ninety-three-year-old child. "Do you suppose it's the hand of the Lord come down to write 'WASH ME' on the tailgate?"

She offered us a quick dance step, her sneakered feet and yoga pants-wearing legs prancing happily to us. I could tell that she didn't recognize either of us, but that never upset Maddy. She'd never met a stranger in her life.

"Would you like some tea, Maddy?" I gestured to her cup on the coffee table, where she'd left it.

"How lovely. I was just wanting a cup!"

She sat again, sipping, and looked up with interest when Belinda spoke.

"I can't blame you for the incident at the grocery store, Cyn. I'm too grateful. Honestly. I don't know what I'd do if you weren't here. I can't bear the thought of locking her away somewhere."

I knew what she meant. It hadn't taken the full seven months to fall in love with Maddy. More like seven minutes. "No, you're right. She'd wither in a home. That would be doom to her."

"But I can't expect you to be responsible if she's going to go around shooting people."

Maddy perked right up at that, birdlike and alert. "Who? Who's shooting at people?"

Belinda couldn't fully hide her bitter reaction. She wasn't as skilled as I was at rolling over the gaps in dementia logic. I'd tried to explain that the trick is to never disagree—never to correct. Keep going. Keep smiling. But it was hard on Belinda.

"A friend of mine," I told Maddy. "She shot a stranger the other day, out of the blue." You never can tell when memory will be partially or fully restored. Would Maddy remember anything about the incident at the grocery store?

Maddy was titillated. "My heavens! Whatever is this world coming to?" Nope. She remembered nothing. The mental fog was thick today. "I suppose he did something quite terrible to make her do it?"

"No one knows why she did it."

"No! And what'd she say when you asked?" This was clearly the most interesting story she'd heard in years.

"She didn't say a thing. I think she'd forgotten about it."

"Forgotten about shooting someone? Oh, you're cuckoo."

Being with Maddy lightens my spirit. Yes, she'd forgotten the incident, but her joy was contagious. I exchanged warm smiles with her, loving the way her dimples popped up in her creased face. "Either I'm cuckoo, or she is."

"Or both!" We both laughed at the thought.

Maddy looked over at her daughter without recognition, but she knew the woman on the sofa wasn't laughing. Belinda got her maternal instinct from Maddy. Maddy wanted to figure out how to draw out the stranger on the sofa—to make her a part of our conversation. She studied her own daughter closely.

"You look so much like Azariah's mother. Are you Ginny?"

Poor Belinda. Every time Maddy didn't know who she was, Belinda winced. She was a doctor. She knew the pathology of the disease and she was grateful that Maddy's condition had left her mother happy. But I could see that—yes, it'd be hard to be mistaken for her own long-dead grandmother.

"Oh, Mom," she said sadly.

I put my hand on Belinda's arm and drew Maddy's attention back to me to give Belinda time to recover. "Ginny is your mother-in-law, right, Maddy? Does this look like Azariah's mother?"

Maddy's husband Azariah had died some fifteen years earlier, but Maddy often forgot that. She studied Belinda carefully. "You look a lot like Ginny. But you're older. Are you her sister? No, I think you *are* Ginny!"

Maddy's triumphant identification was hard on Belinda, so I was the one laughing with Maddy as she exalted in her ability to recognize her mother-in-law. I kept a comforting hand on Belinda's arm and rolled with Maddy's interpretation of events. "Isn't it nice that she came to visit?"

"So nice! Az will be home soon. He'll be so glad to see you!"

Belinda mustered a watery smile, which clearly pleased Maddy.

"You just have to go with it," I told Ginny—I mean, Belinda. "She'll be back to normal before you know it."

"I know," Belinda sighed. "But I still don't know how you handle it. Every five minutes you have to have the same conversation over again."

"But she's so sweet. Always completely happy. And, of course, she's not *my* mother. That makes a big difference."

"Who's not your mother?" Maddy interjected.

"This lady I work for," I told her, looking at the lady I worked for.

"Oh." Maddy noticed the cookies on the table and was immediately distracted. "My favorite! What a treat!"

That time, Belinda's smile had more warmth. It's hard to stay upset when someone is so thoroughly enjoying a Milano. Belinda turned back to the police report in her hand.

"This is startling, I must say. She's never done anything like this. She really shot at a guy?"

"Belinda, no kidding, I was terrified. And I wish you could have seen the FBI agent. He moved so fast once he knew what she was doing. And clearly he didn't want to hurt her, but she was taking aim to shoot again."

I mimicked the gesture of the Peanut Butter Cup, swinging the flat of his hand up against my own outstretched wrist. "He had that gun out of her hand in no time at all and wrapped her in this hug so she couldn't move."

Belinda was wide-eyed. "What did she do?"

"She was angry. She wanted the gun back."

"What did *you* do?"

"Burst into tears, of course. The only rational alternative." I felt more self-loathing, but Belinda brushed it aside. "He actually mopped my tears," I admitted.

"He did?" Perhaps she heard something in my voice, because her interest became curiosity. "And was that nice?"

I knew I was blushing. I could feel the heat in my cheeks. "No, terrible. He's so beautiful—you can't imagine. I felt like such a child."

"A beautiful FBI agent." She smiled. "I'd think that would make things better rather than worse."

She didn't understand, and I couldn't blame her. It made no sense that I'd felt particularly uncomfortable around one of the few truly gorgeous men I'd ever met. Damaged self-esteem exacts a heavy price. Time to distract Belinda and myself. "The FBI wants to know if you're going to sue them for the agent losing control of his gun."

"Sue them?" She sat back and thought about it. "Was the beautiful agent negligent in any way?"

"Well, not that I could see. Maybe you should ask a lawyer?"

"Oh, a lawyer is going to tell me to sue. And I think it's

damned lucky my mother hasn't been locked up. No, of course I won't sue the FBI. I'm so glad they didn't press charges."

"Why, Belinda, dear!" Maddy had finished her cookie. "When did you get back, sweetheart? How was Switzerland?"

"Now, how can she remember I was in Switzerland when sometimes she can't even recognize me?" Belinda's frustration, while reasonable, was non-useful.

"Just go with it," I advised her.

"You look tired, darling," Maddy said to Belinda. "Want me to get you some more tea? What about a nap?"

"I'm fine, Mother. But thank you." She regarded Maddy closely. "How are you, Mother?"

"Me?" Maddy was clearly astonished at the question. "Fit as a fiddle, as always!"

"I'm glad to hear it. I wanted to ask you." Belinda gestured to the pile of mail on the coffee table in front of her. She picked up a thick, creamy envelope. "Do you know an H. de Salles Shipman?"

"Gracious, what a name! No, why? Whoever is that?"

"If this letter isn't a scam—and I'll find out if it is—then someone named H. de Salles Shipman has left you a fishing shack on the eastern shore in his will. "

"Left me? Left me a fishing shack? What on earth could you be talking about, dear?"

"I don't know. I found this in the mail when I got home last night. It probably is a scam. I'll investigate this law firm. See if they're legit."

"Oh, I think you'd better," Maddy agreed. "How long are you here for this time, darling?"

"I leave next week. I'm giving the keynote at a conference in Jakarta."

"My! Of course you are! I'm so proud of my girl!" Maddy turned to me. "Cynthia, have you met my daughter? She's a doctor, you know. Epidemiology. Study of public health." Maddy's pride was like sunshine. The creases that had developed on Belinda's forehead smoothed out.

"I have met her," I replied with a smile of my own. "She's terribly bright, isn't she?"

"She gets that from her father," Maddy said with satisfaction.

No doubt figuring that the dementia fog had lifted briefly, Belinda tried to get some answers from Maddy. She sat forward. "Mother, I heard the funniest story the other day. Have you ever heard of the Oatmeal Man?"

For a second, Maddy's lovely smile faltered. There was an unusual tightness around her eyes. But it was fleeting, and her smile returned. "No, my love. Tell me!"

Belinda sighed and used the useful distraction technique of saying "In a moment," correctly assuming that Maddy would soon forget her question. "Did you ever learn how to shoot a pistol? I mean, in all your various travels and occupations?"

"A pistol?" The light from the large windows shifted again as the clouds parted. This time, the "celestial searchlight" sunbeam poured through the window and onto a glass bowl. It made a fairyland rainbow on the wall, and Maddy looked to see if we were as pleased by this as she was. It was clear she'd gone again, mentally, and the conversation had been wiped from her memory.

"We're going to the doctor tomorrow," Belinda told Maddy. "I want you checked out. I managed to get you an appointment with Dr. Krishnamurthi, Mom."

"The neurologist? Oh, I like it there. We play the most interesting games."

Belinda deflated. "Again, she remembers her neurologist. I don't understand."

"Just go with it," Maddy advised her. "Oh! I was wanting a nice cup of tea, and here it is!"

FOUR
RHYS

"Hey, Dad."

I found him in his home office. He looked up at me over his readers, surrounded by books and briefing papers and no fewer than three computers (two of them secure FBI laptops), and I automatically stood straighter under his observation.

He sighed and removed the glasses. "Son. Come on in."

It was easy to read his mood from the doorway. Alas. Not angry —disappointed. Definitely worse for me than if he'd been ticked off.

"I missed you at the Bureau this afternoon." I'd worked up the courage to take my medicine at work, but after my meetings with all my various supervisors, I'd headed for his office and his assistant said he was out for the rest of the day.

"The Joint Task Force had a meeting at Langley. I came home after. So, what did they decide?" He watched me sit in the chair before his desk. I tried not to collapse into it.

"Community service. I'll do it at the Boys' Club of DC. I'm already helping Dash there anyway. Really, it's a slap on the wrist. I got lucky."

"You got real lucky. Losing control of your weapon? Endangering innocent people? Rhys. Son . . ."

"I know."

He rubbed his leg absently where it ended above his knee, massaging above the prosthetic he wore. I was fourteen when he took the bullet that would have killed his partner. He told me later that he hadn't planned it. It wasn't heroism. He'd just moved to protect Carter, but I thought at the time—and I still thought now —that he was nothing less than a hero.

(FBI Agent Danny Carter agreed. Now in the San Francisco office, he would either send my father some exotic bottle of whiskey on the anniversary of the shooting or they would meet somewhere if they could, to hoist a glass together.)

Would Owen Jones, the FBI agent who set the standard for all agents, have lost control of his gun?

Under no circumstance.

"I wanted to thank you. I'm sure I got off so lucky because of you."

"Not a chance," he insisted. "I've stayed far away from this one. No favoritism, you know?"

Now, whenever I sat in his office, the shelf to my left always seemed to have a higher specific gravity. I avoided looking at it. That was where my father had once displayed my shooting trophies, from grade school through college—at least, until the Peterson arrest. After that, I'd asked him to take them down. He'd replaced them with two of my mother's nicer art photos, and they looked very nice there. But for me, the shelf would forever represent the missing right hand of a Milwaukee accountant who'd decided to try to shoot it out instead of accepting his arrest for running a child pornography ring.

I didn't even work for that division. I was strictly legal and financial crimes. But when Peterson began shooting, when he decided to hold four of his coworkers hostage at the accounting firm, the FBI brought in two experts: a negotiator, and the closest sharpshooter.

Who happened to be me.

It was my father who helped most as I handled the reality of the life I'd shattered. Other agents told me to think about the children I'd helped when I shot off that man's "point and click" hand, and the gun he was waving at my brother and sister agents. But I couldn't get the image of the mangled mess out of my mind. Clean paper targets and swift-moving clay pigeons didn't scream the way Peterson had.

My father flew in from DC to sit beside me on the balcony of my Wayzata apartment. I gave him a beer, and we watched the daylight fade and headlights brighten on the highway below, and he didn't say a word. He just nodded at me, and I realized that he remembered screams like that too.

"Learn to live with it," he said as he headed out to his hotel that night. "Let it make you a better agent."

I'd shot at suspects twice since then. One survived; one eventually died of a homemade shiv in a prison exercise yard. But neither of them had shaken me the way Peterson had. You looked at a person and saw an expression or noted a bunched muscle or watched an idea dawn across the face. But you couldn't see that under all that skin was nothing but blood and pulp and screaming, shrieking nerves, held together only by the merest chance of fate.

It was the stuff of nightmares.

And my dad knew those nightmares.

Our relationship shifted after that. I still thought he was a hero (and that I'd never live up to the standard he set), and I still wanted his approval. But he'd begun to see me not just as a son, but also as a colleague.

That made me proud—and sad.

And I was horrified to discover, sitting in his den and ready to confess my sins, that I could see the evidence of his years in his face. All my life, he'd been the most vibrant, vital man in the room.

Dark, curly hair and lively eyes that saw everything, and the kind of body that helped generations of his people survive in Welsh coal mines—small and compact and well-muscled.

And confident. Owen Jones never minded that the Norwegian he fell in love with had topped him by a good four inches. Inger Swenssen was the only woman for him, and she and he remained besotted to this day.

But I realized his eyes had faint pouches under them, and his hair was showing some frost. Not a lot of gray, but some. A flash of guilt hit me. It wasn't easy having such a fuck-up for a son in the Bureau.

"So. Let's have it. Tell me the whole story. Don't leave out any details." He eyed me suspiciously. "Even the ones you didn't tell Harvey about, and the committee."

"Hang on," I protested, "How do you know—"

"Because I know you. Don't we, Inger?"

He spoke directly to me, but he knows my mother as well as he knows me. And he was right. She was lurking in the hall outside the open door. "Well, I want to hear too! Don't you give my *liten gutt* a hard time, now, Owen."

Liten gutt—her little boy. I'd passed my father's height when I was twelve and my mother's about six painful months later, but I'd always be her little boy. She came to stand behind me and put her hand gently on my head. It was a gesture of love that made me remember being a naughty child who needed defending. Felt pretty good, actually.

"Tell us the story, Rhys. What happened?" She sat next to me and watched me with clever eyes. Mom was a freelance photographer. She mostly did catalogs, but some of the work she did on her own had earned justifiable praise in art circles.

I told them about the day before. They both laughed at the story of Maddy, and Dad closed his eyes and shook his head when I got to the shooting of Barry from Winchester. "You were so lucky," he said again.

"I know. The guy ended up with a hole in his jacket from the bullet."

I pulled my own suit coat out to show them and waited for the lecture I definitely deserved. But my father, as usual, surprised me.

"Sounds like you handled a bad situation as well as you possibly could. I can see why Harvey gave you community service and not a suspension."

What? I was left with my jaw hanging open. Dad shook his head and went on.

"You want to do penance. You want to confess. You want absolution. Well, we're not Catholic. You're going to have to live with this, and let it make you a better agent."

He'd said that to me before. I tried not to wince. Emotional, mental growth? Couldn't he just lecture me instead?

"Move on to the police interview. How'd you handle it?"

"No—tell more about the pretty girl." Mom scented something interesting and homed in on it. "Pretty in mind? Or just in face and body? What's her name?"

Dad and I both protested, but Mom was undeterred.

"What? You're not seeing that Alison anymore, are you? I never liked her very much anyway. I'm glad you left her back in Milwaukee. She was far too chilly for you."

She was right. I'd broken up with my girlfriend, another agent, in Wisconsin when I got transferred. Alison hadn't been too upset when it happened. Most of our best dates had been at the shooting range, which in retrospect was perhaps was an indication of the heat and passion of our relationship—or lack thereof.

"That doesn't mean I need help with dating from my mom. Yuck."

"What yuck? Don't be silly. There's a nice girl who lives over the dry cleaner's. She's not married. She works as a graphic designer, and she and I got to talking. I was going to have you to dinner to meet her, but you've got this new girl, so I won't."

"I don't have a new girl. And I don't want you trying to set me up. I mean, thank you. But no thank you." Couldn't she see my forehead wrinkling as I suppressed my shivers of revulsion? Mom-based dating. Nothing would kill my interest faster.

"Don't worry about it," she said soothingly. "This new girl is going to be very good for you. I can tell."

"I don't even know her."

"Doesn't matter. I can tell," she repeated with a knowing smile.

My father and I exchanged looks of commiseration. The odd thing was, Mom often did know. She had flashes of intuition that Dad and I never gave credence to . . . until they came true.

Mom wanted me to get to know the beautiful Cyn, and Dash was angling for that too. Hm. Interesting.

"Stay for dinner, Rhys, my *liten gutt*. I'm making leg of lamb." The perfume was drifting through the house and making my mouth water. But staying for dinner would take hours.

"I can't. My apartment is still mostly unpacked boxes. I really need some time working on it. I just wanted to check in with Dad first."

"Spend the night. Stay here. You can ride with him to work tomorrow."

"Mom."

"I'm thrilled you're both in the same city. It's so wonderful having you here! Are you sure you don't want to give up that apartment? We've got room for you here."

This time, Dad and I both protested together. "Inger, let the boy have his own life. He's earned it."

The words, so easily and casually spoken, set off an earthquake in me. Surprise and pride and confusion and love for the man I worshipped. I stood to hide my reaction, and they both stood with me.

I hugged my mother. "I'd kill you if I lived with you. Or you'd kill me. You know that. And as for Dad, no way. He's all yours."

She winked at me. As I hugged her again, I looked over her head to my dad. He winked at me too.

"Come on, boy," he said, giving me a friendly slap on my shoulder. "I'll walk you out. I still want to hear about how you handled the police."

"I didn't. I shut the hell up and let Dash do all the talking."

"Best thing you've said so far." Dad grinned and we ended up on the front steps. "I've been watching his career. He's a good example for you."

Well, duh. Dash never put a foot wrong, had closed major cases, and had the respect and trust of senior agents. My father was only one of them. "I'm learning as fast as I can," I promised.

He shook my hand and then surprised me by pulling me in for a brief hug. "You're doing fine. I'm proud of you."

Mom was beaming in the door. "So sweet!"

I ducked my head, and Dad turned away too. That was enough emotion for both of us.

"Come tomorrow. I'll give you leftovers. Cold lamb. Delicious!"

"Thanks, Mom. I'll try. See you at work, Dad."

"Bye, Rhys. See you tomorrow."

FIVE

CYN

I WAS DOING AN IMPROMPTU SOCIOLOGICAL SURVEY IN THE hospital waiting room.

This was a huge place. Patients for several services, including Maddy for neurology, ended up here, waiting in long rows for someone to summon them back into the labyrinth of the hospital. There was a magazine rack near the check-in desk and a few copies of today's newspaper scattered about. But most people didn't so much as glance at them. Print publications were on the wane. Instead, we were all always buried in our phones.

Even Maddy, who thought her phone was a deck of cards half the time, was distracted from her magazine, which lay forgotten in her lap. She was happily watching a little blond girl giggling with her mother. Any minute now, either Maddy or the child would notice the colorful fish tank on the far wall, and then they'd both be off to investigate.

Next to me, Belinda was making another call. These days, a communicable disease specialist's work was never done.

I'd pulled up an old favorite on my phone's e-book reader, but it hadn't held my attention. I was checking my email, more to be in the digital groove with the rest of the waiting room than because I was expecting anything interesting to show up in my inbox, when Maddy spotted the fish tank. Off she went, and I smiled to see her so fascinated. Nothing was going to distract her . . . until something distracted her. The little girl spotted her and was right on Maddy's heels.

The mother and I exchanged nods. We were both going to be keeping half an eye on our charges.

My emails were about what I expected. My mother had sent another photo of my sister's adorable two-year-old, along with a few hopeful lies about how well my brother was doing in his new sales job at Yahoo. I was privately betting he wouldn't last more than a few months.

The University of Florida, Yale, and Columbia were all hopeful I'd make a donation to their alumni funds. That was pretty bold of Columbia, given that I'd dropped out of the PhD program when Don's mother was diagnosed with Alzheimer's-related dementia.

Rose had gone through a far more typical dementia progression than Maddy had, sinking into fear and anger before becoming entirely lost in the fog of her own mind. My sorrowful and challenging time taking care of Rose made Maddy's joy all the sweeter.

Maddy and the little girl had found low step stools that gave them both a better view into the fish tank. Maddy helped the girl up before climbing on her own perch.

Then I saw the email. Speak of the devil. Don had sent me a message.

It had been months since I'd heard from him last. Once the papers were signed and our divorce was final, Don had neatly plucked me from his life. I was no longer a part of his world, when once he'd been all of mine.

The last time he'd gotten in touch was to remind me to change my emergency contact information in my phone. Operating in the post-divorce numbness, I'd obeyed his text. I took him out, put in my sister's information—so far away in Florida—and then I'd spent an entire evening sobbing. There may be a more vulnerable feeling than knowing the nearest person who cared about you was hundreds of miles away, but if so, I didn't want to know what it was.

My finger hovered uncertainly over his message. What did he want this time?

And did I really want to read it?

Was it going to hurt again?

Perhaps my revenge fantasies had come true, and he needed me to rescue him.

Would I?

Trapped in anxiety and indecision, I couldn't even open the message. With great relief, I realized Belinda was finishing up her call. I felt the rush of a near miss. *Phew. Can't look now—must talk to Belinda. I'll deal with that email . . . um . . . later. Later will be good.*

Belinda set her phone in her lap. "Good. That's taken care of. I'm glad I got that done before the neurologist could see you, Mother."

She was shuffling papers back into her carry-all and it took her a moment to realize Maddy was no longer seated by her side.

"It's okay." I put my hand on her forearm as she rose in a panic. "I've got her. She's at the fish tank." I nodded to Maddy and her little friend, both exclaiming over the brightly colored fish.

"Oh, Jesus. I thought I'd lost her. I never even saw her go. I'm terrible at this."

"No, you're not," I soothed. "You're trying to do your job and watch your mom. It's a lot. Don't worry about it. That's why I'm here."

"But you're reading." She nodded to my phone. "And you still tracked her."

"That's my job."

"I'm damned glad of it too."

Belinda was always busy, it seemed. She was heading for retirement, she'd told me, but there was still too much more to do in world health. She'd said she'd feel guilty if she stopped working now. I thought she was the kind of leader our world desperately needed. And at this point, she was the closest thing I had to a best friend. Surely I should have other friends?

"What are you reading?" she asked me.

Certainly not Don's mysterious bomb of an email. What book was on the reader again? "It's Calvert's *Moorish Remains in Spain*. A classic."

"Is Calvert your PhD advisor?"

"No," I smiled. "He died back in the '40s. My PhD advisor probably thinks I died too."

"You'll get back to it," Belinda said with more confidence in me than I had in myself. I made a noncommittal sound in response. "Oh, jeez. Where is she now?"

"Toy corner. See? She's helping the little girl with the maze." Belinda heaved a sad sigh that made me want to soothe her concerns. "Go back to your phone calls. Really. I'm watching her."

"I don't know how you do it," she admitted. "My heart breaks a little more every time she doesn't know who I am, or loses track of a conversation, or thinks Daddy is still alive. And then it's like she's still in there somewhere and I can talk to her—for about ten seconds. It's shattering me. How do you stand it?"

"Like I said. It's easier for me. She's not my mother; I never knew her any other way. And I told you about my mother-in-law." Belinda nodded. The experience I'd earned while caring for Rose as she was dying was the reason Belinda had hired me in the first place. "Maddy is an absolute joy in comparison. Was she always a happy person?"

Belinda frowned. "Well . . . I guess so. Not happy all the time like now, but mostly—yeah. She was optimistic. Positive. She was so good for my father. He was as serious as you can get. Totally what you'd expect from a tenured linguistics professor. His pajamas practically had leather patches on the elbows. You know the type? But Mother could make him laugh out loud." Her smile was wistful.

"She's happy all the time now."

As if to punctuate my words, Maddy laughed, her giggle mixing with the little girl's. They were having a wonderful time together.

"I watch her," I said, "and I think I should be more like her. She's got a lot to teach me. You know how long something bothers her?" Belinda shook her head. "Until her next thought. She doesn't brood or worry over anything. And everything she sees is filled with wonder and joy. What if you and I could live like that?"

Belinda and I were both lost in the vision. She was probably thinking about a world where health was abundant. She's a hero. I was thinking about a world in which I could lay down my rage and pain from the divorce, and my confusion about Don. The rat bastard. I wished he had never sent me the email, which I was dreading. It had rapidly become a monster under the bed.

"Well"—Belinda gathered herself mentally—"at least I know she's happy. And thanks to you, I know she's safe."

"We're hoping. I'm telling you, that incident with the gun . . ." I remembered the bright white glare of my panic in the grocery store, and then I was apologizing to Belinda again.

She wouldn't hear a word of it. "Let's wait and see what the neurologist has to say. If she's become violent or unstable, then we'll deal with it."

"Who is violent? Who's unstable?" Maddy had appeared back in her seat without Belinda noticing. She laughed when Belinda jumped.

"Mother! You've got to stop creeping around like that! I should bell you. Like a cat."

"I'd be a good cat. And if I wanted to hunt birds, I'd take that bell right off."

BELINDA AND I WENT WITH MADDY WHEN SHE WAS CALLED, but the neurological team sent us back to the waiting area.

"She'll look to you for answers, and she'll read the right responses on your faces," the tech told us. According to her badge, her name was Kelsey, although she hadn't bothered to introduce herself.

"All right," Belinda said nervously, "but you have to watch her. She's turned into an escape artist. Like a cat."

"I'm going to get a bell," Maddy agreed.

"Ma'am," Kelsey said, with what I thought was an unnecessarily patronizing air, "this isn't my first dementia patient. You can leave her in our care with complete confidence. She'll be fine. When the doctor is ready to discuss our findings, he'll call you back."

She all but closed the door in our faces. We were dismissed. I laughed when, on the way back to the waiting area, Belinda whispered, "Now I hope Mother makes a break for it."

"That'd show old Kelsey!"

We giggled together and trekked back through the maze to the waiting area, only making two wrong turns along the way.

We knew the tests would take at least an hour, and Belinda had gotten back to work. There was no one for me to keep an eye on. There were no excuses. It was time to face Don's email.

I still had a hard time opening it. I'd yet to decide what I hoped it would say. Did I want him back? Did I want him dead? Did I want something—anything—in between?

I told myself it was okay; I didn't have to have the answers yet. Seven months wasn't long in geological terms. A redwood wouldn't grow very much in seven months. The continents would still drift apart on their tectonic plates, the Acropolis would weather slightly in the pollution, Venice would sink a bit more into the canals. But it'd take extremely precise instruments to measure the difference .

. .

So why should I assume I was qualified to make a reasonable assessment of my marriage—what it meant to me, what I needed from it—in a mere seven months? There was no way I had enough perspective yet.

But this was stalling, plain and simple. Either Don wanted me back or he didn't. But I still hadn't decided. Did *I* want *Don* back?

I'd been so socially stunted when I met Don. Too many university degrees, too few friends. He was the only one who'd seen the woman inside the virgin, and I was almost desperately grateful to him for it. But an impartial observer would no doubt note that our relationship and marriage coincided with alarming consistency with his mother's decline and death. And now I needed to face some bitter questions.

Had he married a caregiver so he wouldn't have to hire one?

Had he seen the woman inside the virgin at all?

Did I have any value to him beyond my patience with his mother?

I suppose it made sense that if you poked at a sore spot for long enough, something would snap. That tiny flicker of anger flared bright again. And anger is a far more tolerable emotion than sorrow or shame. What good had Don ever done for me?

Did he like my brain? Did he admire my intelligence? Did he value my company? Did I like to be with him? Did he make me happy? Or was he just the first person to look me in the eye?

My brain was a gerbil running on a wheel in a lab while indifferent scientists made notes on clipboards. Hm. *Very interesting.*

Suddenly the tension was more than I could bear. I opened the damned email and read it.

Lunch.

Don wanted to have lunch on Tuesday. He was suggesting a restaurant near me.

And the bastard gave no clue as to why. Fortunately, all that did was burn away the anxiety and leave me with some nice, comfortable anger. I sneered at my phone.

"Belinda," I said. She was nose-deep in a white paper. "Can I have Tuesday afternoon off?"

"Sure." She reached for her phone. "I'll get the service to take Maddy. Take the rest of the day too. Don't come home until very late, after having a wild experience like a young girl should have. What are you doing hanging around with two old fuddy-duddies anyway?"

She made me laugh. "You're the least fuddy of all the duddies, I promise you that!"

"Thank you. I'm honored. What are you doing on Tuesday?"

Any attempt to appear cool and capable melted in the face of her warmth. I told her about Don's lunch invitation. We'd talked about Don before, and Belinda was kind enough to discuss the implications. "Do you want him back?" she asked.

I shrugged. "I don't know. He hurt me pretty badly. But I—I don't seem to know who I am without him."

"Time will heal that," she said stoutly. "You don't need him. You don't need anyone. Except your friends. Maddy and me."

I didn't resist this time and reached for her, giving her a one-armed hug. My eyes were damp. Hers might have been too, because she stood and made an excuse about going to use the bathroom—and when she got there, I heard her yip in surprise when she opened the door.

"Mother! What are you doing in here?"

Maddy appeared in the doorway, holding out her cell phone. "Look what I found in my pocket! What is this, dear?"

"Mother, that's your cell phone."

Maddy laughed delightedly. "Sweetheart, this isn't a phone. Look at it! Don't be so silly!"

A harassed Kelsey appeared, huffing down the hallway. "Oh. My. God," she spat in irritation. "Where have you been?"

She tried to take Maddy by the arm but instead found herself face to face with Dr. Belinda Root, World Health Organization epidemiologist and eminent leader in communicable and infectious diseases.

"Did I improperly express to you that you needed to watch my mother carefully?" Belinda's rage was all the more magnificent for her icy control.

"No, ma'am," sputtered Kelsey. "I only left her alone for a second—"

"A second. I think it must have been longer than that."

Maddy had spotted me and was toddling over, a delighted smile on her face. I intercepted her and herded her back. Belinda hadn't noticed Maddy was missing yet, and it'd weaken Belinda's position if she lost her mother while thoroughly chewing out Kelsey for losing her mother.

"You'd better take me to your supervisor immediately."

"Oh, ma'am—please. Mrs. Root—"

"*Doctor* Root," Belinda clarified with focused intensity. Kelsey whimpered.

"That's my name, too!" Maddy chirped in. "Not doctor—but I'm a Root! Well, I'm a Carteret, but I married a Root. Oh, he's just the nicest man. So serious. And so sweet." She grinned happily at me and I smiled back.

"I'll take her now," Kelsey said, all but groveling. "And I'll watch her. We have a few more tests, and then I know Dr. Krishnamurthi will want to speak with you." She edged nervously between Belinda and me to gently draw Maddy's arm through hers. "We're going to have a lovely time, aren't we, Miss Maddy? Want to play some more games?"

"Oh, yes. I love games! Do you want to play bridge? I have a deck of cards here."

"A deck of—oh. I see. Very nice. Ha, ha. Maybe not bridge. I have some other games—"

Maddy toddled down the hall, with Kelsey looking back nervously over her shoulder as they went. She scuttled her charge around the corner, and Belinda turned to me with a face-splitting grin. "Do you know, I feel a great deal better now."

"I'll bet!"

MADDY APPEARED ONCE MORE, UNANNOUNCED. BELINDA AND I were meeting with Dr. Krishnamurthi in his office. He was telling us that based on the tests they'd run so far, Maddy showed no signs at all of the paranoia, anger, or fear that most dementia patients grow into, and no evidence of delusions.

"She remains one of the few lucky ones who is affected in an entirely positive manner by her condition," he was saying to us. "And she's quite delightful as a result, I must say—"

Suddenly the delight appeared in the door.

"Oh, hello!" Maddy cried when she saw us blinking at her in astonishment. "How lovely to find all three of you together! Are you having a party?"

"Mother," said Belinda helplessly.

"Mrs. Root!" Dr. Krishnamurthi rose to his feet with a courtly air and took her gently by the elbow. "Aren't you supposed to be with my lab tech, Kelsey?"

"Who, dear? I'm sorry. I don't know that person." Kelsey, I thought, probably hadn't introduced herself to Maddy either. Or, to be fair, perhaps she had. But it seemed unlikely.

The doctor offered Maddy his own chair and then hissed into the phone until a frantic Kelsey appeared in the doorway.

"It wasn't me! She was with Debra!"

"We'll discuss it later." The doctor froze her with his glare. "Please take Mrs. Root to the cognitive lab. Stay with her while she completes her games. Then bring her back to me. Do that now," he said firmly, overriding her protests. She hung her head.

"Yes, Doctor."

Maddy went with her happily, charmed to meet her. Kelsey was not so charmed.

———

THE DOCTOR HIMSELF TOOK THE TIME TO LEAD US BACK TO THE waiting area, assuring us that Maddy's foray into gunplay was more likely a situation of circumstance and not any advancement in her disease that he could see.

Belinda and I sat again, discussing whether we needed to make any changes in Maddy's supervision, when we saw a frantic Kelsey move at a pace that meant she wished to run but didn't want to seem like she was in a hurry.

Belinda sighed. "Madcap Maddy. They've lost her again."

"She's really, really good at it." I felt a burst of admiration and affection for our escapee.

"Don't I know it. Mother is probably doing stand-up comedy in an operating room. To thunderous applause. Okay. You go that way; I'll go this way."

"Right. Stay in touch. Use the deck of cards in your pocket to call when you find her."

Belinda's laughter floated behind her.

SIX

RHYS

Graduating from law school was only one of the possible routes into the FBI, but it was the one that appealed to me the most. However, no one said I had to pass the bar. That was my idea. And I'd come to regret it.

Once Dash found out I actually was a lawyer (and not just a thoroughly overprepared law school grad), he'd been delightedly making a point of assigning me every tedious legal matter. Today I'd driven out of DC to the Alexandria Federal Courthouse to file papers. It sounded easy. But in fact, it involved a lot of bureaucracy and standing in unmoving lines. You'd think the FBI badge would at least buck me to the head of the crowd, but no such luck. Everyone in a courthouse thinks they deserve priority.

Then I was spotted in the halls by the judge we'd pulled on the Phelps case. He wanted an update on how we were doing with the subpoenas he'd signed for us.

By the time I made it out of the courthouse, my head was aching and I was dreaming of the aspirin I kept stashed in the glove box. Should have brought them in with me.

I was sitting in the underground parking garage, waiting for the aspirins to kick in and enjoying the darkness, when my phone rang.

Trust a federal courthouse to have wired their garage for good cell reception. Is there no place on earth where you can hide anymore?

Caller ID gave me no name. I didn't know who it was, but at least I knew who it wasn't, and it wasn't anyone named Dash Ashwood calling to tell me to head back in the courthouse for more legal fuss and froth.

"Hello, this is Agent Jones," I said.

A cheerful voice, brimming over with mirth, answered me. "Agent Jones? Oh, I see! Is this my sweet Peanut Butter Cup?"

"Ms. Maddy?" I asked, smiling. I still had flashbacks to losing control of my gun, but I could hear that megawatt grin in her voice, and I couldn't help the wave of affection I felt for her.

"Yes. It's Maddy! How nice that you recognize me!"

That made me laugh. I'd hardly forget her. "Well, you make quite an impression on a guy."

"Smooth talker. Aren't you the charmer! Why did you call me, dear?"

I blinked at the phone. I hadn't gotten confused, had I? Surely she'd called me?

"Why, I wanted to see how you were doing after your recent trip to the grocery store and the police station, ma'am."

"The police station? Oh, you're such a tease! I'm not at the police station. Am I?"

I felt a tickle of unease. She sounded alert and coherent, but not knowing where she was had raised my hackles. "Is your friend with you?" No sense pretending to myself that I hadn't memorized her name. It was Cynthia Grace Quimby. Cyn of the dazzling tropical-waters eyes. "Where's Cyn?"

"Well, do you know? I'm not quite sure."

Uh-oh.

"Are you at home, Miss Maddy?"

"Oh, goodness no, you silly boy!" Her delighted laughter wasn't easing my growing anxiety. A dementia sufferer out of safe care is no joke.

"Can you tell me where you are, ma'am?"

"I'm in a coffee shop. It's very nice here. The lady behind the counter gave me a cup of coffee. Isn't that sweet? I don't seem to have my purse with me."

"How nice of her. I wonder. Would you be willing to hand the phone to her?"

"The phone, dear? I don't have a phone."

"Hand her what's in your hand. Will you do that?"

"All right, dear. If you like."

Soon I was talking with a curious barista named Carla, who told me that Maddy had wandered in alone. She was in a Starbucks in the Inova Fairfax Hospital, about fifteen minutes from where I was sitting. I started my car and pulled out.

"Carla, will you keep an eye on her for me? I'm going to call her family, and I'll be right there. And I'll pay you back for the coffee."

"Okay. She's really sweet."

"Yeah. She's a love. But she has dementia, so help me keep her safe, will you? If she wants to leave, offer her a pastry. I'll buy."

"Got it."

My next call was to Dash. I told him the situation and got him to look up Cyn's cell phone number for me.

"That's a long way to go to ask a girl out," he teased me.

"Come on—give me the number. Maddy's on her own."

I ignored the fact that I now had Cyn's phone number in my cell. That was not what was important here, I told myself. Sternly. To prove that I was a complete professional in my dealings with her, my call to Cyn was quick and to the point. "This is Agent Jones. We met a few days ago in the grocery store."

"Oh." Her awkwardness made me feel foolishly protective of her. "Agent Jones, I—"

"Are you missing anyone?"

"Oh, Jesus!" she replied.

"She's okay. She called me. She's in the Starbucks at Inova Fairfax."

"Thank God! We're at the hospital for an appointment. I just have to figure out where the Starbucks is. This place is huge..."

"I'm on the Beltway already. If I get there first, I'll call you. You call me if you find her. The barista is watching over her. Don't panic. She'll be okay."

"Thank you, Agent Jones! I'll call you back."

SHE DIDN'T CALL ME BACK, AND I TOOK THAT AS A GOOD SIGN. IF she hadn't found Maddy, she'd have sent up a red flag and I'd have been one of the people she called. Since she hadn't called, I assumed she'd found her wandering charge and was reassuring herself that Maddy was unharmed.

My assumptions were correct. By the time I arrived, Cyn and an older woman were hunched over a table, trying to make sense of what Maddy was telling them.

My pace slowed and the tightness in my chest eased. I paused in the entrance to assess the situation.

I've been trained in observation and analysis, and that training did not fail me now. I saw that Cyn's eyes were even more beautiful than I had remembered. I saw the arch of her neck as she looked from Maddy to the other woman at their table. I saw that as she leaned forward, Cyn crushed one of her perfect breasts casually, cruelly against the table as if it wasn't even important.

My rational analysis told me that the circumstances were calm —and that it was time to admit I wanted to do more than paint Cyn. A lot more.

But that was hardly useful at the moment. I gave myself a mental scolding and checked in with the barista. "Are you Carla?" She nodded. "Thanks for watching her. What do I owe you?"

"Nothing," she said. "That's one nice old lady."

"That's one nice barista."

My best smile just made her blink. Maybe I was losing my

touch with the ladies. A flash of insecurity zapped me and I crushed it, smiling as I moved forward.

"I'm guessing everything is okay here," I said by way of greeting.

Cyn looked up with a flash of gratitude and gestured for me to sit with them. She introduced me to Maddy's daughter, Dr. Root. Daughter was taller than mother. Elegant. Patrician. They had the same coloring. You wouldn't have to change palettes to paint them both, but Dr. Root was more square, more upright. More than coloring, though, the difference was in attitude. Dr. Root was oil paints where Maddy was watercolors.

And when I greeted Maddy, I put one hand over my service weapon, in its holster under my coat. "Maddy, you're not getting my pistol today."

"Bet I could if I wanted to!" Her grin was undeniably cocky, and I made sure the retaining strap was firmly in place. There would be no more loss of weaponry. Ever.

"Now, what's going on?" I asked in mock severity.

Dr. Root said that Maddy told them "a nice man" was taking her to her next round of tests. "But she can't remember how they got separated, and she doesn't remember his name."

"Whose name?" Maddy asked brightly.

"The man who was taking you for your tests," Cyn offered.

"Do you mean Mac?" Maddy asked.

"Was his name Mac?"

"Was whose name Mac, dear?"

"The man taking you for your tests."

"What tests?"

Belinda gave up. "I'm not sure."

"Well, then I don't know how I'm supposed to know either!" Maddy regarded us all with a happy air. "Doesn't this coffee smell marvelous? Would you like some?"

"It's been like that since we found her," Cyn sighed. "We still might get more out of her, but I'm inclined to believe she followed the smell of coffee and ended up here."

"Are there any men named Mac in the department you were visiting?" I asked.

"I certainly intend to find out," Dr. Root said darkly. The loving daughter had been subsumed into the righteous authoritarian. She'd already notified the Bureau that she wouldn't be suing for the gun incident, and looking at her now, I was glad I was off the hook. No big game hunter ever looked more resolved. Let it be another head than mine stuffed and mounted on the wall of her book-lined den.

"Look!" Maddy cried happily. "It's the Peanut Butter Cup!"

Even Carla the barista looked interested. "Hi, Maddy." I smiled. "She calls me that because my first name is Rhys," I explained to Dr. Root.

"Like a Reese's Peanut Butter Cup!" Maddy couldn't have been more pleased. "How many boxes of condoms did you need today, Peanut Butter Cup?"

The barista was definitely more interested. "Maddy," I sighed.

"Thank you for your help, Agent Jones," Cyn interrupted. "I'm so grateful you called." I could have kissed her for her intervention. Well, at least I'd pretend it was her intervention. The woman had distinctly kissable lips.

I put my rational mind back in the driver's seat and set aside the thinking with the little head. "My pleasure. Since everything worked out, I'm going to get back to work now. You keep my number in your phone, Maddy."

"In my phone? Oh, you're so silly!"

I winked at the barista, shook hands with Dr. Root, and restrained myself from lifting Cyn's chin with my hand so I could see those eyes looking at me once more.

Time to get back to defending our nation.

SEVEN
MADDY

"So, I want you to tell me if you think you're having a delusion."

The older lady in the kitchen is watching me, so I smile at her. She looks pleasant, if concerned, and I'd like to see her smile. Certainly there are reasons to smile—there are delicious smells coming from the stove. I'd like something to eat. Something that smells so good. That would be very nice.

She sighs. "It's not worth even saying, is it?"

"What do you mean, my dear?"

She's sad. I put a comforting hand over hers on the counter. She looks quite a lot like Azariah. She might be one of his relatives. I'm so glad she's come to visit. Azariah will be home soon. He'll be so pleased to see her.

"All right." She heaves a sigh and sets her shoulders. "Cyn says I should just go with it. Lunch is in the oven. It will be ready soon. Would you like to eat on the balcony, Mother? I mean—Maddy? It's a lovely day. If you button up your sweater, I'm sure you'll be warm enough. Bring your tea."

I'm already reaching for the cup in front of me. I take a sip and all the flavors burst in my mouth, making me sigh in happiness. "This is so good. Thank you!"

"You're welcome. The balcony?"

"What about it, dear?"

"Would you like to sit out there to have our lunch?"

"That sounds nice." I look at her. She's tall, but thin. "You might need a sweater."

"Good idea." She slips into a light jacket.

"Oh, I like that color on you, Belinda. Don't you look nice!"

She's startled. "Thank you, Mother. Cyn says you often have your breakfast out here. I thought we could have lunch instead, since the sun has come out. It's nice, isn't it?"

"Yes, lovely." The sunlight on my face is a benediction. I close my eyes in bliss. It warms me, first across my cheekbones and then all over, like an enormous hug. "Where is Cyn?"

"She has the afternoon off. Instead of hiring someone from the agency, I thought I'd take the afternoon off so you and I can spend some time together."

"That's lovely, dear! And where is Cyn?"

Belinda is considering her answer. "Her ex-husband invited her to lunch."

"Who?"

Belinda sighs. "Which who do you mean? Damn. Now I'm doing it. Cyn is having lunch with her husband."

"Sin is having lunch with her husband." A wordplay! I laugh in delight. "Now, to whom would Sin be married? Don't tell me: Sin's husband is Evil. Or, no—Bad Intent."

"Cyn meaning Cynthia. She takes care of you, remember?"

"Why would I remember someone I don't know, dear?"

"Right. Okay. Isn't it pretty out here? Are you warm enough?"

"Warm as toast. Isn't the sun brilliant today? Sun in autumn. It's so delicious. And I have a cup of tea! It's so good. Do you want some?"

"I have some here." She seems tired. I don't know why. The sky is brilliant blue and the sunshine is heaven-sent. It's lovely out here.

A phone rings.

"Damn," says the older woman next to me. "I left my phone inside. Are you all right out here by yourself?"

It makes me giggle. "What trouble could I get up to on a balcony?"

"I'm sure I don't know." She sighs as she goes in. "I'll keep an eye on you from inside. I'll be right back."

"Take your time, Ginny. It's lovely here. My, this tea is good!"

But it's not but the blink of an eye before he appears.

The Oatmeal Man.

"Maddy," he hisses at me. "Let's talk about hiding places."

"I'm not scared of you this time, you sneaking rat!" I shake my fist at him and baptize my sweater with tea. "Are you talking about where you're going to hide when I come after you with a gun again?"

He seems startled by this. "You bitch. Are you faking this dementia? You are, aren't you? I knew it. Crafty old bat."

"Watch your language, young man. And what is the matter with that jacket?"

"What's the matter with it?" His rage is towering. I begin to feel small. "You shot it, that's what! Look at that hole!" His big hands form into fists. "You're going to pay for that."

"I don't know what you're talking about. Why are you yelling at me? Azariah! Azariah, come out here!"

I call, but my husband doesn't come, and I don't like being this afraid. The Oatmeal Man is glaring at me like the very most horrible bad dream. What does Mother say to do when I have a nightmare? I put my head down on my knees and try not to cry. "It's not real. It's not real," I chant.

"Mother!"

There's a lady beside me, her hand on my back. I sit up. "Where is he?"

"Who, Mother?"

"That man!" He has vanished.

"There's no one here, Mother. I was watching the whole time."

"There wasn't?"

"You were calling for Daddy. Did you see him, Mother?"

"What?"

"You've spilled your tea. Let's go in. We'll change your clothes. Tell me what you saw, Mother."

"Belinda?" She helps me inside and closes the sliding doors behind us. The click of the thumb latch makes me feel better. "Hello, dear. When did you get home?"

She doesn't answer, and as she helps me change my sweater, she mumbles to herself. "What did you say, sweetheart?"

"I said I'm going to go with it. But you're not going to be out of my sight today."

"Won't that be lovely!"

EIGHT
CYN

I CLOSED MY EYES, TRYING AND FAILING TO BLOT OUT MY world. The clatter of china and silverware at the restaurant still played like the soundtrack to my own personal tragedy. The longing for a glass of wine still whispered its false promises in my head. The scent of Don's cologne—the cologne I had given him for Christmas mere months before he casually shook apart our lives— it was all still there, and two thin eyelids weren't enough to make it all go away. I was nothing more than an out-and-out fool. Self-loathing filled me.

"Babe. Did you hear me?"

I was shaking my head in negation. Anything to erase the words he'd said.

"I'm getting married, Cynthia. Babe. At least acknowledge that you heard me."

I inhaled slowly through my nose. "I heard you, Don."

"I didn't think you'd be this upset. You knew it was over between you and me. I mean, the divorce is almost half a year old now."

Seven months and six days, not that I was counting. The fact that he *wasn't* counting triggered a flicker of anger that was quickly growing until it overrode my shame. He definitely didn't want me back, but maybe—just maybe—I didn't want him back, either. I opened my eyes and took him in.

Cute. Don was definitely cute—although now that my fury had overcome my shock and sadness, I could see that his nut-brown hair was slipping back off his forehead. His father was bald by the time he was forty, and maybe Don was heading that way. I felt a cruel rush of pleasure at the thought.

He reached forward and put his warm, male hand over my smaller, icy one. "Babe, you knew it was over. You didn't think I wanted to have lunch to get back together, did you?" He read my face. He'd always been able to read me. "Oh, babe. I'm so sorry."

A schoolteacher voice in my head announced internally that I had not yet reached a decision on whether I wanted Don back again. The voice was prim and entirely rational, and almost drowned out the shrieks of anger and upset coming from an imagined prisoner locked behind the thick stone walls in my soul.

Don, I realized, was almost secondary to what that screaming prisoner wanted. I wanted my life back. My identity. My sense of self. Now that I was once again unmarried and unloved, I had reverted back to a time when I'd felt perpetually like an outsider in my own life. If Don hadn't come along and swept me up, I wouldn't have known how warm and pleasing it was to be in orbit around someone. Now I knew, and the loss was still ripping at me.

I pulled my hand from under his. The cheeseburger was a cannonball in my stomach. I should have ordered the salmon salad, but Don had been so sure he could order for me that I'd stopped him and impulsively picked a meal that was apparently going to drag me to the bottom of the briny deep any minute now.

"It's not that I want you back," I tried, knowing that he wasn't going to buy it. "I just miss . . . us. Being part of a pair. Having— oh, you know. A life."

This was the kind of helpless, hopeless crap that came out of me when I was with Don, and I cringed even as I said it. But then, perhaps born of seven months smiling and laughing with a sweet old lady with dementia, I had a minor, earth-shaking epiphany.

Maybe it wasn't just me.

Maybe I was like this—pathetic and whining and desperate for attention—*because that was the way Don liked me to b*e.

I was frowning at him, the muscles between my eyebrows still aching because they were bunched into lines. But my mind was suddenly spinning. Was I letting Don play me? Was my self-esteem so low, even back when we met at Columbia, that he'd trained me over time to assume he was everything to me?

Which begged an important question: Was Don *anything* to me?

Don had an ego, no doubt. When we went out, he loved to order for me. He loved to tell me what to buy, what to wear, what to do to please him. And I'd let him. Whatever it took to stay in the sunshine of his good regard.

Hm.

Don loved knowing that he was the only reason I wasn't totally alone.

"Babe." He regarded me with concern—and now, I recognized, a hint of satisfaction too. "Did you sign up for online dating like I told you to?"

I winced. "I'm not ready."

"Babe, you need to do something to get over me. Let's talk about how I can help."

I needed to cut this conversation off. "Why did you want to meet with me? Why now?"

He gave me the puppy dog eyes. It was the same gaze he'd used when he had to work late, when his mother's caregiver service couldn't fill a shift, or when he admitted, regretfully, that he didn't really like what I'd cooked for dinner. It wasn't the cooking. It wasn't me. He just didn't like scallops, see?

"I wanted to tell you about the marriage in person. I thought it was only fair."

No, I realized. It wasn't fairness that he wanted. He wanted to make sure I'd be hurt by the news; he wanted to see the effect of his words. And I'd given him what he'd craved. I'd shown him my pain.

I put the overly emotional, screaming prisoner in my brain on lockdown and straightened my spine. I offered my ex-husband what I hoped was a suitably chilly half-smile. "So you're getting married. Tell me about her."

This was, I reflected distantly, a terrible change of subject. I definitely didn't want to know more about the woman who was taking my "Mrs. Kempthorne" name.

"You don't know her. Her name is Dahlia. She's sweet. You'd like her."

"I doubt it," I muttered.

"I told her—it's my second marriage. I don't want a big wedding. But you know women." Either he'd forgotten who he was talking to, or he was deliberately rubbing my nose in the details. I knew which option I thought was more likely. "She wants the full deal. Church wedding, gown with a train, lots of bridesmaids, big reception, honeymoon in Hawaii." He smiled fondly. He and I had been married by a justice of the peace at City Hall.

"Sounds expensive."

His mood changed and he shifted uneasily in his seat. "Oh. Right. I didn't tell you."

Warning sirens went off in my head. The prim school librarian and the prisoner both quieted down, fixated on his words. My heart sank. More bad news was coming, and I braced.

"Tell me what?"

"Denbigh Construction. It turns out they got the government contract after all."

I froze. He at least had the decency to look embarrassed.

"Don. Are you telling me that"—I gaped, trying to get my mind around the enormity of his deception—"you took all the money you inherited from your mother and invested it in a company that mysteriously went bankrupt before the divorce courts assessed our net worth, and now that things are finalized, the company suddenly gets a big contract?" My veins were icy, and my head was suddenly far too hot. Thermal regulation offline.

"Not all of the money," he tried to protest.

"Don. You hid your assets. You hid your assets, and *then* you divorced me."

"Babe!"

My focus was complete. I saw him. I truly saw him. Not the man I thought I'd married, not the center of my life. But the lowlife scum in front of me. Reaching deep, I pulled out the first, worst thing I could think of. "You skunk." It wasn't very original, but the contempt, I thought coldly, came through nicely.

"I paid off all your college loans, babe."

"*We* paid them off. You and me together. And then you invested the rest."

"It was an honest mistake."

"An honest mistake." I shook my head in stunned disbelief. "Well, I'll be calling my lawyer. We can have a reassessment, you know."

He regarded me with the full puppy dog pout. For once, it moved me not at all. "Please don't do that, babe."

"Don't call me *babe*. You know I hate that."

"Cynthia. Don't do that. Dahlia has two young kids."

I goggled at him. "What does that have to do with me?" He fumbled for an answer. "Why should I care about some stranger's children?"

"Because"—he finally sicked up the last dregs of his depravity —"because they're my kids too."

The cannonball in my stomach rolled. It was threatening to come back up.

"Don." I couldn't think of a single additional thing to say.

"Babe, stay calm now."

"Don." I was dizzy sitting in my chair. I was having a hard time fitting the pieces together.

"Um, drink some water, or something."

"I don't want water." An icy coldness flowed over me—a mercy. "How old?"

At least he had the decency to ape the more obvious signs of shame. He hung his head. "Cassidy is six and Donny is two."

No advanced degree necessary to do that math. "So. You had a child with her before we married, and another during our marriage."

He nodded.

"And she wants you to marry her at last. How come?" I regarded him coldly. He didn't even need to answer. I saw Dahlia's motivations as clearly as if she, too, were sitting at our table. "Your mother died, you got the money, and baby number three is on the way, isn't it?"

Don evaded my stare, looking out the window as if something fascinating was happening on the street. "You're expecting your third child with her, and you're suddenly rich again." I studied my hands. Remarkably, they weren't shaking. Good. I folded my napkin and rose. "Goodbye, Don."

He leapt to his feet and grabbed my arm. "What are you going to do, babe?"

"Take your hand off me. Immediately."

He must have seen something in my eye that he wasn't used to seeing. He stepped back, and I managed to make it to the street and around the corner before bursting into tears.

He'd met me at a restaurant near Belinda and Maddy's condo, which was in a new and very hip neighborhood in North Arlington. Nice people lived there—the kind of people who might, for example, stop a crying woman on the street and ask her if she needed any help.

I waved all three of them off, trying to smile my thanks for their kindness without actually being able to see through my tears. I ended up in a coffee shop where a kind barista kept me in paper napkins and a bottle of water until I could pull myself together.

The truth slowly grew over me like a blinding, blood-soaked sunrise. Everything I'd assumed about my marriage had been a lie. Not just the end of it, when he astonished me by telling me he'd filed for divorce. But even the previous years when I stupidly thought we'd been happy. He'd left me at home to care for his angry, fearful mother while he ducked the noose of being an Alzheimer's caregiver and went off to his true love and their happy family.

Every time he said he'd be late.

Every time he had to travel over the weekend.

It all came back to me now, with a completely different spin. And it left me—that was the right word for it: it left me spinning.

I felt like a fool. And I felt angry.

I'd been duped. I'd let myself be duped.

After my tears had run out, I pulled out my phone. It weighed more than a cemetery headstone. The divorce lawyer's number was right there. Right under my finger. All I had to do was call him—and I would. But I simply couldn't bring myself to hit the number yet. I needed a little time to rebalance my soul and get my confused feet back under me.

I couldn't go back to Belinda and Maddy's yet. Belinda had insisted I take the rest of the day to "do something fun." Perhaps she, too, was hoping that Don was coming to offer some big, romantic move. Ha. The idea now seemed so naive, so childlike.

I couldn't stay in the coffee shop. I'd probably already driven off all their customers by sobbing in the corner, facing a trendy brick wall and hiccupping.

I couldn't call my mother—or my sister, my purported emergency contact—to announce an emergency. What could they do to help me? Nothing.

It was time to decide if seven months of hiding and coasting and keeping numb had given me time to heal. Was I going to curl up and die? Or did I have more spine than that?

Did I, in short, have any self-worth at all?

This was a tiny turning point. This was the first moment when I could make the smallest, weakest choice. I wouldn't let Don's rejection crush me.

I decided that I needed a mental break.

I needed art therapy.

Not exactly Caesar crossing the Rubicon, but in its own way, this was me committing to myself. I decided I deserved some happiness. There was an exhibit I'd been wanting to see at the Smithsonian's National Gallery of Art—*Baroque Art in Genoa*. Lord knows I'd studied the art and architecture of the period with a fervor that now seemed so desperately far away.

But the Smithsonian was a good place to hide. The National Gallery was very soothing. I'd found calm and peace there before. Plus, gorgeous art. It was a nice place to retreat from the confusion and anger I couldn't quite face yet—and it was a place that would make me happy. I could go without excuse or explanation to anyone.

I knew the bus route into the city. There was a stop right across the street from Belinda's building. I was sitting on the bench, grateful that I'd finally stopped crying, when I realized I was looking into the car of the man from Winchester, who Maddy had shot at earlier in the week.

And he was pulling out of the residents' garage in Belinda's building.

He drove past me, unseeing. Was it that guy? Or someone who looked like him? I couldn't be sure. And I clearly wasn't at my best.

Still, while I waited for the bus, I texted the number on the card Agent Dash Ashwood had given me. And yes, I thought about texting Agent Gorgeous, but he was so out of my league, and I was feeling so low that I couldn't face even the memory of his golden beauty.

Agent Ashwood, this is Cynthia Quimby. We
met on Tuesday when my friend Maddy (the
one with dementia) shot at a guy at the grocery
store. I'm sorry to bother you. I know you're
busy. I think I saw the man Maddy shot at
coming out of Maddy's building just now. Is
that interesting? I'm not sure it was him. It was
probably nothing.

I sat in the weak autumn sunshine, waiting for the bus and wishing I had more tissues with which to blow my nose. My throat was tired from crying, and my eyes felt like they were bugging out. I felt hollow. But surprisingly, I did not feel completely pathetic. I was going to have an afternoon of art. I was going to take care of myself.

A text message pinged in from Agent Ashwood.

I remember you, Ms. Quimby. Give me
a moment, please.

He could take all day, for all I cared. The longer I thought about it, the less sure I was that I'd seen the guy from Winchester, whose name I couldn't remember.

The bus had arrived, and we were rolling our slow way across the landscape to end up on the National Mall when a new text arrived. New number. Not Agent Ashwood.

Ms. Quimby, it's Agent Jones. You might
know me as the Peanut Butter Cup.

Great. It was the pretty one. I'd have tensed up automatically, except his text made me smile.

Hello, PBC. I didn't mean to bother

you or Agent Ashwood.

Don't worry about it. You saw
Barry Gambert in Maddy's
building?

Barry Gambert. Yes, that was the name.

I honestly don't know. He was coming
out of the resident's garage, so it probably
wasn't Barry. I thought I'd check in, just
in case. I know you've got more
important things to do.

If you could see what I was doing, you'd
realize you've thrown me a lifeline.

Why? What are you doing? Not
action-packed FBI stuff?

Financial research. Important. (Don't tell
anyone I said it was tedious.)

Ha!

I'll look into Barry's address and get back
to you. Can I text you in the next few hours?

Heading to the National Gallery now. Baroque
Art in Genoa. I think my cell phone will
work in there.

Great exhibit. You'll love it. I'll get back to you.

Thanks.

It was silly to feel excited about waiting for a text, but even the slightest attention from the Peanut Butter Cup was acting as an antidote to the rage that Don had inspired in me. Don had been having an affair for all four years of our marriage. And really, if he and Dahlia had a child even before Don and I married, then technically, I was the other woman.

Christ. I wanted to hide in a hole and withdraw completely. Or relieve Don of certain key pieces of his anatomy.

There had been times over the past seven months when I'd thought about moving home to Tallahassee, where my mother and father would greet me with warm, if confused, arms. They're lovely people. They just never understood how they managed to have such a book-learning daughter. They didn't know why I'd gotten all my degrees; they didn't understand my marriage. They certainly didn't understand why my marriage had ended—not that I had either, until now. *Dahlia,* I thought with venom.

I didn't begrudge my sister her happy marriage. My emergency contact had a darling baby and a loving husband and a home easily six hundred miles away from my existence. She knew who she was. My parents understood her. Her life made sense. It threw the disaster of my failed relationship into sharp relief. No, going home would be the ultimate failure, and I wasn't ready to concede yet.

I deserved something better, even if I didn't quite know what it was that I wanted. I strode into the museum, thinking that my visit was at least a good start.

The Peanut Butter Cup was right. The exhibit was wonderful. But more than looking at old masters, it was the architecture of the museum itself that soothed me.

High ceilings, stone walls, cool air, perfect lighting. By design, a museum is a place where emotions are contained. The passions and anger and envy and spite are neatly framed on canvas. You can examine them closely or walk on past. There is bliss in that.

I finished the exhibit and was planning on sitting for a moment in the equally serene garden courtyard.

And who was sitting on a nearby courtyard bench, waiting for me?

The Peanut Butter Cup himself.

NINE

RHYS

PHELPS HOLDING'S ACCOUNTS PROVED TO BE ENTIRELY fascinating. The guy was a wizard at hiding his ill-gotten gains. But that was academic. The subpoenas I'd scored were paying off. Phelps was good. I was better.

I was so deep into my investigations, hunched over my computers in my cubicle at FBI headquarters, that everything else had blurred into the background. Impromptu conversations in the aisles, formal meetings in the conference rooms, the hum of justice clocking busily around me was nothing. I didn't pay attention to the text alert tone from Dash's phone from his cubicle across the aisle—

—until he rolled his desk chair back and waved his phone at me. "Hey, lover boy," he called.

As conversation starters go, I had to admit that it did get my attention. "What? Are you talking to me?"

"I just got a text from your girlfriend."

Alison in Minneapolis? This confused me. Not only was she no longer my girlfriend, but why would she be texting Dash? A guy she'd never met?

He tossed me his phone. I fumbled it but caught it before the phone hit the carpet.

Nope. Not Alison. The delicious Cyn. *Hello.* She'd written to Dash about spotting the man Maddy had shot at. My eyebrows went up.

She wanted to know if spotting the guy was interesting. Yes, it was. I remembered the guy, and he'd been adamant that he'd never seen either woman before.

Also interesting because it was contact with Cyn. First fate (and a casual desire for a lunch of protein-rich scrambled eggs) had thrown us together at the grocery store. Then Maddy had called me when she'd wandered into the hospital Starbucks. And now Cyn was wondering if she'd seen something interesting, and Dash was playing Cupid.

But it was faintly embarrassing to have Dash grinning at me like he was capable of arranging my life. We were all just pieces on a large, Dash-sized chessboard to him. I tossed the phone back to him. "She texted you, not me."

He gave me a pretty-boy pout, clearly mocking me. "We can fix that."

He texted her back, and then threw me the phone again. This time I fielded it neatly and read the message asking her to "give him a minute."

"Go on," he said. "You're taking this one, not me. I'm far too busy with the Phelps case."

"What the hell do you think I'm working on?" I gestured to the laptop in front of me. "I'm tracking all these invoices. The guy is dirty."

"I know. Send me what you've got, and I'll take it. You go take her." He gestured with his chin to his phone. "You've got her number. Text her back. Take the rest of the day off. You've earned a break."

It felt awkward, but Cyn's eyes had been appearing with alarming regularity in my doodles. I was going to have to copy over some of the books I took notes in. Those could *not* be included in case records.

"You sure do want to get me laid," I grumbled as I tossed his phone back to him. He was not fooled. I wasn't hiding my pleasure at all well. I pulled up my notes on the case to refresh my memory. Cyn's number was in my phone, so I texted her, hoping that referring to myself as the "Peanut Butter Cup" would earn me her smile.

There was a pause and I saw with a jolt of pleasure the three dots that meant she was replying.

Hello, PBC. I didn't mean to bother
you or Agent Ashwood.

A little shy, a little retiring . . . but the "PBC" for Peanut Butter Cup was cute.

Don't worry about it. You saw
Barry Gambert in Maddy's
building?

I honestly don't know. He was coming out of the resident's garage, so it probably wasn't Barry. I thought I'd check in, just in case. I know you've got more important things to do.

She was definitely worth a mild bending of the truth, so I exaggerated my boredom a bit.

I kicked back in my chair as we texted back and forth, forgetting to suppress my satisfaction. This felt like a conversation. This felt like flirting. And I was in favor of that.

I got a swift buzz of electricity when she said she was heading to the National Gallery. She was going to my favorite DC museum, to see an exhibit that I'd loved. Clearly, she was the ideal woman.

We ended our conversation. I put my phone down, and of

course Dash was standing at my cubicle smirking at me. "I gather that went well," he said.

I raised my eyebrow and considered my words carefully. "She's the ideal woman for me. Perfect. I'm going to marry her."

"Go for it, lover boy. I'll be your best man."

"Deal. I told her I'd get back to her. I've got to look up this Gambert guy."

"Have at it." He went back to his desk with an undeniable swagger. The FBI Cupid. I shook my head at the image of Dash dressed in nothing but a diaper and wings, pulling back his bow to shoot darts of love. Direct hit when it came to Cyn.

Barry Gambert had a record, but it wasn't terribly interesting. He showed an address in Winchester, Virginia, and before that, in New Jersey. I jotted down the salient points and picked up my phone . . . but then I thought about it.

If she was at the National Gallery, she was a few blocks from FBI headquarters. Dash had given me the afternoon off, and it was a nice fall day. A relaxed walk and I could be sitting in the handsome inside courtyard, where she'd have to exit.

I looked up. Dash, with his uncanny "ace FBI agent" senses, was already watching me.

"Go," he said, not waiting for my excuses or bluster.

I got a little zip of excitement. Why deny it? "Okay," I said. "I'll go."

I forwarded my work to him, grabbed my jacket, and walked out with an undeniable spring in my step. Going to see a pretty lady on a "playing hooky" kind of afternoon. Life felt pretty sweet all of a sudden.

She took her time in the exhibit. I liked that about her. The selection wasn't huge, but I knew from personal experience that it was powerful. Each painting deserved its moment of focus—some absolutely demanded it. So I waited on a stone bench amid the palms, trying to imagine I was touring the exhibit with her. Would she see the same things I did? Would she admire the same techniques I wished I could duplicate? Which paintings would she move on from quickly? Which would hold her interest?

It was a surprisingly enjoyable interlude, and all the rat fuckery of the Phelps case drifted away on the cool museum air. The shame of losing my weapon to Maddy further lost its grip on my psyche. The hope that I wouldn't screw up too badly and disappoint my father. The still mostly unpacked apartment. The desire for a less-crowded pool for lap swimming. Whether or not to head back to Minneapolis for Pike's annual birthday bash weekend. The to-do list that included inevitable trips to the Department of Motor Vehicles to change my license. All my anxieties, large and small, got lighter while I was waiting for her.

When she appeared at the exit, I realized I hadn't remembered her quite right. She was so slight—so graceful. Tiny, really, but bursting with vitality. She was lost in thought, which didn't surprise me; the exhibit could do that to you. When her eyes slid across me and then swiveled back to verify that she'd seen something unexpected, my breath hitched. The color and shape of her eyes was simply mesmerizing. I hadn't gotten them right in any of my sketches yet. I needed further study. A lot of further study.

I smiled at her and held up empty hands to signify from across the room that all was well. She moved toward me uncertainly.

As she approached, I clenched my hand on my notepad, suddenly remembering the numbers of pages I'd covered with sketches of her eyes. She'd think I was an insane stalker if she saw them.

"Hi," I volunteered, and then wondered at such a pedestrian beginning. All that time sitting there awaiting her and I couldn't come up with a better opening? I was trying not to stare too obviously, but she moved with an unconscious grace that was a pleasure to watch.

"Agent Jones?" She was surprised, and once again her instinctive awkwardness made me want to protect her. "What are you doing here? Is everything okay?"

I patted the bench next to me and she sat nervously. "It's fine. I didn't mean to frighten you. Please call me Rhys."

"Barry from Winchester isn't going to jump out and abduct me, is he?" She was trying for a lighthearted joke but was too tense to pull it off.

"Seems unlikely. No, the National Gallery is one of my favorite places, and I'd had it with financial research, so I brought you what I found instead of texting you. I hope you don't mind. You were a good excuse to get out of the office. Did you like the exhibit?"

I gestured toward the show she'd come from. She blinked as if she'd forgotten why she was here. "Very much. You've seen it?"

"Twice. I came when I first moved to DC, about six weeks ago, and then I couldn't stay away. The compositions of the Baroque period blow me away. So dramatic."

The frown line between her eyebrows eased up. "Beams of sunlight through black clouds. Finger of God stuff," she agreed.

"Or through a dark window. It's night everywhere else except where the angel is, come to speak the truth in broad damned daylight."

She brightened, and the tension in her shoulders began to ease. "Exactly! Did you see the Castiglione? That angel might as well have been holding a spotlight on the Virgin."

Yes, I thought. *Yes. You stopped in the right place. You saw what I loved. You're for me.* "Infant swathed in titanium white with highlights in zinc." I nodded. "It almost burns the eyes, it's so bright."

She regarded me with sudden suspicion. "You're an FBI agent?"

I laughed. I'd slipped too far into the part of me that responded to art. "I'll prove it. Here." I flipped open my notepad (carefully skipping past pages of her eyes) and recited what I'd found.

"Barry Gambert, born Gamberetti, in Bayonne, New Jersey. Thirty-four years old. Moved to Winchester, Virginia five years ago. Has a rap sheet and served time for con jobs and grifts. Nothing major. No violence on his record. Drives a black 2012

Mercedes, which he bought used two years ago. Was that the car you saw leaving the parking garage?"

Her mouth had fallen open. She was caught up by the history of a stranger. "Um. No. I think that car was blue."

"You didn't notice a license plate?"

"No. I'm sorry."

"That's okay. Sedan? Sports car? Truck?"

"Like, a sedan. I think. I didn't really pay attention."

"Did you get a good look at him? How sure are you that it was him?"

"Um . . ." I'd interviewed witnesses before and saw her hesitation. She wasn't sure she'd seen him, but it was a close enough match that she felt compelled to get in touch with me. Well, with Dash. But same thing.

"I wouldn't worry about it," I reassured her. "Let me know if you see that guy again. But it's unlikely that Barry came back so Madcap Maddy could shoot at him some more. How is she, by the way?"

She huffed a little laugh. "Maddy is fine. She's always fine. She has no past to regret and no future to fret over. There's only now for her. I'm taking her as my role model." She ducked her head and glanced at me. "Except for the shooting at strangers part, of course."

"Good plan."

She gave me the side-eye again, clearly uneasy. I needed to make my move.

"For myself," I said, "I'm glad we aren't looking to Barry officially. If you or Maddy was part of a case with the FBI, then I couldn't ask you out."

She squeaked, "Ask me out?"

"Absolutely. Dinner tonight. Why not?"

"Oh. No. No, no, no." Her recitation of the negative seemed to be peculiarly calming to her. She relaxed. "That's not happening."

She was making me smile, even as she rejected me. "Why not?"

She looked me full in the face for the first time that day. "Why not? Well—look at you."

Paranoia crept in. Did I have lettuce in my teeth from lunch? Had adolescent acne made a vicious comeback? I'd showered after my run, hadn't I? "Something wrong?"

"Yes, there's something wrong. You're way, way too pretty for me. There's no way I could date you. I'd be a nervous wreck the entire time."

That was better than acne or spinach or BO. I grinned. "A nervous wreck. Not relaxed, like you are right now."

My teasing went right over her head. "No, I deserve a short, balding man with a paunch belly . . ." Her words trailed off as if she'd realized something. I took advantage of the pause to leap into the argumentative fray.

"Would it help if I told you I was *this close* to being fired?"

She telegraphed her disbelief. "You're not. From the FBI?"

"Oh, yes, ma'am. Not so intimidating now, am I?"

I put a hand under her elbow and stood. She came up with me without even realizing it. I walked her through the courtyard. "Yes," I went on. "You're strolling with a man on his last professional legs. It's a sorry tale of bitter stupidity. It would make the angels weep. It would make a Castiglione angel howl in the darkness."

We'd reached the stairway to the side entrance and she let me lead her, all of her focus trained on me. Horror washed across her face as an idea dawned. "It wasn't because of Maddy and the gun, was it? Oh, God. I'm so sorry."

"Oh, don't worry about it." We were moving down the broad stone stairs. "That was just the latest in a string of disasters for me. My bosses have gotten to the point where they just shake their heads at me."

I held the door for her, and we emerged in the fading light of a late October afternoon. "Where are we going?" she finally thought to ask.

"To dinner. Aren't you hungry?"

She stopped, confusion written across her face like a Picasso. "No, Agent Jones—"

"Rhys, please. Or Peanut Butter Cup, if you prefer. Don't you want to hear how badly I've fucked up my career as a law enforcement officer?" I held out my hand as she conducted her internal war. "It's sordid and stupid, I promise. You'll love it."

I'm not sure she consciously reached for me, but I tucked her hand into my elbow, and we were walking down the street before she figured out how to renew her protests.

"Okay," she said in wonder. "Let's go on a date."

TEN
CYN

We walked along broad city avenues as the sun set. Washington, DC, owed so much of its handsome architecture to the ancient Romans, with style updates drawn from the Italian Renaissance. And yes, I was aware that I was focusing on architectural history to avoid the feel of his elbow under my hand, of his long legs kindly slowing down so I could easily keep up with his stride. He moved next to me with the grace of a panther—like a large, well-oiled beast that I had no business being with.

He smelled wonderful.

How odd this is—how very odd. Is this my life I'm living? Or have I slipped somehow into someone else's? Someone who lived a different life, where handsome, tall people floated lightly and laughingly through beach volleyball and après-ski cocktails in the hot tub. A world where bold, confident women walked through cities arm-in-arm with stunning male models.

Whoever's life it was, it was unquestionably exciting.

He led me to a nearby restaurant. "Lebanese okay?"

I nodded and found myself ensconced in a booth with a view of the darkening city street. He told me what he thought was good on the menu and I, mindful of the ill-advised cheeseburger at lunch, ordered lightly. Then, true to his word, Rhys unfolded for me what he clearly saw as a bitter and stupid work history, and I forgot to feel awkward as the details spooled out.

"My first offense was a speeding ticket," he said. He was smiling, but there was a shadow behind the amusement.

"Just a speeding ticket?"

"We at the FBI are supposed to uphold the law, not break it so ruthlessly."

"How ruthlessly?"

He winced. "Ninety-four in a fifty-five."

Yeah. That was pretty ruthless, all right. The oddness I'd felt—the sense that I was in someone else's life—had faded. "Damn."

"I know."

"Were you chasing someone? Was it—you know, FBI stuff?"

"It was a friend with a new Porsche that I wanted to drive. He was howling his encouragement in the passenger seat, and then howling with laughter when I got pulled over." He was laughing, but his face had reddened. The handsome man was blushing. I tried not to smile as I teased him.

"Oh my God. It was peer pressure. Were you in high school?"

"Oh, shut up."

"And the cop wasn't impressed with your badge?"

"Not when I was that far over the speed limit, he wasn't. Usually, locals cooperate with us. Not this time. He was so angry his face was the color of a damson plum. The only reason the judge didn't take away my license was because the Bureau intervened."

"Ouch. That was humiliating."

"Nothing but the truth, ma'am. Utterly humiliating. But you can't have an agent without a valid license. So it got put in my file, I got called on the carpet, did a year of community service, and pulled every shit detail my bosses could think of."

Our drinks arrived. I'd wanted a glass of wine, but he'd ordered iced tea, so I had sparkling water. Living wild, I'd asked for a lime in it.

"Even that I could have survived if the next profoundly stupid thing hadn't happened."

I raised my eyebrow at him. My anxieties had faded, and I decided that he wasn't just dazzling to look at; I also kind of liked him. More, I was beginning to believe that maybe he liked me too. The realization buoyed me. As the waitress set down a plate of hummus and a basket of bread, puffed-up and almost too hot to touch, I had a burst of confidence and a "nothing ventured, nothing gained" moment. I boldly tore off a rip of pita, regardless of the heat—it would've been nothing to most people, but it was a gesture of giddy freedom to me—and dipped it in the creamy mixture. I was rewarded for risking scorched fingers; the mouthful was heavenly, and I licked my lips to capture every atom of that delicious flavor. Rhys was staring at my mouth.

His appreciation gave me a thrill that went like lightning to my crotch. I could lick other things with as much delight, I thought— and then was startled by how quickly such a racy fantasy had crept up on me. We both blinked. Time to get back on track.

"The next stupid thing," I reminded him. "What happened?"

"I was accused of being inebriated at work."

"Shit," I said. "Were you?"

He shifted in slight agitation. But sharing his errors had been his idea, and whether he knew it or not, it was working. I was far more comfortable with him than I'd ever expected. Plus, I was thinking entirely lascivious thoughts about his body. *Keep talking, big man.*

"Yeah," he said on a sigh.

"You were a drunk FBI agent at work?!"

He held up a hand. "In my defense, it was another endless day of research. I wasn't going near any civilians. And I wasn't drinking on the job. I just hadn't sobered up from the night before."

He was quite puffed up about his excuses, but I wasn't fooled. That was bluster to hide his shame. The humor overtook me, and I was unable to stop my giggles.

"You're kidding."

"I'm not. A girl I was dating had a birthday, and we went out. We had some drinks. Is that such a crime?"

My giggles got bigger. "It is if you're an FBI agent!"

"Yeah." He deflated, bluster all used up. "That's what my bosses thought too."

"So why didn't they fire you outright for that?"

He nodded resignedly. "The guy assigned to test me claimed he couldn't get a test for a couple of hours. In the meantime, he sent me out to run around the city with one of those hydration packs on my back."

I had an inappropriate vision of Rhys in nothing but black running shorts and sweat. He looked good. *Focus, Cyn.* Back to the decorous conversation. "Does running sober you up faster?"

"Well, constantly drinking water while running does dilute the percentage of alcohol in the bloodstream. Just enough, in this case."

"How long?"

He looked into the distance without seeing anything, remembering. "I ran for two hours and seventeen minutes."

"Shit." I was laughing even harder. "And then did you have to go to the emergency room?"

"I run marathons. That wasn't the bad part. The worst was how painfully my head was pounding the whole time."

That cracked me up. It wasn't kind of me to laugh at his misery, but the idea of a drunk man determinedly running for longer than it took to watch a movie, do the laundry, change the sheets, and still have time to lounge around? Yes, that was absurd enough to give me a fit of the giggles. When my laughter tapered off, I leaned back in relaxation. "You're still pretty, but I find I'm a lot less intimidated by you. Thanks for sharing."

"Oh, you think I'm done?"

"There's not more? You're a disaster, Agent Jones."

He stopped and leveled a smile at me. His voice dropped. "Please say my name, Cyn."

This time, I was the one blushing. "Rhys," I murmured, my eyes going back to my lap. He sighed peacefully and I lost my heart.

He gave a shake and went on. "The third one on my list of disasters was stupid. I made a joke during an arrest."

"Just a joke?"

"I swear, it really wasn't even funny. All I did was tell a businessman that he should have gone to Club Med while I was handcuffing him. That's it."

"That's it? That's not even a joke. It's just stupid."

"I know. But after the speeding ticket—"

"And the drunken debauchery—"

"Yeah. The Bureau doesn't find the defense of justice funny at any time. I was told to lose my sense of humor, they transferred me to DC, and I was given a legendary super-agent as a partner. Dash Ashwood. You met him. He's awesome."

"But Rhys, that doesn't sound like a punishment." Saying his name gave me a tiny thrill. It was a step into intimacy. "So if things are so bad, why do you still have a job?"

A reasonable question. He clearly thought so too. "There are two reasons. No, three."

"Hit me with them." I toyed with the chicken shish kebab on my plate, more interested in what he was saying than in what I was eating.

"Well, I have a genetic gift. No, two, really."

"Stop counting things and get on with it."

"I have a sharpshooter's eye."

"What's that mean?"

"It means I'm really, really good with a gun." My eyes dropped to his jacket. I'd forgotten about the gun that Maddy had seen instantly. He saw my gaze and read my nerves. "It's okay. I have the thumb latch on. It's not coming out unless we want it to."

I was struck again with lasciviousness. Was he talking about his gun or his cock? The thought made me blush even more vigorously. Wait—was his face reddening too? Were we sharing a naughty thought?

"So you're good with your pistol." I winced as I said it. So much for ignoring the implications. Why didn't I just do a striptease and sit on his lap?

"I am," he said, hopefully unaware of the direction of my thoughts. "And that makes me valuable to the Bureau."

"But if you spend all of your time doing financial research . . ."

"Every now and then we all have to draw our weapons. And when we do, I'm the guy they assume can disable a gunman."

"Can you?" My eyes were wide again. All thoughts of naughty pistol chat were forgotten. And that was a good thing. Wasn't it?

"Usually."

"Have you ever had to?"

"Uh, yeah."

"Don't want to talk about it?"

"I'd rather get back to making you blush over how good I am with my gun."

"Oh my God."

"Yeah. Just like that. You have skin made for blushing."

I was flustered. This was definitely flirting. He'd been reading my mind. Was I embarrassed? Or excited? (*Why not both?* asked the prim librarian in my brain.) *Okay. Let's walk this back a bit.* I needed to give my heart time to slow back down to normal. "Go on with why they don't fire you outright."

"You mean my second genetic gift."

"What is it?"

"My father."

I cocked my head in confusion. "What about him?"

"Special Agent Owen Jones. A hero and a legend at the FBI. My father was injured in the line of duty when I was fourteen. He lost his leg above the knee and has held a desk job at the Bureau ever since. My continued employment at the FBI is unquestioned, blatant nepotism."

"What? You think you have a job because Daddy is watching out for you?"

My disbelief must have felt a tad harsh to him. He leaned back from the table and his shoulders came up. Big man on defense. "You don't know my dad. He's an amazing man. Everyone loves him. Of course they want to keep him happy and protect his fuck-up son."

"Hang on." I was beginning to understand. And even with the brief overviews of his disasters, I was seeing a pattern here that he hadn't caught onto yet. I eyed him, forgetting I was ever intimidated by his beauty, his size, his big, sleek body. "That doesn't sound right. Not in this day and age. Was it your father who delayed the blood alcohol test until you could sober up?"

He scoffed. "I was in Minneapolis. Dad works here in DC."

"So he had nothing to do with that one."

"They were keeping him happy."

"Sounds like someone wanted to keep you on the team, regardless of your father."

He scratched his head. "No. They all want my father to be okay with their decisions. He's risen really high in the Bureau."

I regarded him skeptically. For a smart, observant man, he definitely had a blind spot when it came to his father. "He's a law-and-order kind of guy, huh? Brought you up to be honorable and truthful?"

"Yeah. He just didn't plan on me being so stupid."

I ignored that as a comment not worthy of consideration. "And everyone knows he's all about justice and fairness?"

"Well, yeah."

"So if your father learned that someone had covered for you when you were drunk, would he praise them? Or write them up? Seriously?"

My alternate view of his past was making his forehead wrinkle. That was a good start. I kept pushing.

"Seriously. What would your father do if he knew agents were covering for someone who was drunk on the job?"

He scrubbed his eyes with his fingers. I was pushing him off-balance, but I was getting through to him. "He'd fire them."

"That's what I figured." I sat back, triumphant. "So it's possible your guys were protecting you, not your father."

"Jesus."

"Do we need to reexamine the speeding ticket too?"

He blinked at me. I knew the feeling of having your past rewritten in a moment, and I felt a burst of empathy for him. "Everyone knows I'm a fuck-up," he said, trying to gather the tatters of his identity back around him.

"Maybe you're not as much of a fuck-up as you think you are."

The noise that came out of his mouth was a combination of disgust and confusion. "Boy. We've gone deep, here. No soul-shattering revelations on a first date, please. That's not fair."

I dropped my eyes again. "I forgot this was a date."

"Well, it is. At the end of the evening, I'm going to plant a kiss on your silky cheek and ask you out again. And I'm going to aim for further back, towards your ear so it's more sexy and I leave you thinking good things about me."

I shivered at his words, my eyes going wide at the thought. "Wow."

"Good answer," he said with evident satisfaction. "Now tell me why the thought of a balding man with a belly made you grind to a halt back in the museum."

Twilight turned to darkness outside, and we lingered over our meal as he slowly teased out of me all the background information on Cynthia Grace Quimby, once Cyn Kempthorne.

And because I liked him—and was beginning to trust him—I told him about growing up smart.

"I graduated from high school at sixteen because I refused to leave at fifteen. I was through college by eighteen, and I had my master's by the time I was twenty."

"In what?"

"Architectural history, from Columbia."

He whistled in appreciation. I made a face.

"Sounds good, doesn't it? The truth is, I'm no smarter than anyone else. But studies show that some kids develop focus at an unusually early age. They're no more intelligent than anyone else. It just looks that way because we keep leapfrogging through school."

This was a source of pride and confusion for my family, and a very tough road for me. I loved learning, but I never had the same childhood most other people had. "Mostly what it meant was that I never had a friend. I was too young for every cohort I was with. I was always physically small, but it was more glaring as I began skipping grades. Everyone else grew up; I always looked little. I was known as a fourth-grader in fifth grade, I was the eighth-grader in the tenth-grade classroom. I never went to a prom, never had a sleepover with 'the girls,' never went to the mall to giggle at boys. I'm not looking for a pity party. I'm pointing out that I was a hopelessly overeducated virgin of the highest order when I met Don."

I shook my head, lost in memory and sadness.

"Don was sweet and funny and swept me off my feet. And I'm beginning to understand why."

I checked his reaction. Was this too much? He was sitting with his chin in his hand, watching me with an intensity that flattered and unsettled me. "Go on," he said. "What did you come to understand?"

"Well . . ." I took a moment to gather some of the thoughts that had hummed along in my lizard brain all afternoon. "When you're a teenager, you say you want independence and to be yourself. But really you want to get into a group and disappear in the anonymity of being a princess, or a goth, or whatever."

"Or a jock," he agreed.

"Was that you?"

He nodded. "Shooting competitions. Baseball team. Some football, but only if it didn't get in the way of shooting. Go on with you. What group did you blend in with?"

That was the point. "I didn't blend in with anyone. I was always the outsider. Always. And when you get trapped in that mindset, it's really hard to break out of it. I was still a kid when I went to college. I didn't know who I was—I didn't even think to ask who I was. My job was to learn and to keep my head down."

I sighed. There was so much I should have done, so many tentative extensions of the hand of friendship that I now recognized, but which I'd ignored at the time. "And along came Don, and he saw me and told me what my identity was. Which was, eventually, to be his wife. Of course, I found out—today—that Don also had a child with a woman named Dahlia. Dahlia!" I spat the last word, my sorrow fully flipped to anger, which I liked much more.

"He had a child?"

"He did. And he kept seeing Dahlia after he married me. I know that because I found out—also today—that Don and Dahlia had a second child while Don and I were married."

"The fucker."

"No doubt."

"What did he want with her when he had you?" His unquestionably pro-Cyn question made me smile.

"A better question is, what did he want with me when he had Dahlia?"

"Well?"

It was all so clear to me now. How could I have missed it before? "He had a mother. Rose. She had dementia and three million dollars that he wanted to inherit. He married me and persuaded me to put my PhD on hold and care for his mother in her home so she wouldn't persuade a lawyer to let her change her will. I cared for her for three and a half years."

"That's why you're so good with Maddy."

I smiled. "Maddy is a dream compared to Rose. Dementia took Rose in a far more typical way. Rage. Confusion. Fear. Suspicion. Maddy is a vacation in comparison. I adore Maddy."

"Me too." We shared a smile.

"Peanut Butter Cup." I smiled at him. "Anyway, when Rose died, Don got the money. And to be fair, he did pay off all my student loans before divorcing me."

Rhys hissed in sympathy.

"He was my whole life. I spent twenty-four hours a day with an old woman who was locked in a perpetual nightmare, and my only light was Don. He was my partner and my lover and my guide. I built my entire life around Don and his mother until I didn't know who I was. And then she died, and he threw that away. He threw me away."

He laid his hand over mine, and his simple act of support blurred my vision with unshed tears. I was angry. But more, I was ashamed. I'd been the victim of a flimflam man.

"I'm sorry," he said. "You deserve so much more."

I took a deep breath and then turned my hand until my fingers wrapped over his. "I deserve a million and a half more. But once he inherited his mother's money, Don invested all of it in his buddy's company."

"Oh, wait," Rhys said. His fingers tightened gently around mine. "Now you're in my territory. Let me guess. The buddy's company went belly-up before your marital assets could be calculated." I shook my head, but he knew I was agreeing with him. "And then once the divorce was final, the company magically roared back to life."

"They got the government contract they thought they'd lost."

"Hallelujah!" he shouted, startling those at nearby tables. "It's a miracle!"

"Shh," I hushed him, but I couldn't help but smile.

"A tale as old as time," he said with a shrug. "I'm sorry to say. You know you can sue for a reassessment of your assets."

"I know. That's why Don told me—today—about his two little children, who need the money. Oh, and that he's marrying Dahlia. And they have a third baby on the way."

"Fuck that. That's money you earned by caring for his mother."

"I know. And I'm going to call my lawyer. Tomorrow. I couldn't face it today."

"I'll get you the names of some good forensic accountants if your lawyer doesn't have someone they recommend. It'll cost you some, but what do you care? You'll be richer by a nice chunk of change." He smiled at me brightly, and an answering smile crept across my face. The tightness in my chest eased.

"I do feel bad for his kids, though. Daddy is a rat bastard."

"Not your fault."

"I know. But more money might make their childhood more bearable. Maybe."

"Christ. You're a saint."

"Oh, I'm so not." I let go of his hand and he grabbed me back, lacing my fingers with his.

"You are," he insisted.

"If you knew the near-death experiences I've planned for him in the last seven months, you wouldn't say that."

"If you knew the sniper bullets I've planned for him just during this conversation, you'd run screaming." He grinned to let me know he was kidding. Mostly.

"Hm." I considered him, and he stroked my hand with his thumb. It sent a rush of warmth up my arm and then down my body. "Good thing you're so honorable and upstanding."

"And determined," he agreed. "I'm following in my Dad's footsteps in the FBI, come hell or high water. And no rat bastard like Don is going to make me screw up my career plans."

"Right! Me neither!"

"Atta girl! So what are you going to do now? Back to the PhD?"

I sighed. "A doctorate in fourteenth-century Moorish architecture seemed like such a good idea at the time . . ."

"Wow."

"Yeah. I don't know what I'm going to do. But like I said, I'm trying to be more like Maddy. Stop frowning over yesterday, stop worrying about tomorrow. Be in the now, man." I faked a big, sunny smile and he returned it. I felt him imprint on my DNA.

"Okay. What do you want to do in the now?"

I regarded him. "Kiss on the cheek. Near the ear so it feels sexy. I need someone a lot better than Don. I deserve someone a lot better than Don."

"I'll get you Dash Ashwood's phone number."

He made me laugh, and I found a new burst of confidence in the heat of his regard. "You're stuck with me. How are we getting out of here? Metro? Uber? I've had a long day and I want to go home and dream about how handsome you are, Rhys."

He bit his lip, a definitely lascivious light in his eye. Wow. Was I ready for what I was apparently getting into?

What I was getting into was an Uber. We chatted politely with the driver, and then Rhys leaned over to me and murmured in my ear.

"Let's do this now so it doesn't get awkward later." Then his lips pressed gently to my skin, in front of my ear. Heat. Warmth. Lust.

I put my hand on his, where it laid on the seat between us. Then, gathering my courage, I sat forward and turned to face him. Like a strange sea creature moving in slow motion, my far hand came floating up and gently took his chin. I turned his head enough so I could lean over and kiss him in exactly the same spot. He repaid my bravery with a sigh that verged on a low moan.

"So nice," he said as I sat back. "You know, this is the third time we've met."

I paused to consider. "When Maddy shot the guy, when Maddy got lost, and now. That *is* three times."

His far hand was caressing my head with smooth, warm strokes. "If we counted all three as dates, we'd be way far behind in what to expect."

I was definitely tingling in several eager places. "But can you really call it a date if someone gets shot at?"

He smiled, and I could feel the muscles in his cheek flex against my fingers. "Okay. Let's call it two dates. Doesn't that call for a real kiss?"

I couldn't help but bite my lower lip in anticipation, and he watched me do it. "Here. Let me do that."

And then the space between us was gone and he was kissing me —so softly. So slowly. Just lips. No tongue. Yet I was sizzling with excitement.

Then his mouth opened, and he nibbled on my lower lip with his teeth, and I couldn't help but utter a delighted laugh at his boldness.

"We're here," the Uber driver said, uninterested in the bliss he was interrupting.

Already? That was the fastest trip out of the city ever. I put my hand on Rhys's chest when he moved. "Don't get out of the car. This was the perfect goodbye. I had a wonderful date. Thank you."

"I'll call you," he said, holding my hand as I got out of the car until our arms were stretched out straight between us. Then he gestured to the door of Belinda's building. "I'll watch until you're inside."

I smiled. He'd left me feeling both excited and protected. I could get used to this.

ELEVEN
RHYS

I could have dismissed the Uber and gotten out with her on the sidewalk. My apartment building wasn't ten blocks from where Cyn lived. I could have walked it easily. But I understood why she'd wanted me to stay in the car. If *she'd* been standing on the sidewalk and *I'd* been standing on the sidewalk—as keyed up as I was by her?

Lip to lip was only the beginning of what I wanted. I was aching to feel her belly against mine, her breasts pressing to my chest. Yeah, there would have been some major public display of affection if I'd left the car with her. I let the Uber driver finish the trip.

And I waited a whole half hour before texting her.

> I'm playing it cool. Not going to call you for THREE WHOLE DAYS to prove how casual I am and how easy this is going to be.

Her reply came quickly.

How easy WHAT is going to be?

Tease. I grinned.

Me seducing you.

Oh, is THAT the plan.

Absolutely. But the campaign doesn't
start for three days. Because I'm
so casual about it.

I think the opening battle has already
happened. The campaign is
on, Big Man.

You're not supposed to know that yet.

After that Uber ride? Your cover is
blown. What are you planning on
saying to me in three days?

I thought, a movie? A little necking
in the back row?

You find me in a peculiarly
vulnerable mood. Ask me now.

When can you go to the movies?

I'll check tomorrow. Belinda has travel
coming up, but she'll be home the next
few evenings. I'm not going to sleep
with you on a second date, you know.

First of all, why not? And second of all,
I'm not expecting you to.

First of all, I'm not sure, and
second of all, good!

You're a temptation, Ms. Quimby.

You're a terrible temptation, Agent Jones.

Text me tomorrow when you know. Let's
shoot for Friday?

Date night. How unusual for me to
have something to do.

How unusual that the rest of the male
population has left you alone for me.

I always thought so. Good night, Rhys.

Good night, Cyn. Sweet dreams.

I think you've already assured that!

Then my job here is done. I retire
victorious from the battlefield.

Until tomorrow!

Delicious. This was definitely the girl for me. I took a hot shower and jerked off joyfully to the memory of her lips under mine. I came with a yell and then a stupid smile. That girl lit me up. Friday night couldn't come soon enough.

WHEN FRIDAY CAME, I TOOK HER TO DINNER FIRST. I LIKED that she tried to insist on paying, but I wasn't having any of it. "You can take me out once you get your $1.5 million. How's that going?"

"I called my lawyer, which was horrible." She shook her head. "Reliving the divorce is too damned painful. Every time I talk to that guy, I'm right back to where I was in March. Just shattered."

I leaned over and slid my hand around her arm at the elbow to let her know she wasn't alone. She smiled and put her hand over mine. "I'm much better than I was then," she said. I could tell it wasn't just a brave front. This was a woman who was doing some healing. "Really. I've discovered that I'm pretty mad at Don, and that maybe this fiasco wasn't entirely my fault. Plus, Maddy and Belinda have been a big help . . ."

She glanced at me, suddenly shy. "And a date with a hot guy on a Friday night? That didn't hurt either." She grinned. "So make sure to remind me of all the good you've done to my psyche when you blow me off later."

I sat back to regard her with amusement. "Who says I'm going to blow you off? You and I are getting married on a mountaintop in a hot air balloon. Then we're going to float away from everything and never come down."

"Sounds chilly." She grinned.

"Imma keep you warm, girlie." I waggled my eyebrows at her and she laughed. My cock twitched.

"Thank you for the names of the forensic accountants. My lawyer said he'd check them out and get back to me."

"Dash's recommendations. I've got a few friends in the business, but they're all back in Minneapolis. Dash has been working in DC for years. He knows the really good ones around here."

"Pass on my thanks, please." She dove into the pizza when it arrived, risking a burned mouth from the bubbling cheese. "Oh, lordy," she sighed. "That's hot. But it's so good!"

I took my own slice but was caught up in watching her relish hers, my own forgotten before me. "Christ, you've got a beautiful mouth."

I'd caught her mid-chew. It was a singularly inelegant moment, and I burst out laughing. She swallowed and joined me, coughing until she cleared her throat with a sip of her wine. I toasted her with my beer. Friday night. Just like it was supposed to be.

And then somehow it became something more.

It was the conversation. It began easily. I told her about the pick-up basketball games I'd been getting into with other FBI agents. She told me about her sister's picture-perfect life. And then, somehow, we were in an engrossing discussion about the intersection of art history and architecture. I was fortunate to have some great friends, but none of them could have kept up with this passion of mine—much less expand on it and make me see an entire cultural history in a building.

Google Images got a real workout. We were both summoning examples on our phones, gesturing madly, arguing with a spice that left me hungry for more. We came very close to missing the movie entirely, but Cyn pulled us back to the real world and got us both going so we could make it on time.

The movie was an action thriller that opened with a court case. The flagrant inaccuracies immediately ticked me off, which at least helped me to stop thinking of other artists I wanted to ask her opinion of. So instead of thinking about her brain or watching the movie, I focused on the shape and length of Cyn's fingers. I picked up her hand and twined her fingers with mine. She was so small— fragile. Like porcelain. But also so strong. She wasn't afraid to speak her mind. Her approach to life blew me away, and I loved that she was willing to fight Don for what he'd hidden from her.

She was watching our fingers too. "Is this where we make out in the back row?" she whispered.

"Have to wait at least until act two," I murmured in reply. "I'll have blue balls for the rest of my life if we start any sooner than that."

"You don't like just making out?" Her look was definitely coy, and it made me want to bite her lip again. And nibble on a lot more than that.

"I love making out," I said, turning in my seat to gather her close. I'd deliberately picked a theater where we could lift up the center armrests, so I could draw her right up against me. "When the hero kisses the heroine, that's when I'm going to kiss you."

"How do you know he'll kiss her?"

"It's Hollywood. Of course he'll kiss her. In manly fashion. Watch the movie."

"I hope he kisses her soon," she whispered as she nestled into me.

"Act three," I groaned. "It's always act three."

I almost made it, too. I had an arm around her. Her head was on my shoulder, and her hand was distressingly high on my chest. I longed to cover it with mine and slide it down, down, down to where my cock was on alert. But this was a second date, and we were in a public movie theater. I settled for running my hand up and down her arm so that the useless, nerveless outsides of my fingers could brush along the side of her breast. It was so much like high school that I wondered if I had baseball practice tomorrow.

And when I couldn't stand it any longer, I moved to kiss her and found her rising to meet me. Our mouths met in a tangle, and without a moment's hesitation, our lips opened and our tongues slid against each other in heat and wetness and the thrill of finally —finally—tasting her.

I had to come up for air. "It's coming back to me why high school was such a challenge," I muttered as I reached to catch her under her knees and pull her legs across mine. Her calf pressed against my steely cock and I groaned at even that simple sensation.

"Mm," she said and scooted into me another inch, pressing her leg against my groin and making me see stars. "I wouldn't know. Do stop talking."

Then she was kissing me again, and it was a good thing we really were in the back row, because I'm sure someone behind us would have objected to how little attention we paid to the movie and how much to each other.

"Tell me again why you won't sleep with me on a second date." I tried to mask the gasp in my breath as I crooned into her ear.

"I really don't know why," she breathed. "It's just—I don't know. Moving faster than I think we should go."

"Do you want to?"

She pulled back. "Well, my body does."

"But you're not sure if your brain does." I needed to regain control and let her have more time. Restraint. More and more like high school. But I could do it.

She leaned back into me. "Maybe my brain does too." She tried to kiss me deeply again, but I gentled the kiss.

"Take it easy on me, sweet thing. We're going to wait until your brain is absolutely sure. There's no hurry here." *Except in my balls. There was a definite sense of urgency there.* But I could master that.

She smiled at me. "Really?"

"Really." I tucked her head under my chin and pointed out that the hero and heroine were kissing. It didn't look as good as she'd felt. I told her so.

"Ooh, Rhys," she said, but didn't follow it up with anything.

"What?" I asked.

"I don't know. I think I like you."

"Good. I like you too. Maybe you couldn't tell that before, but I do."

"Some things a girl likes to hear for herself."

I WALKED HER HOME AFTER THE MOVIE ENDED AND PULLED HER to me in the shadow of her building. By then it was clear to me that I had a very bad case of Cyn, and I wanted to see more of her. A lot more of her. "What are you doing tomorrow?" Pulling her entire body against me was magnificent, delicious torture.

She wound her arms around my neck. "Belinda leaves tomorrow. I'm with Maddy, and the caregivers' service couldn't find anyone for Saturday night, so I'm on duty."

"Bring Maddy. Come with me. I'm doing my community service at the Boys' Club of DC. They'll love her, she'll have a great time, and you and I can spend the day together. Will you come?"

"To the Boys' Club? What will we do there?"

"Only be the center of attention from the moment you arrive until the moment you leave. Come with me. Let me show you off."

She liked that. "Okay."

We made our plans, and then I tasted her tongue one last time, not sure I could let her go. But I knew it was going to be easier to stop than to try to keep going. So I set her from me with a groan. "Get away from me, you hussy," I said with a grin. "I'm going to be walking funny for days now."

"Poor blue balls," she said with a hint of delighted cruelty. Her tone gave me a rush of excitement. Then she switched back to being prim and proper. "Thank you for a lovely evening, Rhys. I'll see you tomorrow."

I couldn't help but grope her caressable ass as she swung away. She yipped and looked over her shoulder at me in mock outrage. Then, checking to make sure we were still in the shadows, she hinged forward, stuck her ass out at me, and did a genteel little bump and grind. I growled, she laughed, and our date was over.

Phew. That woman got me hot.

TWELVE
CYN

BELINDA WAS PRETTY GOOD AT THE SILENT EXIT WHEN SHE HAD an early flight to the other side of the world, but on the morning she left for Indonesia, I wasn't sleeping anyway, so I heard her when she got up.

I found her drinking coffee in the kitchen, her wheeled bag at her side, watching the progress of her Uber driver on the app.

"Ramon," she said, gesturing to me with her phone. "He'll be here in ten minutes, and he knows all the good shortcuts to Dulles. Did I wake you?"

"You know all the Uber drivers in the area now?"

"Seems I know all the ones who will pick a person up at 4:30 in the morning and take them to the airport. Why are you up?"

No matter how much of a friend my employer might be, it didn't seem right to tell her I'd been awoken by the haze of bliss at the end of a very erotic dream featuring the Peanut Butter Cup. Did women have wet dreams?

"Ah," she said with a smile. "Your blush says it all. Going well with the FBI agent, then? I'm glad. You deserve better after that reprobate you married."

My smile faded as the memory of the warm, Rhys-laced dream was replaced by the chilly memory of Don's betrayal.

"You don't think," I asked Belinda, "that it's going too fast with Rhys? I mean I just figured out how deep Don's river of crap runs. Am I bouncing from one guy to another?"

"A reasonable question." She regarded me thoughtfully over the rim of her mug. "Do you feel like your identity is defined by how Rhys sees you?"

Did I? My brain was filled with him at the moment—by his big blondness and his warmth and his easy grin . . . by his passion for the Italian Renaissance . . . by the feeling of his large hand coasting up my ribcage . . . but did that mean I was letting him define me?

"That's a tough question for so early in the morning," I hedged.

She tipped me the ghost of a wink and put her mug in the dishwasher. "Well, think about it. If you decide you want him to make all your decisions for you, then it's too soon. If you want to be with him without wanting to crawl inside his life and hide, then it's not too soon." She gathered up her suitcase and bag. "Either way, use a condom. Take it from an epidemiologist."

"Good advice. Have a good flight."

"I'll be back next week, and you have the number for Maddy's caregiver agency. Keep me posted on any more sightings of the Oatmeal Man, will you?"

"I will."

I walked her to the door and saw her out. "And I want to hear about today's date. Send me an email tonight. Let me live vicariously through your handsome FBI agent."

We muffled our laughter in deference to the neighbors, and then she was gone.

I spent the next few hours doing laundry and thinking about her question. Would it be smart to slow down my relationship with Rhys? Was I attracted to him because, in the aftermath of Don's departure, I was longing for someone else to define my life?

Or was it that man's beautiful runner's ass?

These questions were like a hamster on a treadmill. They could get going pretty quickly, but they didn't ever seem to get anywhere. Still, by the time Maddy woke up (as sunny and happy as ever), I'd decided that Don had offered me the illusion of a relationship so I'd be his mother's caregiver. Rhys didn't seem to want anything from me, other than the hopeful, fearful possibility of a relationship and the near-certainty of the wondrous sex I'd only experienced through books or movies.

It came down to trust. Did I think he'd use me the way Don had?

And was I too naive to answer that question in time to avoid another psychological shellacking?

Maddy and I ate our breakfast and chose her outfit for the day. Even though we'd discussed today's plans the night before, she had, of course, forgotten about them. Maddy was surprised and delighted to learn that we had a date.

"A date! How exciting! What will Azariah say?"

"It's okay," I told her with a smile. "He said he didn't mind this once." Her loyalty to her husband, dead for more than fifteen years, was touching, and inspired definite envy in me. Who wouldn't want such a caring relationship?

Maddy clapped. "Isn't Az the dearest man? What a sweetheart! You're so pretty in that sweater. The blue really brings out your eyes."

"Thank you!" She made me feel pretty. "And the rose of your sweater makes your complexion glow."

"We're two beauties, aren't we?"

"Oh, we are!"

"And what shall we two beauties do with this gorgeous day?"

I hooked her arm companionably through mine and walked her to the garage elevator. "What about a date with some handsome men? Does that sound good?"

The appreciation of our sweaters had wiped her memory clean again, and the news of a date was a fresh source of excitement for her. "A date with handsome men! That's my very favorite thing to do! Shall we bring Belinda?"

"Oh, she'd love to go. But she left for Jakarta this morning." I checked Maddy's seatbelt and started the car. Every journey with Maddy, from the most mundane to the most exotic, became an adventure. My mood had lifted, and all my concerns were left in the slipstream as we pulled into traffic. Rhys was a handsome, kind man, and I was a single, available woman. What more did I need to know for now? I chanted the Maddy Mantra: *Be in the now. Forget yesterday—enjoy today.*

"You're very sparkly today, my dear," Maddy said to me.

I couldn't suppress a smile. "Do you know, I feel sparkly!"

"Lovely! How come?"

"Well, Maddy, I can tell you." And I could. She was all but guaranteed to be happy for me and then immediately forget whatever I told her. "Last night, I had a date with a really good-looking guy who turned out to be nice too."

"A rare combination!"

"I know it!" We headed into the city. "And then he kissed me at the end of the evening and asked if you and I would meet him today."

"Oh, how exciting! What did you say?"

"I said yes. I know you'll love him."

"Now, where did he kiss you?"

She was eager for girlish gossip. "Um—outside the front door to our building."

"No, I mean, your hand? Your cheek?" She waggled her brows at me. "Your lips?"

The heat coming off my face was inspired by the memory of him all but pulling me onto his lap at the movie theater, but there was no need to share with Maddy anything more sensational than a G-rating.

"My cheek," I said. It was true, after all. It just wasn't the whole truth.

"Do you think he'll try to kiss my cheek?" Maddy was beginning to sparkle too. As usual, the world, even at its most dreary, was edged in gold for her.

"He might—and maybe close to the ear, too, so it feels a little extra—"

"Sexy," she finished. Her eyes were wide and delighted.

"Oh, yeah. And then he'll say 'Good night,' but he'll say it before he pulls away, so his voice is all low and growly in your ear."

She bounced in her seat and clapped her hands. "That's the best kind of kiss on the cheek! What's his name?"

"His name is Rhys."

"What, like the peanut butter cup?"

"Exactly like the peanut butter cup!" She and I laughed delightedly together.

Traffic heading into the city was light for a Saturday morning—surprising, given that the day was beautiful. The fall leaves were shining in the sunlight, and clouds were drifting across the bright blue sky. A paradise for tourists coming to visit all of Washington, DC's many sights.

Of course, we weren't heading to the National Mall. In fact, the GPS led us to Anacostia, a part of the city little seen by visitors. A lot of residents never ventured that far east, either. The neighborhoods we traveled through were older and less polished than the tourist spots, and it was clear that the history here was less wrapped in glory and patriotism and more grounded in repression and poverty.

We turned into the parking lot and found a space. "Here we are," I said to Maddy.

"Where, dear?"

"At the Anacostia Boys' Club." I pointed to Rhys, handsome in jeans and a black T-shirt, who was already crossing from the door to meet us. "And there's our date for the day, coming to walk us in."

"Goodness. Isn't he lovely!"

"Yes, he certainly is." I unbuckled and got out. He intercepted me as I went around the back to help Maddy out. His warm hand was suddenly in mine and he leaned in for a kiss that was entirely brief and appropriate. And yet I'd been so keyed up by our make-out sessions that just that kiss was enough to send a shiver through me.

He saw it, of course, and favored me with a contained leer. "I don't know about you," I said to him primly, "but I'm on duty." I looked pointedly at Maddy's door.

His leer became a grin. "Me too. Hi, beautiful." That last was to Maddy, who was extracting herself from the car.

Maddy, as usual, defied expectation by recognizing Rhys immediately. "Why, Peanut Butter Cup! Oh, it's a pleasure to my eyes to drink you in! You give me a kiss, please!"

He leaned in and kissed her cheek, and she breathed in delightedly. Rhys smelled like soap and pine. No surprise Maddy wanted to fill her lungs with him. "Hello, Madcap. Are you planning on any adventures today?"

"Oh, you sly thing. Every day is an adventure. Don't you know that?" She clung to his hand, clearly happy to be next to him. Looking around, she saw me. Again, the fog of dementia lifted, and she recognized me as well.

"Oh, Cyn! How lovely to see you! Is this your house?" The three of us examined a building that could have been used as "Classic Elementary School Number One" on a movie set; it was that iconic. "Is it a school? It looks like a school."

"It was, a few decades ago." Rhys's deep voice drew her back from her examination of the building, and the distraction had worked its typical effect. She no longer knew either of us but was unconcerned. Maddy's life was a very happy one.

Rhys walked us to the school, one arm around my shoulders and the other hand gently holding Maddy's. She peered at me across his broad chest and raised her eyebrow delightedly. Maddy had spotted a budding romance between me and our escort, and it was clear she liked the view.

Rhys told us about the school and how it became the Boys' Club.

"There's a Girls' Club too. The goal is to provide a safe space for boys or girls without the social strain of the opposite sex. So you'll be welcome to volunteer, but don't be surprised if there aren't too many other women here today."

Maddy suddenly came to a halt, a thought blooming across her face. I was reminded once again that her dementia hadn't reduced her intelligence—it just stopped her from being able to put her thoughts together in a normal order. Rhys and I stopped too, to watch her and see what she had to say.

"This is why you buy all those condoms," she said, squinting up at him. "You buy them for the teens at this club. Not for you. I'm disappointed in you, Peanut Butter Cup. I thought you were having wild dates all the time!"

He laughed at her and recaptured her hand. "The Boys' Club doesn't get *all* those condoms, Maddy. I do keep a few for myself." He grinned at me with undisguised interest. Maddy turned to me, and I—not nearly as cool and calm about this as the two of them—found myself blushing. I ducked my head and got us moving to the door. Where was a Maddy distraction when you needed one?

Ultimately, Rhys took pity on me and drew Maddy's attention by gently waving his hand, her tiny fingers still enclosed in his. "A lot of FBI agents volunteer with the Boys & Girls Clubs. There's Dash over there."

He gestured to the open lot next to the school, where the handsome Dash, blade-straight and agile, was leading a group of boys in a rough-and-tumble game of football.

"Let's go play!" Maddy was captivated immediately. She had more stamina than anyone in their nineties ought to have, and given the chance, I suspect she'd have run and run with the football players until she collapsed in happy exhaustion.

But her Peanut Butter Cup put a restraining hand on her arm. She smiled at the warmth and gentleness of his touch. "Hang on,

Maddy. I have something better for us to do. Come inside, will you?"

He led us into the school. The difference between the bright sunlight and the dim hallway wiped the memory of the football game from Maddy's mind. The sounds and scents of this dim entrance to the building triggered her memories.

"Oh! I remember this!"

I'd have put a hundred dollars on a bet that Maddy had never before been to Anacostia, but I understood her observation. There was something about a school that was hard to forget. Graham crackers, institutional cleaners, the ghost of the floor polisher's hum, perhaps the echo of a brassy, ringing bell. That atmosphere was probably common around the country.

But I checked with my aged client just the same. "You grew up in Connecticut, didn't you, Maddy?"

She looked at me without recognition, but with admiration. "Why, you look just like a pixie. So cute! And you're so bright and clever too! You're right—I did grow up in Connecticut!"

"So do you really remember this school?"

"What school?"

I know she didn't do it on purpose, but whenever she yanked the conversational rug out from under someone, she did get a fit of the giggles at the confusion she created. And both Rhys and I were looking decidedly off-balance. Soon we were all laughing together.

The sound from the first room off the hallway reached out to draw us forward. It was the chatter of young voices, the occasional raised tone, a random burst of laughter. The Peanut Butter Cup walked us into a large, sunny room crowded with a microcosm of the large, diverse city around us. Boys and young men from every ethnicity looked up as we entered. Some were smiling, some were frowning; all were watching us with great attention.

Maddy peered past Rhys's arm and hooted in delight. With a merry wave, she called out. "Aren't you lovely!"

"This is the art room," Rhys said. He'd dropped his arm from my shoulder and tucked Maddy's hand into his elbow. He led her to a long table spread with butcher paper. Markers and crayons were scattered across it and several boys were coloring, either right on the paper or on separate sheets. "Would you like to paint or draw with us today, Maddy?"

The rainbow colors had caught her eye, and her fingers unconsciously opened and closed with the longing to select a favorite color and make her mark. "Yes! Oh, what fun!"

"Excellent. Mario, will you share your pencils?"

A stunningly beautiful boy with enormous liquid eyes nodded shyly and moved over. He laid down a clean sheet of paper in front of the empty seat beside him and gestured to the pencils. "Come on, lady. Everybody gets to draw here, and no one will make fun of you. That's the rules. What color do you want to start with?"

"Oh!" Maddy was completely focused on the opportunity before her. She took up a pencil the color of warm, rich chocolate, and another one in orange. "I'm going to draw a peanut butter cup!"

Mario nodded solemnly. "Good choice. I like them too."

I suspected that Maddy didn't know exactly why Rhys and I were both laughing, but it didn't matter. She was happy so she was laughing too.

THIRTEEN

CYN

MADDY WAS FULLY ENGROSSED IN HER DRAWING. ONCE AGAIN, her immediate acceptance of joy was a reminder to me to let go of my fears and concerns. The Maddy Mantra.

Still, I did have a job to do. "We'll have to watch her," I whispered to Rhys, who leaned down to hear me. My sudden proximity to his handsome head gave me a thrill. "She's become a tremendous escape artist. The first thing to distract her, and she'll be off."

"I have the perfect solution," he replied.

He introduced me to the other adults in the room. Kyle was an FBI agent, Damien was a community volunteer, and Angel, Bobby, and Tyrone were identified as mentors. "Gentlemen, our guests today are Maddy and Cyn. Maddy has memory issues. You understand?"

They all nodded, and Tyrone shared that his grandfather had the same issue. "I know what it's like," he said to me with intense sincerity. "We'll help to watch over her."

"They will too," Rhys confirmed. "This is a great group here."

We all smiled and nodded. Rhys led me farther in the room. He was greeted with shouts as we moved. Half the boys wanted him to look at what they were doing, and he had praise and suggestions for all of them.

I'd seen Rhys in his official capacity as Special Agent Jones of the FBI. And I'd gladly explored a more personal side of him . . . both mentally and physically. But it was clear that I was seeing a different version of him in this art room, and it took me time to figure out what had changed.

He was moving with the same cat-like grace, lacing his big body easily between tables and chairs and the sprawled limbs of boys and teenagers. He had the same smile that lit up his face. His laugh was low and warm and friendly.

So what had changed when he walked through the door?

I finally realized that he looked fully at home. Like his skin fit him better. His spine wasn't as straight, his shoulders had come down a touch, and even at rest, his mobile lips were turning faintly upward. He was happy here, talking with kids and alternately teasing and encouraging them. It was a good look for him, and I decided he'd look even better if he let the precise, tidy FBI haircut get a little longer, a little shaggier.

We ended up at a table that held sticks of charcoal and a large pad of newsprint. It was open to a page that showed the rough outline of a sketch. I saw immediately which of the boys was the subject.

"That's amazing," I said. "Did you do this?"

"It's just a scribble." He looked uncomfortable but also distantly hopeful.

"It's a little better than a scribble." He'd captured movement and life in a few simple strokes; it was mesmerizing. "Can I look through the pad?"

He shuffled his feet but didn't stop me.

The first pages were more sketches of the boys. Some were clearly pages where he'd been instructing others. They were mere lines on the page. And then I flipped to a recent page and saw . . .

My face.

"Sorry about that," he mumbled. "I don't seem to be able to stop drawing you."

I was shocked. And fascinated. He'd captured something in his image of me that was both wistful and proud. He made me look . . . beautiful.

Through the lines he'd drawn on the page, I wasn't childishly small—I was delicate. I wasn't woefully flat-chested. I didn't wear the astonished look I feared was my default setting, of an alarmed deer caught in the headlights.

He'd made me look smart. Funny. Sexy.

Like someone you'd want to spend some time with.

The image on the page was like me, and yet so unlike me, that I was rendered speechless.

"The eyes aren't right," he offered. "I keep working on them."

"You do?" I squeaked.

That made him laugh. "My notepad is covered with attempts. It's absolutely the wrong thing for an agent to have in his record. I'm probably going to have to copy the entire book over before I file it. Those notes often show up in court records, and endless efforts to capture the curve of your eyebrow wouldn't help my reputation at all."

He reached out with his thumb and lightly traced my eyebrow, a wholly innocent gesture that nevertheless sent an electrical flash through me. I lost the ability to do anything other than blink.

"I'm lucky there aren't pencils or paints at work," he teased, clearly trying to lighten the mood. "I've been imagining color combinations ever since the grocery store. They'd put me in the loony bin."

I stared at him, speechless. "Too much?" he asked. "Are you freaked?"

I gulped. "Flattered. Confused. Why would anyone want to draw me?"

But I turned and looked at his sketch again, and saw how

pretty I was to him . . . and I thought maybe he was seeing something that no one else ever had. "Wow."

"Yeah. Sorry. Okay. Let's get this back on track. How would you like to take over the session today?"

"Uh—" The abrupt subject change would have floored me anyway, but what he was offering gave me more of the dog-who-can't-figure-out-where-the-sound-is-coming-from tilt to my head. "What?"

He gestured to the kids all around us. "They're all ages, with all levels of skill. And they're already bored with my plan for the day, which was to copy images from the National Gallery."

He held up a handful of the copies you could buy in the gift shop. One of the Thomas Cole *Voyage of Life* paintings, a French flower seller, a brawl between Italian armies.

"I was thinking maybe you'd have an idea for something they could do today that would keep them entertained and not fighting with each other."

My first instinct was to demur. To gesture back to him so he'd make the decision. What did I know about keeping these kids happy? Hell—any kids happy? I didn't even have a typical childhood to fall back on, as I was almost always in academic camps or clubs while my peers were doing whatever kids did during non-school hours.

On the other hand . . .

Here was Rhys—the man I'd feared I was going to lose myself in—offering me the chance to take the lead. He wasn't trying to fit me into his concept of what I should be doing. He was standing by, ready to support me if I ventured an idea of my own.

He really, really wasn't Don.

It seemed silly that I had this realization, which should have been obvious from the beginning. It was like a balloon escaping my fingers and lifting off blissfully into a wide-open sky, to be tugged and led by any passing breeze in a smile-inducing dance.

This internal monologue took place over the course of mere

seconds and Rhys was still looking at me hopefully, ready to surrender his leadership if I wanted him to.

Did I want to take the lead?

I realized I did.

"Okay. I have an idea, I think."

It didn't sound like a freedom manifesto, but it certainly felt like one.

"Oh, good!" He clapped once, a gunshot that got the attention of every pair of eyes. "Gentlemen, we have a visitor today. This is Cyn."

Maddy, who had looked up from her drawing at his clap, waved. "Hello, Cyn, darling! How nice to see you! Don't you look just like a pixie!"

Rhys turned to me. "What would you like to share with the group, Pixie?"

"You didn't even want to hear the idea first?" I gulped.

"No need. If it doesn't work, we'll go on to something else. This is supposed to be fun, right? So what do you have? Any thoughts from fourteenth-century Flemish architecture?"

"Moorish," I corrected automatically. "That's not what I'm proposing. Okay."

I stepped forward, nervous but hopeful, and addressed the sea of young faces watching me with varying levels of interest and suspicion. "Let's say you had all the money in the world."

Many hoots and jeers greeted this statement. "That's never going to happen," one young artist called out.

"I know, but in here, no one makes fun of you for ideas. Right?"

They agreed.

"So for fun, to put on paper: Let's say you have all the money in the world. Can you design your ideal house? What would it have?"

Already they were thinking. Several reached for paper. I kept talking, hoping to open up their creativity and inspiration. "Would you build it over a river so you could have a boat in the garage? Would you have an entire movie theater in your living room? What about your family? Are you giving them room in your house, or do you live there all by yourself? Do you need a helipad on the roof?"

Some of the boys were grinning. Some were frowning. Some were shouting out their ideas and some were drawing with their arms curled protectively around their papers to hide their brainstorms. They were all thinking, and most were already drawing. Even the mentors were talking to each other about their dream homes.

"Work on your ideas for a while. Draw a picture of the front of the house, and then I'll show you how to draw a floor plan. Don't forget, money is no object, but you can't ignore the rules of reality. You can't live on a cloud, and 'down' is always below 'up.' We'll talk about load-bearing walls and the importance of grouping plumbing later. Okay?"

Rhys and Damien were grinning, and Kyle the FBI agent was already in deep discussion with a kid about how much room you'd need for a family of tigers.

Rhys took my hand as I passed him. "You just pulled that out of nowhere? I ambush you, and you light them up like no one else ever has?"

I ducked my head at his praise. "It's a favorite mind game of mine. I'm glad they like it."

He looked at me, a smile playing around his mouth. "You're like a pixie. Something impossible and mythical."

I blushed under his admiration—and his support. And the room was filled with heads bent over papers. Even Maddy was scribbling a house on her page. She and Mario were talking with great passion about having a wishing well in the front yard. She was in favor. He was leaning more toward a vast water park.

It was one of the most enjoyable days I'd had in . . . forever. Lunch was provided (sandwiches, milk, and a cookie in a paper bag) and Maddy became everyone's adopted grandmother—or girlfriend, depending on where she was in time at any particular moment.

She lay down on a dilapidated sofa in the art room after lunch and took her regular nap, happily snoozing through the cacophony. Then, she and the boys went outside for a run as if it were recess, while I watched nervously from the window. Dash, who by that point was working with a group of older boys on defensive and offensive plays, greeted her like an old friend. Of course, she didn't remember him, but treated him like a bosom companion just the same.

The afternoon sunlight was bright, and the air was cool. The volunteers kept her outside for perhaps fifteen minutes and watched over her with gentle care. She returned to the art room unharmed, her cheeks flushed and her eyes laughing.

By the afternoon, many of the boys had drawn up magnificent palaces that would make high-priced architects grind their teeth for not being the first to think of such brilliant ideas. And Rhys was sketching me.

He brushed aside my protests. "It's much easier to draw you when you're in front of me. Keep doing what you're doing. Don't mind me."

So he captured me explaining to a boy named Xavier about roof lines. He did a quick, fluid sketch of my discussion with David (who liked trains) about trestle bridges. He drew me laughing with Maddy, a drawing that was so alive and true I demanded it on the spot, knowing that it would make me cry once she died—may that be many, many long and happy years from now.

"She really does have it right, you know," Rhys said to me. "You really do look like a pixie. A lovely, fantastical creation. How can you be real?"

I blushed and covered my shyness by leafing through his sketchbook again.

"You absolutely astonish me," I admitted. "You're an incredible artist."

"Thanks. It's something to do in off-moments, though."

"Really? Because I think this is pretty good."

"Nah. I'm an agent. I have a job. I'm giving this up. It's getting in the way."

"Giving up what? Art?"

"Absolutely. It's one or the other—art or agent. I clearly can't do both, and I knew I wanted to be an agent when I was fourteen. So, that's that."

"You can just give this up?" I looked at the inspiration all around me, almost breathless at the idea that he could turn his back on such a gift.

"Did I explain to you about having to copy over my notebook?"

"But Rhys. Look at these." I found the one he'd drawn of young Jeong. "Boy. That's something. You really see people, don't you?"

"Now, why should that surprise you?" He regarded me with the light of challenge in his eyes.

"I don't know. It's just that—"

"Yeah? It's just that what?"

It took me a moment to wrangle my emotions into words—and the emotions weren't going to be very flattering to him, so I chose my phrasing carefully. "Well, it's been my experience that really good-looking people don't actually see those around them. Life's been easy because they're attractive. They don't really know how to . . . I don't know."

He was staring at me, and I was flustered.

"You think I can't see what others need? I only care about myself?"

"Well—no. When you put it like that—"

He stood and took my hand. "Kyle. Damien." He got their attention, and Rhys forked his fingers at them and then at Maddy. "Cyn and I are going to hit the supply cabinet. Got it?" They nodded, and he tugged me from the room.

"Are you mad at me?" I asked, unsure of myself.

He grinned down at me without slacking our pace. "I'm not mad, Cyn."

"Then what are we doing?"

"I'm going to get charcoal dust on you. Doesn't show on this black T-shirt, but it's going to show on that blue sweater."

"What?"

He stopped and unlocked the door to what was either a very large closet or a very small office. Supplies filled the shelves on either side, and a high table held a paper cutter and a printer.

He pulled me inside, shut the door, and bodily lifted me so I was sitting on the table. "I'm proving to you that I can know what other people need."

My heart pounded as he stepped between my knees and boldly came up flush against my crotch. I tried to think of something clever to say, but I was speechless with nerves and anticipation.

"And what I think you need, Cyn, is for someone to give you one hundred percent of their attention. Not in a cab or a movie theater or outside your door. I mean right here, right now. To show you that you're magnificent. Magnetic. I think you need me to prove to you that I can see to your needs." One of his arms was around my waist and the other hand cupped my chin. "So if you don't want me to prove that to you now, speak up."

He leaned in and tipped my head to the side so he could kiss my cheek exactly where he had the other night. The feel of his mouth against me, his breath in my ear, made me tighten my grip on his biceps.

"Now I understand that for many people," he murmured, "silence implies consent. But I'm afraid that's not good enough for me. I'm a lawyer, and I'm going to need a verbal authorization to proceed, ma'am."

He drew back and the loss of his heat and weight against me left me afraid that I'd float away. "Ha?" I said.

"May I kiss you, Ms. Quimby? Here, hidden away where we won't be disturbed? I mean really, really kiss you. Yes or no?"

"Oh." His eyes were warm like the richest coffee. His hands were strong and firm on me. "Yes. Yes, please."

He gave a grunt of satisfaction and then laid his lips on mine in a surprising whisper of a kiss.

This was unexpected. Our past make-out sessions had surely propelled us past gentle seduction . . . hadn't they? I offered a mewl of protest and I could feel him smile as he leaned in closer, slowly increasing the pressure of his mouth on mine.

I was the one who, sliding my hands up to draw his head down, finally left gentle behind and found the weight I needed. It was my tongue, not his, that made the bold foray into enemy territory. And then the battle was on, and we licked inside each other with increasing eagerness.

He groaned and shifted against me. I could feel his cock through both our jeans and knew my panties were getting wet. I arched my back to press my breasts against him and he growled in approval.

Desperation was welling up, threatening to overwhelm me. He'd taken me from "what's going on" to "please fuck me on this table" in the space of a single kiss. The realization sobered me. He felt my resistance and drew back.

"I was going to make some kind of clever comment," he said, breathing heavily. "Something about understanding your needs. But I can't remember what I was going to say."

"Jesus," I said. "Wow."

"Yeah. Wow."

He looked edible. "What happens now?"

"Now you have to figure out how to get the streaks of charcoal off your sweater, and I have to go back into a room full of boys with a raging boner."

"Do you want me to . . ." I looked at his groin with mingled timidity and interest, not entirely sure what I was offering.

He shivered for a moment and touched my lips with his thumb, but then turned it into a caress and dropped his hand. "Nah," he said with a gentle smile. "Not in a supply closet. This went further and faster than I thought it would, and even if we're fully alone, I don't want to make you moan here." His arm tightened around me, suddenly pulling me into his chest. "Although I could. You know that, don't you?"

"I do know," I breathed. Nothing could have been more clear. I'd gotten a case of the overexcited giggles. "I never got taken into the cloak room by the prom king in high school, but I bet it was like this. Exciting and hot."

"Mm." He nuzzled my neck. "I was the prom king, you know."

"I'm not at all surprised." The top of my head was lifting off as his lips followed the tendon under my ear.

"And I feel like I've finally gotten my impatient hands on the sexy teacher." I could hear his grin. "Smart and clever and way out of my league, but she's letting me get away with naughty things in the supply closet—"

We didn't really need any fantasies, but spinning unlikely high school stories was increasing the juice between us.

"Shit," he said against my mouth. "I have *got* to calm down."

He pulled back and laid his forehead against mine. We both panted as we recovered. "Let's you and I take a little walk, okay? Put some daylight between us. Don't worry," he said, forestalling my protest. "They'll take good care of Maddy. We don't need to go far. I'll calm down in a minute. You could use some time too, you know. You're a little flushed yourself."

I put my hands to my fire-hot cheeks. "Wow. I'm so hot."

That made him wink at me. "Stop that. I'm trying to calm down."

Which made me flush all the harder.

He untucked his T-shirt from his jeans, which maybe camouflaged his condition slightly, and helped me jump down from the table.

"Hang on." He spotted a roll of paper towels. With focused attention, he blotted the outlines of his hands that he'd left all over my sweater in charcoal, and then turned me around to dust off my backside. Bearing the marks of his lust on my body—it was thrilling. Inappropriate, but thrilling.

Then he was done, and I was presentable. "Good date so far?" he asked with a grin as he opened the door.

"Good date," I agreed.

"So you'll go out with me again?"

Boy. Would I!

FOURTEEN
RHYS

I'D PROMISED CYN SOME DAYLIGHT BETWEEN US. BUT I couldn't let go of her hand.

She glanced back to check if she could see Maddy through the art room window as we walked out the front door and down the path to the street. It wasn't hard to interpret her concern. Her relationship with Maddy was clearly more than a caregiver to a patient, and knowing the eternally cheerful Maddy, I could see why.

"Kyle and Damien will take care of her, and we won't be gone long," I assured her. "This neighborhood can be dicey, and my gun is locked in my car."

She darted a glance at me, her eyes laughing. "Wait. Are you telling me they didn't teach you kung fu or anything at the FBI Academy?"

The sparkle in her eyes lit up the afternoon. Cyn in a teasing mood took my breath away. Then again, Cyn in just about any mood took my breath away. "If you must know, I did complete the required coursework in personal defense, but if you don't practice that stuff every day, it's really not much more than book learning."

"And you don't practice every day?"

"I go to the shooting range every day. We all focus on what we're good at, you know?"

Her eyes went to my mouth and her blush flared up again, spreading a wash of rose across her pale skin. That could only be captured by pastels, I thought distantly, even as I adjusted my gait to make room for the renewed interest from the below-the-belt brain.

"Cut that out," I said. "I'm trying to calm down."

"What? I didn't say anything!" Her blush became even more rosy. I knew her cheek would feel heated against my lips and realized I was gripping her hand to keep myself from reaching for her.

"You didn't have to say anything. I can hear what you're thinking."

"Oh, Jesus. I hope not!" She was fully embarrassed, and I was fully hard.

"Let's talk about something that will help me cool off," I suggested. We were strolling down the sidewalk, the October air cooling our heated skin as the school disappeared behind us.

"Like what?"

I thought about it. "Your ex-husband. Tell me all about him. I want to kill him. That will take my mind off of what you're thinking."

"Yeah, well, it'll take my mind off what I'm thinking too. Do we have to?"

"I honestly can't figure out how any man could prefer someone over you. Especially someone named—what was it, Daisy?"

"Dahhhhlia." She drew the name out, scorn and pain dripping off the word.

"Dahhhhlia," I repeated, hating the sorrow below her anger. "Who names a child Dahlia, anyway? Who gets a bundle of darling baby and says, I know what we should name her. Dahlia is the perfect name."

"No kidding!" Her smile was tentative, but it brightened my mood.

"You've never met her?"

She shook her head. "Never. I thought about searching social media for her, but—you know. Eww." She frowned at me suddenly. "Don't you do any research either. You know—FBI research. Like with Barry from Winchester."

"I won't," I promised. "That kind of shit can get you into serious trouble. Dahlia's not worth it. Neither is Don. Anyway, I'm sure she has frizzy red hair and smells like wet dogs."

"Oh, please." Her shoulders were relaxing a bit. "She's undoubtedly a six-foot-tall supermodel with blond hair and a big rack."

You can tell so much about a person by how they describe others. Cyn's image of the unknown Dahlia as an impossible super-hero type was pure insecurity rearing its ugly head. She was describing the kind of woman she'd envied all her life. "And you're small and dark-haired and have perfect breasts that I really want to nibble on." Shit. That got out of hand fast. So much for good intentions.

She gasped and dropped my hand, her blush back in full force. "Oh my God. Don't say things like that."

"Why not?"

"I'm definitely not used to hearing things like that!"

I took her hand again firmly and kept walking. "I could kill Don for not making sure you understood how desirable you are. He's a complete fool, and he deserves a thrashing at the very least. He should have told you every single day that you are—you're art walking. You're stunning. I can't take my eyes off you."

Her eyes were huge. She was overwhelmed.

"Boy," I said, trying to bring her back to earth. "It's really easy for me to forget you weren't experienced before Don. You're the kind of woman every man would want to be with. And what's so great about him, anyway? Is Don the type who could attract a supermodel?" She offered a laugh. "Seriously. Does he drive a Ferrari? Wear Armani? Does he have money to burn, and is he a social media influencer? Why would a supermodel want to date Don?"

She shook her head at each suggestion and was offering huffs of laughter by the end. I felt like I'd won a prize.

"I don't know. Aren't supermodels famously stupid?" she tried.

"I'll have you know I modeled a bit in college."

She uttered a scornful sneer. "Of course you did. You're gorgeous enough."

"Thank you. It's a lot harder than you think."

"Right." She didn't believe me. "Born with amazing cheekbones and bedroom eyes and that jawline. I'm sure it's every bit as tough as digging a ditch."

"Madam. I'll have you know that I gave up modeling because it was too damned hard. No, I'm serious. Beer makes your eyes pouchy. Hang out in a pool hall for an hour, and your skin dulls from the smoke. And eat a brownie? Under no circumstances. Not only can you not afford to gain even a pound—and they check, believe me—but a single pimple could lose you a series of gigs for being 'unreliable.' The camera click takes a second. The lifestyle is absolutely twenty-four hours, with no time off."

"Really," she said. "You're pretty passionate about it, huh?"

"I'm saying, have some pity for Dahlia the supermodel. First, her life is brutally hard and filled with rejection. And second, she's going to marry a worm like Don. Think about it. Doesn't that deserve pity?"

I hit her with the bedroom eyes, and she laughed out loud. "Okay. I guess she does deserve pity."

"That's right, she does." We were about as far from the school as I cared to get, and I drew her across the street and onto our return voyage.

We walked in companionable silence for a while. I was thinking about the fleeting period in the art room, when it seemed like she expected me to decide what the kids were going to try next. And when I didn't decide—when I gave her the room to make up her own mind—there was a moment when I felt like I could see into her secret self. This was a remarkable woman who'd never been encouraged as she grew into adulthood. She'd had to make do as best she could.

I was determined to show her all the support I could and give her the time she needed to decide what she was doing with her life. Hopefully, she'd leave room for me to fit into it too.

Of course, this was far too deep for casual, flirty chatter on the sidewalk. So I stopped fixating on futures and plans and possibilities. Instead, I smiled down at her, walking at my side as naturally as if we'd always been together.

She caught my smile. "Better now?" she asked, discretely glancing at my crotch.

"Entirely respectable, thank you." I might even be able to tuck my shirt back into my jeans.

"So, let me try a topic of conversation now."

"Lay it on me," I said.

"How come you can't be an artist and an agent?"

I frowned and considered how I could explain. "Those two jobs need two different brains. Art is . . . art is all about emotion, and then you try to bring your skill to bear to make a vision into a reality."

"Makes sense."

"But law enforcement, that's logic and law and experience. Emotion—well, it's not wrong to use emotion in law enforcement. You have to understand motive, and that's pure emotion. But for the most part, emotion isn't helpful."

"Oh." She and I both thought about that as we walked along. "So the three things you told me about, when you got in trouble. Those were about emotion, huh?"

Hm. Wanting the exhilaration of a fast car, leading to a speeding ticket: emotion. Wanting to celebrate a girlfriend's birthday, leading to being drunk at work: emotion. Making a stupid joke at an arrest: emotion. "Yeah," I said. "I guess you're right."

"So being an agent means denying your emotions?"

"Argh!" I called out my frustration. "Can we not confront the blackness of my soul at every turn?" I leered at her to take the sting from my words. "Do you make it a habit to psychoanalyze your dates?"

"Doesn't everyone?" She grinned back at me, and I forgave her for attempting to make me face up to a point of confusion in my life: Could I be as good an agent as my father and still be me?

"Okay," she said. "Let me try a different topic." She looked shy again, and I pulled her closer.

"I hope I have a better answer for this one."

She was at a loss for words for a moment. "When we, you know —make out. I mean . . . I don't know. It seems that together, we're pretty, um—"

"Hot? Incendiary? Sexy beyond belief?"

She blushed again. I wanted to keep her blushing like that until the end of time; she was so pretty. "Yeah. Is that, like . . . normal?"

Tricky question to answer. I didn't want to look like some kind of man-slut, but I'd kissed my share of women, and was definitely in a good position to rate the power of kissing Cyn. But she deserved a straight answer. Even if it did make me look like a himbo.

"Not normal. Definitely not normal. I don't mean to push you too fast. I swear I don't expect anything from you. I should have given you something more controlled and respectful this afternoon. You were so cute, and I've been watching you all day, and then we were in the supply closet, and . . ." My cock was like steel again. "Shit. All that calming down has just been wasted."

She came to a halt and I swung to face her. She looked positively guilty. "I'm so sorry."

She was a magnet and I was iron filings. I stepped into her and slid my hands around her waist. Her hands came up instinctively, and I shivered at the feel of her. "Don't worry about it," I said before I leaned down and captured her lips once more.

We were on the street and possibly in view of the windows of the school, so I tried to hold on to my hunger. The kiss was slower and softer, but there was no denying that I rocked my hips into her for the bliss of feeling her soft belly against my cock.

Her hands were in my hair, her tongue was in my mouth, her warmth and scent surrounded me. How could something so little unbalance me so effortlessly?

I pulled back far enough to rest my forehead against hers and we breathed deeply together.

"This isn't going to help your condition," she said softly, rocking her hips forward and making me gasp.

"This *is* like being in high school," I admitted. "I'm afraid I'm going to have to duck into the teachers' bathroom and do something unmentionable before I can go back into the art room. Don't blush at me like that. I might make you come with me, and that would be a seriously horrible place to make love to you for the first time."

The sting of her unconsciously fisting her hands in my hair felt like bliss. She was as turned on as I was. "Rhys! How can you say things like that?"

"What?" I watched her glorious eyes. "Do you want me to point out that you're in every bit as desperate a condition as I am, but yours isn't as visible?"

Her answer was a blink and a gasp. I kept whispering to her, unable to restrain myself.

"If I were to slip my hand beneath the waistband of those jeans and slide my palm over the naked skin of your pretty ass, when I got to the center of you, I'd find you wet and ready for me. Wouldn't I?"

"Oh my." Her eyes were clenched tight shut, and she shivered.

"That's what I thought. You're one sexy pixie." I leaned down further and inhaled the warmth of her scent before kissing her neck. "So now who needs to calm down?"

I released her regretfully. "Me," she admitted. "I'm like putty in your hands."

"That could be fun," I grinned. "Come on. Let's go back in."

"Oh, fine for you. You've got a bathroom to duck into."

"Well, there's a girls' room, if you want it." I waggled my eyebrows at her and she sniggered.

"I'll pass. I think I can control myself."

"That does beg a question, though." This time I pulled her hand into the crook of my arm so I could feel her more closely at my side. "I'm not expecting anything. But just in case you'd be so inclined, how should we arrange our next date? How long is Dr. Root out of town?"

"She's gone for two weeks. I never minded that until this very minute."

"I'm less than eager to make out with you while Maddy sleeps in the next room. That would be too much like I'm going after the babysitter in the basement rec room."

She nodded. "Agreed. I wouldn't feel right having a 'sleepover' while I was responsible for Maddy."

There was no denying that I really wanted to get this woman under me. All the cues to her personality pointed to her needing space to make her own decisions, but by this point, I wanted her pretty badly. I tried (and probably failed) to modulate the adolescent horniness in my question. "Is there any time when you're not on duty?"

She thought, chewing her lip. The sight almost brought me to my knees. "Belinda has a service for evenings, but I generally try to be nearby when she's with them. I don't have to be. I just like to know she's doing okay. Oh," she said, remembering, "she works out with her trainer twice a week, but that's an hour, and I'm usually right there."

The thought made me laugh. "Maddy has a trainer?"

She nudged me to make her point. "What, you think a ninety-three-year-old woman could climb into a shopping cart if she didn't stay flexible and strong?"

"She's healthy as a horse," I agreed. "It's impressive."

"It is. Everything but her memory. She and her trainer even do some modified yoga."

"Good on Madcap Maddy. That's awesome."

"It is. But it makes anything more than a noontime quickie pretty unlikely for you and me for a while."

"And a quickie definitely won't do. I want to take my time exploring you, my pixie."

She licked her lips and shivered. "We could go to dinner, I suppose. If the service could send someone Maddy has had before and likes."

"I don't want you feeling anxious. Want to talk to the service and get back to me?"

She liked that I wasn't pushing too hard. I could tell that by the way her shoulders came down. And she definitely liked that I was attracted. Just by luck, I was threading a needle and it was working. Bull's-eye.

"I'll call them first thing on Monday," she said. "I'll find us a time. I'd like to do some exploring of my own, you know. I just love to lick a Peanut Butter Cup. Slowly."

We were at the stairs to the front door, which made her reply particularly painful, since we were definitely in sight of any number of impressionable boys and young men, and I thus was constrained against grabbing her again and kissing her until she was moaning my name. But I wanted to. Oh, how I wanted to. My cock leapt, and her smirk looked particularly triumphant. It was going to be fun helping this girl become brave.

"Go on," I growled as I led her inside. "You head back. I'll be there in a minute."

"Just a minute?" she said coyly.

I swatted her ass and she laughed as she moved to the art room.

The teacher's bathroom was as unromantic as it could possibly be, and the toilet stall even less so. But she'd gotten me so worked up that it took about three tugs before I came, biting back my groan of release. Not at all what I wanted, but it would do for the moment. I cleaned myself up with a handful of rough paper towels. *Just like high school*, I thought ruefully. Who would ever have imagined I'd be back in those highly hormonal days?

I walked back to the art room, as respectable and in control as any FBI agent should be. Cyn wasn't far from the door, chewing on her thumb as she watched Maddy. The heat that had flushed her damask cheek was forgotten, and I mourned its departure even as I sharpened my focus to see what had her concerned.

The old lady was sitting in the window, apparently having a conversation with the open air outside.

Cyn angled her body to mine when I came up behind her—not in attraction but in an unconscious yearning for support. "She's never had delusions before," Cyn said. "First the grocery store, and now this."

Maddy laughed brightly and said, "Oh, Timmo. That doesn't seem right. I think you're very smart. Don't you listen to your brothers!"

"You're sure there's no one out there that she's talking to?" I asked Cyn.

"You and I were out there. Did you see anyone?" She turned her huge eyes on me, her concern obvious.

"No, but I wasn't very focused on other things . . ."

"Well," she said, her attention going back to Maddy. "Is there anyone here named Timmo? Or maybe Timothy?"

"Not that I know of. I'll go look outside."

"Thank you, Rhys."

A quick scan of the bushes against the school revealed nothing at all. The street was quiet. Nothing but rusted trucks, burned-out cars, and a grandmother pushing a toddler in a stroller. Dash and his football players were finishing up. They had nothing to report about anyone near the windows. I went back in.

Maddy was back at the tables, delighted to meet Mario and praising him for his drawing of a peanut butter cup. The boy gravely thanked her and offered her a new sheet of paper. "It's clear outside," I told Cyn.

"I'm worried about her, Rhys."

"The neurologist said she was okay?"

She nodded, not particularly appeased by that reminder.

"Well, let's keep her away from guns." My inept sally earned me a smile. "I'm sure she'll be fine."

FIFTEEN

CYN

I DRIFTED BETWEEN UNCONSCIOUSNESS AND WAKING UP. Everything was woolly and vague. Dark. It was nice.

Except . . .

My hip hurt.

And if I was taking a slow inventory, my hip didn't hurt as much as my head.

Once I recognized the pain, the woolly, unconscious state began to slip away.

I was lying on my side, too curled up. I wanted to stretch, but my muscles wouldn't obey. I had been still too long. But not everything was still. The world was moving, and I could hear . . .

. . . the low, steady rumble of a car on the highway.

I tried to straighten my legs, but something was in the way. Something was in the way all around me, but on one side, the obstacle was warm and alive. Everyplace else—even above my head —was hard and dark and cold.

My eyes snapped open, but it didn't help. I was in darkness.

My hands panicked before my mind understood. I patted around me, finding the limits of the space. The ceiling was inches above me, and I bumped my aching head when the car hit a pothole.

Waking up had come slowly, but clarity slapped away the last vestiges of calm.

I was in a trunk.

I've watched soap operas. I've seen TV detective shows. I knew this unlikely but undeniable truth: I was locked in the trunk of a moving car. The very thought simultaneously offended, horrified, and astonished me.

And the soft, lightly breathing shape at my side . . . was Maddy.

"Oh my god," I breathed. "Maddy? Maddy!" I shook her gently in the darkness, terrified that she'd been injured. "Are you all right?"

I almost cried with relief when she answered me in her bright, just-woke-from-a-nap voice.

"Now, this is an entertaining game!"

"Maddy, are you okay? Are you hurt anywhere?" I was patting as much of her as I could reach, and she was giggling.

"I'm fine, you big silly! Where are we? We're in a car, aren't we? I can tell. It sounds like the highway."

"We're in a car. But I can't remember why. Can you?"

"I think we're playing hide-and-seek. This is a wonderful hiding place! My, you smell good! It's a purple smell. Like lavender. Or maybe lilacs."

She nestled into me and I wrapped my arms around her, terrified but determined to protect her from whatever was coming.

My mind was racing, and my heart wasn't far behind. What on earth had happened to us? More to the point, what was going to happen to us? I stared uselessly into the darkness, desperate for something to seize on—a point of light, a good idea, whatever.

"It's a good thing you and I are both so little," Maddy whispered in delight. "A bigger person wouldn't fit!"

I'm not claustrophobic, but her comment triggered an internal radar and suddenly my lungs were cramped. I couldn't get enough air.

"Maddy," I said in a deliberate attempt to calm down. "You and I are locked in a trunk."

"Yes! Isn't it grand? We'll never be found in here! Where do you think we're going? What an adventure!"

I laid my head back on the rough carpet, crammed up against the wheel well. I willed my muscles to relax, which made the headache leap to the fore of my attentions again. "Oh, my head."

"Darling," asked Maddy, "do you have a headache? I wish I had an aspirin for you."

By wiggling and pushing hard, she managed to wriggle onto her back, even if her knees were still canted over toward me. Even Maddy couldn't raise her knees in this trunk.

"Maddy, really. You don't have a headache? Are you okay?"

"Oh, certainly. I'm just fine, dear. You know, I've never been afraid of the dark. How cozy we are together! And you smell very good, I must say!"

I imagined I smelled like fear and adrenaline, but she was fixating on my shampoo. I couldn't decide if I wished she were panicked with me, so at least I'd had some company in my terror. But then I immediately realized this was better. Happy Maddy was far less stressful than upset Maddy, and her serene tranquility was grounding me.

Once again, the Maddy Mantra proved its value. *Be in the now. Don't worry about what happened. Focus on what's going on now . . . and what I can do about it.*

I ran my hands over my jeans. No surprise, my pockets were empty. "They've taken my cell phone. Aren't cars supposed to have a latch in the trunk?"

This time my hand-by-hand survey of our space was far more deliberate. If there was a lever in this trunk, I was going to find it, even as I repressed the certainty that Maddy was right: We were on a highway. Popping the trunk would allow us to wave for help, but we certainly couldn't slip out the back and run away while the driver was distracted by . . . something.

Maddy was laughing as I patted the walls around her. "Ooh, that feels funny!"

"Sorry. I'm trying to get us out of here."

"You're very clever!"

I sighed. The space was tiny—more and more like a steel coffin for two as the minutes ticked by—and it didn't take long to come to the conclusion that we weren't in a car that featured a convenient handle. No wrenches or tire irons either, which I could've used to clock whoever eventually opened the trunk.

Assuming someone would. Eventually.

No, I chastised myself, *that's not a useful line of reasoning. Of course someone will come for us. Calm down.*

I relaxed again in despair. "I wish I was clever enough to find a trunk release. But just in case, can you feel anything, Maddy? Reach around."

"I feel you. Are you ticklish?"

"Maddy. Stop that!"

"Oh, you're ticklish!"

I bumped my head on the ceiling trying to wriggle away. Then I suppose I was simply overcome by our experience and went through a stress-relieving, temporary insanity:

I tickled her back.

This occupied us for several minutes until we were both warm and giggly and tired.

"Thank you, Maddy. I feel better now."

"Certainly, dear. So, no trunk latch?"

"I can feel carpeting and you, and that's it."

"I can't even feel wires or anything. I saw a movie once where the person locked in the trunk pulled the wires to the taillights, and the police saw and pulled the car over. Wasn't that smart?"

"Smart," I agreed woodenly. Unlikely, more like. Why didn't

Hollywood give us better information in these crazy circumstances? "And my headache's worse than before."

"Well, if I had an aspirin, I'd definitely give it to you. All I have is a deck of cards."

I froze. Hope rose in me. It almost choked me. "A deck of cards? Where is it?"

"Right here. In my pocket."

"Maddy." I breathed a prayer. They'd searched me and taken my phone, but who would've thought that a ninety-three-year-old lady had a phone too? Could it be? "May I have it, please?"

"Certainly, darling. Just a moment."

She fumbled about—the space was too cramped to make any movements simple—and I heard something thunk to the floor. But there was no way I was letting this precious "deck of cards" vanish. I fumbled around to retrieve it. At last, I had it in my hands and touched the home screen.

The light from Maddy's phone was so bright I blinked. Better than any rescue searchlight. I gasped when it worked.

Maddy, startled by the sudden light, immediately forgot what we'd been going through.

"Why, Cyn! Hello, love! Are you playing hide-and-seek too? We found the same hiding place!"

My silent prayer became a babble. "Jesus, Mother Mary, help me here . . ."

I was going to push 9-1-1 on the screen and throw myself on the mercy of whoever answered, but then I realized there was one person who made me feel safe. One person who I thought might actually be able to mount a rescue . . .

And there he was. In her contacts list. She'd neatly typed his name and phone number from his business card and somehow saved it all, dementia notwithstanding.

I had a moment to entertain the sudden thought that she might have put absolutely any phone number under his name—and then Rhys picked up.

"Madcap Maddy, what are you up to now?" said his lovely male voice.

I squeezed my eyes shut to cut off the tears that threatened to gush out of me, and Maddy, her head almost as close to the phone as my own, called out happily.

"Is that my Peanut Butter Cup?"

I shushed her, and suddenly the words were pouring out of my mouth.

"Rhys! Thank God. Maddy and I are in trouble. I think we've been abducted."

There was a startled silence, and then he spoke again. "Is this a joke?"

"It's not a joke. You have to help us! We're in a trunk. The GPS on Maddy's phone says we're going north on 270 to Frederick."

"Shit. Don't hang up. Hold on."

Maddy angled her head so she could hear too, but the sounds were muffled. He must have had his phone pressed to his chest. "Do you think he's wearing that nice charcoal pinstripe?" Maddy asked me. She noticed that my eyes were wet, and she reached out her tiny old lady hand and laid it gently on my cheek, wiping the wetness with her thumb. "It's okay, sweetie. Even if it's not the pinstripe, I'm sure he looks lovely."

Even now, Maddy could bolster my spirits. I gave her a watery smile. I was ready to do violence to whoever had taken us—to anyone who threatened to hurt this dear old lady.

"Miss Quimby?"

It was a new voice. I clutched Maddy's deck of cards to my ear. "Yes?"

"This is Agent Ashwood. Can you confirm what you told Agent Jones?"

He wanted confirmation, so I took a deep breath and made a determined effort to repeat our information as clearly as I could.

"All right," he said calmly, as if this was something he did every day. Maybe it was. "We can track you by the cell phone. How's the battery? Do you have plenty of power?"

I checked and praised whichever god happened to be watching out for us. "We're at ninety-two percent."

"That's great. All right. We're alerting the Maryland State Police. Don't panic. We'll have you out of there very soon. I want you to make sure there are no other apps running that might drain the power."

I checked; nothing else was running. He continued, his calm voice soothing me.

"Can you tell me anything about the car you're in, or who's driving?"

"I wish I could, Agent Dashwood. Maddy and I both woke up in the trunk, and I have the most awful headache." Although the headache had begun to ease as soon as Rhys answered the phone.

"Those aren't very good answers," Maddy whispered to me. "Let's make up something better."

I laid a cool finger gently across her lips, and she nodded and winked. She probably decided we were playing hide-and-seek again and needed to stay quiet. Worked for me.

"Tell me the last thing you remember before you woke up in the trunk."

"I—I'm not sure. I don't really remember."

"I remember!" Maddy called. "Azariah and I went to the hardware store."

"Thank you, Miss Maddy," his calm voice said. "That's very helpful. How about you, Ms. Quimby? What do you remember? Do you know what you had for breakfast this morning?"

Slowly he walked me through our day. Breakfast on the balcony. Making beds and putting the dishes in the dishwasher. Taking Maddy to her hair appointment, and then to our favorite bench across from the school so Maddy could watch the children play.

"Then we went to lunch . . ."

I knew we'd been to lunch. That was our plan, and Maddy

always liked eating out. But somehow, I couldn't quite remember where we went.

Of all people, it was Maddy who remembered. "We went to the diner," she said. "I had the meat loaf special. It was delicious."

That's right. I did remember that, the way a person remembered a dream a few hours after waking.

"All right," said Agent Dashwood. "That's a good starting point. It sounds like you probably got to the diner at about noon and were slipped a sedative in something you ate or drank. I'd estimate you've been on the road for no more than two hours."

Simply putting the pieces together was helping to balance me. "Thank you for helping us. I suppose I should have called 9-1-1."

"Not at all. We've alerted the police already. The minute you were taken across state lines from Virginia to Maryland, this became an FBI matter anyway. But I hope you understand that Agent Jones can't work on this."

I could hear Rhys in the background, and I wanted to join in his protests. The thought of Rhys holding me in his arms was all that was keeping me together, but Dashwood wouldn't hear of it. "Absolutely not," he said to Rhys, and I knew he wasn't talking to me, but the message got to me anyway. "You're dating her. You're entirely compromised on this matter."

Maddy stirred as she listened eagerly. "Who's dating who?" she asked with new curiosity.

"Agent Dashwood!" I cried.

Maddy laughed and said, "Everyone knows he's Dash Ashwood, not Dashwood, silly!" But I had no focus left over to pay her any mind.

"Agent, we're slowing! I think we're taking an exit! Yes! The GPS on the phone says we're pulling into a rest stop. I have to hide the phone!"

"I see your GPS. Remain calm. Local police are putting together a response. Twenty minutes should do it."

"I'll call you back."

I turned off the deck of cards and tucked it firmly into my bra. That made Maddy laugh. "Bet you wish you had bigger fronts now!" she teased.

Then the car stopped. The driver's side door opened and closed—footsteps walked along the car—and then, in a rush of blinding light and chilly October air, the trunk was thrown open.

Maddy and I peered up. I was fearful, but there was real curiosity too. Who had taken us? Why?

A man I'd never seen before stood looking down at us. He was scowling through a bristly, black beard. He looked like a mountain man, or a cartoon of a bear made human.

"You look just like a grumpy Yogi Bear," Maddy said with a chuckle.

He wasn't amused. "I gotta pee." He even had a growly voice. "I bet you do too, and I don't want you pissing in my trunk."

I tried to sit up, but he reached for Maddy, and his huge hand easily wrapped all the way around her arm.

"There's no one else here. You can use the restroom one at a time. But if you try anything, I'm going to hurt the other one. Bad."

"Oh, please," I pleaded.

"Shut up, both of you. You're not even supposed to be here, girlie. You go first, and I'll hold on to this old lady. Go on if you're going."

"I have to go to the bathroom too, Grumpy Bear," Maddy said.

I knew there was no way Maddy could be sent to the restroom by herself. She'd get distracted and forget who we were. She could wander off, or . . . or get abducted, I thought, as if we hadn't already been kidnapped by Grumpy Bear. "Let me take her. She can't keep track of things. I should be with her. We won't try anything. I promise."

Indecision crossed his face and I tried to look as meek and small as I could. Innocent. No trouble at all. Finally, he pulled Maddy out of the trunk. "All right. But I'm going in with you."

"My heavens!" Maddy said. "What a scandal! What will people say!" Her happy laughter rippled across the empty rest stop, and Grumpy Bear gave her such an annoyed look that Maddy's laughter became guffaws.

"She has dementia," I said. "Please don't hurt her." I was clambering out of the trunk after her, and he let me do it.

"You're responsible for her," he growled, and then marched us to the restrooms.

I tried to take as long as I possibly could to give the police time to catch up to us, but at last he jerked me away from nervously combing Maddy's hair in the mirror.

No one had pulled into the rest stop. Where was everybody? Where were the police? And although I couldn't wrap my mind around the reality of returning to captivity, he put us back in the trunk. I *let* him put us in the trunk, and I'd never felt so helpless. Maddy wrapped her arms around me in the darkness. "Aren't you lovely and warm!" she sighed in contentment. I was listening for sirens, but the serene landscape was entirely siren-free.

"I'll be back in a second. You stay quiet now." Grumpy Bear slammed the lid, and I heard him pace away from the car.

I wrapped Maddy more tightly in my embrace. "The police will be here soon. Don't worry."

"Why would I worry?" she asked me. "Isn't this fun?"

I retrieved the phone, and soon I was talking to Agent Ashwood again.

"We're in a white Ford sedan. I couldn't see the make, but the license plate is from West Virginia."

"That's good. That will help."

"The driver is maybe fifty. He's a white guy with a big black beard. He's wearing a flannel—"

Then I heard the most god-awful noise. It sounded like a big, metal mistake of a screech. Hastily I shut off the phone and hid it again. And then there was light pouring in once more. A handsome preppy man was looking down at us, holding a crowbar.

"Hurry up! While he's in the bathroom!"

Salvation—it was a Good Samaritan. My heart was pounding, sure that Grumpy Bear would come out of the bathroom like a nightmare before we could get away.

The man helped both of us out of the trunk. He stood in thought for a moment while my panic threatened to overwhelm me, and then, quite violently, he stabbed the back tire of the car with his crowbar.

I gasped and Maddy cooed. He had to hit the tire several times, but finally there was a hiss and the tire started to go flat. His eyes were darting back to the restroom as often as mine were. Our savior was as scared as I was. At last, we ran with him to a blue minivan parked in the next space. It had a cherry air freshener hanging from the rearview mirror and an empty child's seat in the second row. An unlikely getaway vehicle, but I was far from being picky.

He shepherded Maddy across the front of the van to help her into the front seat, and I climbed in behind the driver's seat, next to the stiff shell of the child's seat.

I was dancing with fear—"Hurry!"—and he was breathing in terrified gasps as he buckled Maddy into her seat. But Maddy was oblivious to our panic.

"I love being in the front seat," she confided. "It's absolutely my favorite place. You can open the window and roll your hand in the wind. Just the flick of a finger pushes your hand up—swoosh! And then down again. It's like flying."

He was fighting to get Maddy's seat belt attached, watching the door to the restroom over his shoulder, when Maddy recognized him.

"Why, Mac!" she said. "How nice to see you again! How's work at the hospital going?"

SIXTEEN
CYN

It's hard to remain calm when panic is fizzing every nerve ending. I was thanking the stranger for rescuing us and also urging him to go faster—"Get in the car and drive! Drive!"—when Maddy's words stopped me short. "What?" I asked. "Maddy, do you know this guy?"

He shot a nervous look at me and closed Maddy's door. Suspicion bubbled up through my fear. As he rushed around the front of the van to get in the driver's seat, I asked again.

"Who is that guy, Maddy?" How could she possibly know the stranger who rescued us?

"Isn't he a love? Look at him go!" She beamed her affections on our rescuer as he hurriedly fastened his seat belt and started the car.

"Oh, shit!" He was looking in the rearview, and I turned to see Grumpy Bear tearing ass towards us like the monster that finally decided to come out from under the bed. "We gotta go!"

His minivan lurched into motion, and I felt a hot burst of adrenaline—a combination of victory and terror. I turned in my seat, keeping my eye on our abductor as he grew smaller through the rear window. He was running for his car. Running and howling in rage. "That guy is really mad," I said unnecessarily.

"Keep an eye on him. Tell me what you see."

Maddy clapped her hands. "Oh, isn't this exciting!"

We were moving along the access road, building up speed for the highway. But not quickly enough. I couldn't figure out why my hand hurt and discovered that I was pounding on the seat in front of me. "Faster! Go faster!"

Already the white sedan was coming after us, a screaming Grumpy Bear at the wheel like something from a *Mad Max* movie.

"Oh shit, oh shit, oh shit." Our driver was keeping up a steady litany.

Then something changed in the car behind us. I gasped. "No! It's okay! His tire is coming apart!" Just before we pulled onto the highway, Grumpy Bear's car slewed to the side and came to a halt in a ditch, long strips of tire rubber trailing behind. As we raced farther and farther from him, he shook a furious fist out the window.

I screamed in victory and pounded on the shoulders of the driver in front of me. He jumped and swore some more.

"You did it! You did it! Oh, Lordy! Thank you!"

"Oh my God! I thought I'd have a heart attack," he said in a half-laugh.

"You're a hero!" I couldn't help but cry. "Just keep going on this road. The police are going to catch up to us in a few minutes! I'll call them." I was fishing Maddy's phone out of my shirt when he spoke again.

"The police? Oh, fuck. We've got to get off this road."

"What?" I watched in astonishment as he veered across the highway to take the exit we were passing. "What are you doing?"

"I'm sorry," he said. "I can't let you go to the police."

"What? Pull over. Pull over right now! Let us out!" My relief— my overwhelming relief that we'd literally been rescued from the trunk of a car—became confusion, followed rapidly by a tidal wave of fury.

"Sorry. Sorry." He kept apologizing and kept driving. "I have a few questions for you, ma'am." He looked to Maddy, who was bright-eyed and happy in the passenger seat. "And maybe a trip."

"A trip!" she replied. "How wonderful! Where shall we go?"

"Chincoteague," he said shortly.

"What?" I was aghast. "What the hell are you talking about? You mean like the children's horse book?"

"Oh, I love Chincoteague! What fun!" Maddy was bouncing in her seat, her eyes shining. I was in a nightmare, and she was having a wonderful adventure.

"Pull over right now!" How much adrenaline did a human body hold? I hadn't gotten over the rescued-from-the-trunk burst when I was swept up in the every-muscle-ready-to-fire mode, because a meek guy in a minivan was also apparently kidnapping us. Every inch of my skin was superheated. My nerve endings were shining silver. I had to move. And the movement I settled on was leaning forward and wrapping my two furious hands around the throat of the stranger in front of me.

"Pull over!" I was shrieking.

He reached over and grabbed Maddy's arm.

"Let go of me. Sit back and be quiet, and I won't have to hurt her. Let go. Let go! You don't want us to crash, do you?"

The world was running at half-speed. Maddy turned her head—so slowly—confusion blooming in her eyes. She tugged at his hand on her arm and I saw that his knuckles were white. He was squeezing her.

He was hurting her.

My hands came off his throat as if I'd been electrocuted. Defeated, I sat back, shocked and newly terrified. We were being kidnapped by a guy from the J.Crew catalog. "Who are you? What is this about?"

"It's quite a long drive to Chincoteague," Maddy offered with a sunny smile. "Isn't it lucky that my darling Cyn has a deck of cards!"

Holy smokes. I'd forgotten. That's RIGHT. I did have a deck of cards!

The phone was a sleek square against my chest. I fished it out and eyed the driver. He couldn't see me texting. The empty baby seat was in his "glance over the shoulder" zone. I was seated directly behind him and he couldn't see my hands. I switched Maddy's phone to "silent" and began texting the FBI again.

> Now in a blue minivan. Can you still see the GPS coordinates?

A flare of grim satisfaction hit me when the text went through. I'd regained some control, and that helped me stabilize my emotions. I felt more balanced. What should I do next? How could I help us get out of this mess?

Gather information. Figure out what was going on.

The driver didn't look like he was well-versed in a life of crime. He looked like the assistant coach of a Little League team. In fact, he was acting as upset and nervous as I was. I eased my tone as far back from furious as I could. "Is your name even Mac?"

We'd come to a red light amid endless strip malls, and he reached out to grab Maddy's arm once again, presumably so she and I didn't coordinate leaping from the van.

"Of course it's Mac," Maddy said, patting the hand that was restraining her. "Mac like my initials. Madeline Alice Carteret. People call me Mac too! Did I tell you that?"

No one I knew had ever called her Mac. Given that her last name was now Root and she'd been married for decades, probably no one still living ever had. He nodded, removing his arm as we picked up speed again. We were coming to a highway entrance ramp.

> Rte 70 heading Baltimore. Can
> you see us?

"You told me your nickname was Mac, Miss Maddy. At the hospital. Remember?" He was calmer now that we were moving again.

"I remember, dear. We were going for coffee. Where did you go?"

"Where did I go?" He laughed briefly as he merged into traffic on the highway. "Where did *you* go?"

My mind was reeling. Maddy hadn't "escaped" at her neurologist's appointment. Apparently, that had been the first time someone had attempted to abduct her.

And—my headache was back—it was clear that Mac wasn't the only one trying.

I was stretching my brain to envision any possible scenario under which both preppy Mac and flannel-clad Grumpy Bear would both want to kidnap a ninety-three-year-old woman with dementia when the phone in my hand vibrated.

> Still see your phone on the tracker.
> You switched cars?

> We switched kidnappers.

Keeping an eye on Mac, I texted my reply to Agent Dashwood. "She lost you in the hospital, huh?" I said cynically. I had no sympathy for our abductor. This was a man I was destined to loathe. Mac might look like the vice president of the PTA, but he was also a kidnapper. Apparently twice. He was a bastard.

"Shit," he replied shortly, shaking his head. He was keeping the car just above the speed limit. We were traveling fast but not so quickly we'd attract the attention of cops with radar guns. Smart. Maybe he was better at a life of crime than I'd assumed.

Agent Ashwood was taking his time with his reply, but it finally arrived.

CLARIFY

Oh. Poor guy. The FBI agent was frustrated by the goings-on? Please. Get in line.

COME GET US. Blue minivan.

State police already deployed. I'm about to head for the helicopter. Are you safe?

"Maddy's tricky like that," I said, hoping to keep Mac talking while I texted my reply.

"Yeah. I know that now. That damned hospital is a maze. I got lost." He seemed to want to unburden himself to what he may have thought was a sympathetic audience. Maddy, at least, was listening to him with great attention. "I went out a fire exit. She follows me, ducks back inside, the door slams shut, and I'm locked on the wrong side. She just slipped out of my grasp. I couldn't believe it."

Another one I had no sympathy for. Poor baby.

Safe for now. Driver is white, in his 30s, brown hair. Doesn't seem to have a weapon. Has threatened violence but seems more scared than anything else. My phone is on silent. Don't call.

First name maybe Mac?

Keep texting. Tell me what happened.

"I remember that day, Mac, dear. I smelled coffee. Didn't you smell the coffee?"

"No, Miss Maddy," he sighed. "I sure didn't."

"I love coffee. Let's stop and get some now, shall we?" She looked at him eagerly, the world's oldest bright-eyed schoolgirl.

"Um . . ." To his credit, he was treating her gently. For a kidnapper. There were no marks showing on her arm. Perhaps he hadn't grabbed her hard enough to bruise her fragile skin after all. Did that appease me? Distantly, I decided it didn't appease me at all. I was still burning with anger, and the man remained scum of the lowest sort.

Jones wants to know if it's Mac
from the hospital.

Of course he did. That man didn't miss a trick.

Tell him YES. Maddy seems
to know him.

"I like my coffee with just a little cream. Do you have any of that hazelnut creamer, Mac? That's so tasty, don't you think?"

"Well—"

"You might like it black. Azariah takes his black, but it keeps him awake. Not me. I sleep like a baby! I love to sleep, don't you?"

At the wheel, Mac was overwhelmed. I felt a certain smug satisfaction as Maddy worked her madcap ways on our preppy abductor.

State police setting up roadblock.
Remain calm.

Calm. I'm calm. I'm angry, but I'm calm.

Clarify: Was "Mac" the driver of
both cars?

Maddy was tangling Mac's thoughts with a long discussion about the best kind of pillow to sleep on. I had time to text.

First driver was Grumpy Bear.

WHAT DOES THAT MEAN

I was being driven down a mostly deserted Maryland highway into the unknown by a man who had threatened my charge with bodily harm, and still I was struck by the absurdity of what I'd stupidly texted to the people I was trusting to rescue us. A slightly hysterical giggle escaped me, and I shook my head in frustration. I planned on declaring temporary insanity if questioned about it.

Sorry! Maddy names people. She named
that first guy Grumpy Bear. I don't know
another name. Mac is the second abductor.
They're definitely not working together.

Maddy was playing with the radio. Mac was beginning to look a little wild-eyed. Okay, a little *more* wild-eyed.

Jones says Im to say to you PEANUT
BUTTER CUP. Is that code?

Things were ridiculous enough that I actually felt a grin blooming.

It's code in Maddy-speak.

To make sure I'm following, you've

been abducted by a second,
different kidnapper?

> Yes. I'm sorry. I know it's confusing. I'm
> confused too.Mac rescued us from Grumpy
> Bear. Then it turned out that Mac was
> kidnapping us too.

We'll figure it out. You're coming up
on the police blockade. Just in case,
is your seatbelt fastened?

I was texting my reply—a brief "yes"—when suddenly all the airbags in the van exploded, and I was jerked sharply into the baby seat next to me. The phone flew out of my hand and the sound of a crash filled my head.

"The fuck!" screamed Mac, who was wrestling with the wheel. We were being pushed inevitably off the road by the black car on the other side of my window.

"Whee!" cried Maddy, her hands in the air like she was on a roller coaster. We came to a halt on the side of the highway, deep in the grass. "Do it again!" she demanded.

The windshield had been shattered into a million fragments of safety glass by the impact, so it was hard to see more than the outline of the man who stood in front of the van. But it sure looked like he was holding a gun.

"Get out of the van. All of you. Right now."

He fired a shot—yep, it was a gun—into the grass before him. Mac and I jumped, and Maddy applauded. She scrambled for her door. Mac and I were slowed down by the large black car wedged up against our side of the van. We clambered out after Maddy.

She was the first one out and the first one to get a good look at the new participant. "Oh! You damned OATMEAL MAN!" Maddy shouted, suddenly enraged.

Openmouthed, I watched as she launched herself, a tiny guided missile of fury, at Barry from Winchester.

Barry from Winchester, whom she'd shot at in the grocery store. This was the Oatmeal Man? "Never seen either of those women, officer," he'd said, and now here he was, on the receiving end of about a hundred pounds of geriatric rage.

Mac grabbed her as she went past. "No!" he shouted. I thought he was protecting her, and I felt a rush of gratitude for the man who looked like he taught night classes at the community college. That is, I felt grateful until he finished his statement. "I've got her! She's mine!"

"Not anymore, she isn't!" Barry grabbed Maddy's arm, but Mac refused to let go. Barry was bigger than Mac, and there was no way to know whose side Maddy was on.

I was still fighting my way out of the back seat—my foot was caught in a seat belt and deflated airbags—and the maddening buzz of panic built in me again. As I struggled, I watched as the three of them slowly but inevitably crab walked to Barry's car (a black 2012 Mercedes he'd bought used a few years ago, I remembered uselessly from Rhys's report), with Maddy giggling and adding in dance steps that both men got tangled in.

"Oh, dear. Neither of you are very good dancers. That's all right. I can teach you," she said.

I'd made it out of the back seat and onto the shoulder of the road. Running to get to Maddy was like a nightmare. I couldn't move as fast as I urgently, desperately needed to.

And then the black circle of nothingness at the end of Barry's gun was suddenly as big as a house and pointed right at me.

"You—stay back. You—open the door. Get in!" Barry shouted. He jerked his head at Mac, who surrendered to the gun and pulled the driver's side door open. Barry pushed Maddy in. Since she was clinging to Mac like a limpet, he also pushed Mac in. "Move over! I'll shoot him. I don't care."

"Well, I don't care, either," Maddy protested. "Quit your shoving! Oh, you bad-tempered, evil man!"

"Shut up! Just stop talking!"

As they drove away, leaving me standing helpless on the side of the road and swamped with fear and frustration, I could see that Maddy had leaned in front of Mac and was lecturing Barry from Winchester. She'd have been pinching Barry's ear to keep his attention if she'd been able to reach. There was nothing but rage in Maddy's face.

Mac, on the other hand, looked past Maddy to me as they pulled away, his jaw dropped in open-mouthed astonishment.

Day not going quite how you planned it? Join the club, buddy.

What the hell was going on?

SEVENTEEN
RHYS

MY FATHER TOLD ME YEARS AGO THAT IT WAS MY SENSE OF CALM that helped me in shooting competitions. Even as a preteen, a cloak of stillness fell over me when I focused. I could block out everything around me until there was nothing but the target ahead of me and the gun or rifle in my hand.

"You're either born a sharpshooter or you aren't," he told me, "but not everyone with the eye can bring the focus to bear. You've got that, son. It's a rare combination."

I lived for that man's praise. But as I sat next to Dash in the helicopter, flying over the thick of DC rush hour, I realized that calmness during a competition was easy. There was no cost. I'd never really cared about the target before—its emotions. Its fragility. Its captivating, beautiful eyes, set in a head that was, if you thought about it, such an amazingly fragile thing.

The cloak of calm had deserted me. I was faking it so Dash would continue to let me tag along . . . but in my soul, I was shrieking.

And what I was shrieking was *FLY FASTER*.

My phone lit up in Dash's hand. I was on such a hair trigger that I noticed it immediately. I was itching to take it back, but it was a miracle he'd let me onto the helicopter. There was no way I was going to get to talk to Cyn during this madness.

Dash was on the radio with the barracks captain of the Maryland State Police, arranging the roadblock, and hadn't noticed the phone was lit. Certainly he couldn't hear the ring in the helicopter's noise.

I did not lunge and grab it out of his hands because I was calm. Calm. Not at all frantic. So I nudged him to get his attention. And when he looked at me, I gestured with my chin to the phone in his hands.

What a cool customer I was.

He answered the phone, but of course couldn't hear anything but the roar of the helicopter. "You don't have a headphone jack for this, do you?" he asked over the headsets we were wearing.

The one thing I could have done to help, and my pockets were empty. I cursed myself but simply answered him with a fully controlled "Sorry."

He held the phone up and shouted into it. "Cyn, we're in a helicopter. I can't hear you. Text me. Can you hear me? Text me."

The phone went dark as she disconnected. I spent the next few moments praying to a god I didn't believe in to keep her and Maddy safe. At last the text arrived. I leaned toward Dash to read it.

Maddy kidnapped again

Motherfucker! This had to be some elaborate joke. Dash was texting for information when her next text arrived.

Barry from Winchester. Has a gun.

My blood went icy. Dash and I exchanged frozen stares. The return of Barry—whom Madcap Maddy had called the Oatmeal Man.

CYN & THE PEANUT BUTTER CUP

And he was armed.

With that news, I was relieved to feel a measure of icy calm descend over me at last. I coolly marshalled my resources for action would surely be needed soon. An armed kidnapper meant an armed response might be necessary. I suddenly felt as if I'd have a keen eye and steady hand if I had to protect my Cyn—and darling Madcap Maddy.

Cyn was texting again.

Black Mercedes. Going north on
Rt 27 Ridge Road. Left me on the
side of the road.

ARE YOU THERE?

Dash was already on the commlink with the Maryland police again, updating them as to the new location. I talked to the pilot about shifting our landing point further north, and then took the phone from Dash's unresisting hand. Even the ace FBI agent was willing to break protocol for this one.

We're heading to you now, pixie. Hang on.

PBC?

It's me. I have the phone for a moment.

Thanks for coming for me. But don't
come get me. Get Maddy. Please?

We'll get both.

Being able to communicate with her calmed me somewhat. I was still worried about Maddy and almost insane to discover why two different people—no, now it was three—wanted to abduct an old woman. But Cyn staying safe by the side of the road, and far from the lethality of a bullet? Yes, that eased something inside me that had been pulled tight.

> How long since they left?

I waited for her reply, but it didn't come. Dash looked over and reviewed our conversation. When she didn't answer my question, his frown deepened. He took back the phone, and with great self-discipline, I let him.

> Miss Quimby please check in.

That high-tension wire in me drew tighter again when the screen remained dark. I couldn't make the helicopter go any faster, and suddenly couldn't think of what to do with my hands—

And then I saw the three dots that meant she was texting. I exhaled my relief sharply beside Dash, and he grimaced at me. Then he was taut as a wire, too, once he read her text.

Got my own ride. Heading north
after them with Mac's brother Will.

> Excuse me?

Dash was growling at the phone. I'd have been able to hear his curses even if I didn't have headphones on.

> Miss Quimby GET OUT OF THAT
> CAR leave this to us

No longer up to me. Sorry. Appears
Will is kidnapping me.

Now my curses were as loud as Dash's. There were simply too many people to keep track of, and Cyn was back in danger. Dash was shouting with the pilot, and then, blessedly, sent a final text to Cyn giving her a new phone number to call.

When the phone rang, the pilot was able to hook the call into the intercom system so we could talk to Cyn instead of texting. It was an immeasurable relief.

"You'll let me do all the talking," Dash said to me sternly. "Not a word."

I mimed zipping my lip. It'd be enough to hear her voice.

"Miss Quimby? Are you there?"

I could hear scuffling on the line and then Cyn's voice, strong as it could be. "You're not getting this phone. Just shut up and let me talk. You drive. Agent Dashwood?"

I felt a burst of pride for my pixie. She was clearly fighting mad. Dash grinned despite himself when she got his name wrong again. "Are you all right, Ms. Quimby?"

"I'm fine. This guy is going to get quite a headache if he doesn't step on it. Long pedal on the right, Poindexter! Let's go!"

"Miss Quimby," Dash said impotently, but Cyn was focused on this new character— Will. Brother of the . . . second abductor.

"The Oatmeal Man isn't going to violate the speed limit, chum. Believe me. I've been through this twice. He doesn't want to get pulled over for speeding. YOU CAN CATCH HIM. Go! Go faster!"

Even the pilot winced when her shout came through the headset. "Who's kidnapping who?" he was foolish enough to ask no one.

Dash glared at him. "Patch this call to the head of the police barracks right now. Ms. Quimby!"

"What?" Her focus returned to the phone call. "What is it? How close are you? Can you stop him?"

"Tell me about the car you're in, please."

"The car I'm in? Don't worry about me. Get Maddy! She's in a black Mercedes with one side totally crushed in. It shouldn't be hard to spot. Are you going after her?"

Dash got calmer as others got more frantic. It was part of what made him such an invaluable agent. He refused to be distracted from his question. "Tell me about the car you're in."

"Oh, Christ, you're stubborn. Minivan again. This one is maroon. What? Thanks. Will says it's a Dodge Caravan."

"And your phone's GPS is still working, so I know you're still going north on Route 27."

"The Oatmeal Man wouldn't have turned off this road, would he? We're in the middle of nowhere. Agent, you have a helicopter, don't you? Can't you get ahead of us and find them?"

"We're still about half an hour out from you, but I've got the state police setting up a roadblock. The third roadblock in an hour, I might add." Dash shared a look with me that begged for commiseration. There's a natural territoriality between locals and feds, and working so inefficiently with the state police wasn't helping that relationship. Still, it seemed an inappropriate time to bring it up with one of the kidnap victims.

Cyn apparently agreed with me. "Don't get snippy with me, Agent Dashwood." Cyn's anger soothed me. She wasn't too frightened to be righteously outraged. This was not a fearful woman. "It's not my fault that three separate people have kidnapped us today! What? Oh, thank you, Will. He says four, although why he wants to be counted, I cannot imagine. Go faster!"

"Miss Quimby, please secure your own safety. You're endangering yourself by driving at high—"

"There they are!" she shrieked. "I can see them! Rhys! I see them!"

The pilot, Dash, and I were hanging on her words.

"Hurry up, Will! That's your brother in there! No, I don't know what to do. How would I know? Figure it out. Well, drive him off the road! What? Shut up! I don't care about collision insurance.

You drive him off the road right now! No, they'll be fine. Look at that car. It's a tank. Yes, you can. YES, YOU CAN."

"Cyn, baby." I couldn't help but interject. "You don't want to have a crash at that speed. Please leave it to the state police."

"Rhys, this isn't a high-speed chase. We're going thirty-seven miles an hour. This guy is a total wimp. Wait. What the hell is that?"

Even the pilot looked back to exchange his surprise with us. What the hell *was* that?

"Well, pull over. Let him pass. Rhys, there's a big old pickup truck coming up fast behind us. My God. Look at him go." She began spitting out information. "Red pickup Ford West Virginia plates, driver is huge has a big black beard."

"Is it the same guy?" Dash asked her.

"No!" she shouted. He was distracting her. "Different guy. He's holding—LOOK OUT, WILL—ohmygod, that's a rifle. The driver is holding a rifle."

We could hear the shot through the cell phone, and then another one.

"He just shot out his own windshield! Oh my God. His own windshield! He's got Barry's tire. Or the engine, or something. He's pulling over. They're both pulling over. Pull over, Will! Don't go past them. Don't you dare!"

After that, she clearly dropped the phone. It thunked to the ground and relayed the sound of doors opening and feet running. In the theater of my mind, horrific scenarios played out.

"How much longer until we're there?" Dash asked the pilot.

"Fifteen minutes. If they stay still."

"She never does stay still, does she?" Dash said mournfully to me.

Sure enough, as we watched the screen, the red dot that was Maddy's cell phone began to move again. The fumbling sounds came through the phone and we could hear Cyn screaming. "Fuck your brother! He's nothing but a kidnapper! You drive this car! You get us out of here! Rhys? Rhys, are you there?"

"I'm here." I couldn't be more relieved to hear her voice.

"I've got her," she said in triumph. "We're heading east. Is it east? Shut up, Will. Drive, you pathetic wimp. You're definitely going to get caught now."

"We can see you on the GPS, Cyn." I tried to make her hear me, but she was too busy berating Will, who was advocating for going back for his brother.

"He'll be fine. Barry and the other guy are totally focused on killing each other."

"Timmo," said Maddy's bright voice. "That was the Oatmeal Man and Timmo."

"Who's Timmo?" The question came simultaneously from Cyn, me, Dash, the helicopter pilot, and the head of the police barracks, now tuned into the call. I flashed back to our date at the Anacostia Boys' Club. Maddy had been having what we'd stupidly assumed was an imaginary conversation with someone out the window—someone named Timmo.

And the Oatmeal Man was Barry Gambert from Winchester.

Players had been circling Maddy for days, and we didn't realize it. I'd let her down. I should have noticed. And clearly, whatever was going on in this series of kidnappings, at least some of it was obviously premeditated.

Maddy, chipper as ever, answered our universal question. "Timmo? He's my friend. You know Timmo."

"I certainly do not." Cyn spoke for all of us. "He's terrifying."

"Oh, don't be such a silly pixie, darling. He's not terrifying. He's a love. His brothers say he's slow, but I say they're meanies."

Cyn had lost interest in the question of Timmo's intellectual assessment. "Maddy, let me look at you. Are you okay?"

"Yes, sweetheart. I'm fine. Like always. How are you, dear?"

"Miss Quimby," Dash interjected. "Is anyone with you armed with a weapon? Any guns or rifles in the van?"

Cyn interrogated Will, who protested that of course he didn't have a gun. Dash and I both relaxed slightly. Dash got Cyn's attention again.

"Miss Quimby, we have the state police chief on the phone. Chief Hendricks, you've been monitoring the situation?"

A new voice joined the cacophony. "I have, Agent Ashwood."

Cyn, still on the cell phone, muttered, "Ashwood. that's right. Not Dashwood. Damn."

The police chief continued. "After setting up roadblocks in Frederick, Mt. Airy, and Westminster, fully half the Maryland police force has diverted all traffic off of Route 795 in Reisterstown —which happens to be the exit to get to the Baltimore County Police Department, Precinct Three. You're covered, ma'am. You should be coming up on the traffic jam now."

"We're in stop-and-go traffic!" No one had ever been as happy before to be caught in a horrific jam. "Keep going, Will! Oh, don't be such a baby. You're stuck on this road. Where else are you going to go?"

"We'll be here to meet you, ma'am, when you arrive."

"We will too," said the pilot. He pointed through the twilight to where we could see the headlights of a massive traffic jam on the road below us.

"We're on our way, Cyn," I promised.

"Is this like a horror movie?" she asked, and maybe I could hear the hint of tears in her voice now. "Is something going to leap out and grab us now that we think we're safe?"

The returning chorus should have heartened her, as the police chief, the pilot, my partner, and I all protested. "Not this time!" "No way!" "You'll be okay." "We've got you."

"Thanks," she said, and this time I heard the tears.

THE PILOT LANDED ON THE GRASS NEAR WHERE THE TRAFFIC WAS being diverted along an access road and back onto the highway. Only one minivan in the massive queue of cars was happy about rolling forward at no more than walking speed, but the joy I felt at seeing Cyn waving at me undoubtedly outweighed the resentment and bitching of the hundreds of drivers who had been momentarily detained.

She fell out of the van and into my arms, and unsurprisingly, burst into tears. I cradled her against me and let her sob. I was overwhelmed by gratitude. To hold her again, whole and unharmed, was precious. I pushed aside the memory of Peterson, the Milwaukee child pornographer I'd shot in the hand—the violent, stomach-turning result of a bullet piercing vulnerable human flesh. But no one had been shot today. Cyn was whole and warm and trembling in my arms, and I decided I wasn't ever going to let her go again.

Dash took Maddy's arm as she clambered sprightly out of the van. "Hello," she said, not remembering meeting him at the police station or the Boys' Club. "Aren't you handsome! Are you coming to Chincoteague with us?"

"Ma'am?"

"Oh, yes. We're going there now." I watched over Cyn's head as Dash led her gently away from the van. She happily babbled to him, and the state police arrested Will.

"It's over," I whispered into the fragile shell of Cyn's ear. "I've got you."

So, of course that's when the shooting started.

All the cars in the backup were filled with screaming citizens. I'd ducked behind the van with Cyn before I consciously thought about taking cover. "That's a rifle," I shouted to Dash.

"From the vacant lot," a state trooper shouted, pointing.

Past the off-ramp in a deep field of untended grasses, a ratty, old, red pickup had parked broadside to us. Behind it, an enormous bearded man was holding a rifle. He was big enough to be shooting over the top of the cab, not just over the hood. Seeing that he'd captured our attention, he roared to us.

"Give me back my brother!"

Various law enforcement representatives called out their identifying branches, telling the shooter to stand down, which made no difference at all.

"Now, who the fuck is *this* guy?" Dash asked.

"He wants his brother?" There was only one pair of brothers we'd come across so far, but it didn't make sense. "Does he want Will? Is that Mac?" I was incredulous. Will looked like a banker, and this was a mountain man.

"I'll bet that's Grumpy Bear's brother," Maddy called from her hiding spot two cars back.

"Keep your head down," Dash chided her.

Beside me, Cyn peeked out. "I'd guess that's right. There is a resemblance to Grumpy Bear, although this guy is bigger. A lot bigger."

"But this is a different truck and driver from the one who shot at Barry?" Even as I asked her, I knew the answer. Barry's attacker had shot his own windshield out, and the truck parked on the hill across from us was unscarred.

"Different guy," Cyn confirmed. "How many people are in on this? I can't keep track."

That made two of us. At least two of us.

The police captain, on his radio, passed on that Will (already in a police cruiser trying to make its way past the traffic jam to the police precinct) had no idea who the guy was. He *did* confirm that it definitely wasn't the brother of the only person we had in custody.

"Well," Dash glared, "who wants to tell him we don't have Grumpy Bear?"

"You've got one minute!" came from the field.

"We don't have your brother," called Dash, but the big guy's reply was a spectacular shot through the engine cowling on the helicopter, which responded with a high-pitched whine, a plume of smoke, and immediate silence. The pilot howled in dismay. The gunman howled too, but he had more words than the mourning pilot.

"My brother! You give him to me now!"

Dash moved up to crouch next to me. "Rhys, let him know we're armed too."

"What? You see all these staties here and you think he believes we're unarmed?"

"Go on. Give him a taste."

"A taste? Are you kidding? There's nothing sticking out but his head. I could hit him. I could kill him."

"He started shooting, not us."

"In case you haven't noticed, the guy's a pretty good shot. He's not trying to kill anyone."

"Yet." Dash glared at me. "I'm not saying kill him. Just let him know what he's up against."

"Christ, Dash." Despair filled me. Especially after just getting Cyn back whole and safe, the idea of putting a bullet anywhere near another human made my skin crawl. Beside me, Cyn was wide-eyed.

"Do it, Agent." Dash wasn't using the "we're friends" voice. That was the senior partner giving the junior partner an order. I had a nanosecond to decide how badly I wanted to be an FBI agent. I had a brief vision of the prosthetic strapped to my father's leg and made my decision. If I could stop anyone else from being harmed, I had to do it.

"Shit. Yes, sir." I stood against the van, my arm braced on the windshield. "Please God, don't move, brother," I whispered. Waiting until I was between heartbeats, I squeezed off my round.

The dirty white Stetson flew off the mountain man's head, and we could hear him cursing.

"Sweet shot!" a trooper called.

The mountain man clearly decided that discretion was the

better part of valor. He threw his rifle in the truck and started the engine, taking off across country.

"Can we get him?" Dash turned to the state police.

"Every cop for miles around is at this roadblock, and your helicopter is disabled," the man replied with a shake of his head. "It's going to take us a few minutes." He was clearly trying to rally himself, if not his troops. "But we'll get him."

"Huh." Dash didn't seem convinced. "All right. Now can we figure out what the hell is going on around here?"

That's when Cyn beside me gasped. "Maddy!" she cried.

I looked back. When Dash had come forward to join us, he'd left Maddy alone. A simple mistake. Easy to make…

But a woman with purple hair had pulled up next to Maddy on a powerful motorcycle.

"Hey, mama," she said. "Want to ride?"

"Do I ever!"

And as we watched in horror, Maddy clambered nimbly on the back of the bike, which circled around and took off back up the ramp. Going the wrong way through the traffic jam, the bike wove between stopped cars filled with innocent people. I had no shot, especially as Maddy was shielding the driver from my aim. At the top of the ramp, we could see the biker cut through traffic to get to the open land on the other side.

Maddy was gone.

EIGHTEEN
MADDY

I'm flying!

I think that maybe I'm dreaming—it feels like a dream—but then we bump on the field and swerve around a bush, and I shout with laughter because this isn't a dream. This is real, and so much fun!

There's a woman in front of me. I know it's a woman because long hair pours out from beneath her motorcycle helmet. Her hair is lavender. Or maybe lilac. It's so beautiful.

I can pet that hair. I'm pressed to the back of her black leather jacket. We're as close as sisters.

When I stroke her hair, she glances back at me. "Cut that out," she says.

Ho, ho! She's prickly! And I love to play.

So I hold my hands up innocently. "It wasn't me," I call.

Then, when she turns around, I stroke her hair again. It's so silky soft!

"Knock it off!" she growls. Hee, hee!

We bump hard over a curb. We're on a road and she goes faster. Oh, how wonderful it is!

And then, ba-dump, we're up again on the grass.

It's a baseball diamond! "We should stop and play! Do you have a ball?" I point to the field but she doesn't hear me.

Then we go through some parking lots and another street and a backyard where a dog barks at us and then—oh, this is so funny! We ride along railroad tracks and I call out "Aaaaaaaaahhh" as loud as I can, to hear how my voice bounces as we bump over the logs. I sound so silly!

Then we're off the bumpy tracks and—swoosh!—down an embankment and into the darkness of the woods. The woman keeps pressing something in front of her, so I lean over to peer around her.

She curses. "Sit still. Even someone as small as you can turn us over."

It doesn't matter. I see that she's trying to use her phone in a clever holder on the motorcycle. "You have a phone!"

She grunts in acknowledgment. I hear a voice saying, "Leave a message."

"I've got her, you asshole. Pick up. Damn it, where are you?" She punches at the phone again.

The sun's setting, but there's enough light for me to see that she has the prettiest hair. I reach out to stroke it, and she swats at me. That makes me laugh. She can't reach me from there! I'm a clever monkey, clinging to her back!

Then we get to a road and she starts to go faster, and I forget everything in the thrill.

"Oh! Oh!" I call in delight. "Oh, faster!"

I reach my hand out like through an open car window, and the wind catches my arm and pushes the whole thing up, up, up, to my shoulder like I'm waving at the sky. This wind is so much stronger than in the car!

The motorcycle swerves and the woman curses. "If you're going to do that, use both arms at the same time. Or don't do it at all. But nothing on just one side."

Oh, the bliss! I'm flapping my wings. "I'm a bird!" I call to the darkening twilight sky. "I'm flying!"

"Well, fly on, grandma," she says. "Knock yourself out."

That makes me laugh. As if I'd knock myself out by flying!

I flap and flap and laugh and feel the wind on my face. And then in a passing streetlight, I see that this woman has the most beautiful hair, the color of lilacs. Or maybe lavender.

Fascinated, I reach out. It's so soft!

"Jesus," she says. "What the hell. Go on and do what you're going to do, granny."

Granny! She's so funny.

I can braid hair. I braid mine every day for school. So I plait hers.

Or I try. Somehow the wind is too strong and it gets tucked into the fringe on the back of her black leather jacket. That looks nice, so I keep trying to add it in. Then something gets knotted and I can't do any more. "There," I say happily, patting her back.

I look around. "Look! Look at that house, all lit up with lights!" I'm so pleased to see it that I stand up on the pegs, and that makes the woman howl.

"Sit down!" she says. My, she certainly has an attitude! I stick my tongue out at her and the wind dries it so quickly. This air is wonderful.

She's pushing something on the motorcycle. "It's my phone," she says to me. "Don't try to look at it."

Oh. A phone. Cyn has one of those.

"Cyn has one of those," I say. "Let's call Cyn! Let's tell her how much fun we're having!"

"I don't have Cyn's number," she says shortly.

"That's okay. Just open the phone. It's in there."

"No, it's not. Not in my phone."

"Well, hand it to me. I know how to do it. I'll call her."

"You can't. Not with my phone."

"Yes, I can. I know how..." I was going to explain, but then a voice told us to leave a message.

"Tell Cyn to join us," I shout, but the driver tells me to hush.

"I'll meet you in York," she said. "You better be there, you dick."

"I'll be there," I assured her. "Don't worry. I'm never late. Everyone knows that about me. Oh, look at your hair! It's so pretty!"

"Sure, lady. Whatever."

I fly in the night wind because it's such a joy, and she tells me not to use one arm. Two arms are even better! What a beautiful ride I'm having!

I talk to her and sometimes she answers. Then she says, "There. We're in Pennsylvania. All those Maryland cops that are after you will have to suck an egg today."

Suck an egg. I love that expression! It makes me hoot in the cool wind.

We drive through a town so quickly the lights are blurs. "Faster!" I cry. "Go faster now!"

"You're my kind of nut, lady," she says, and then the motorcycle seems to leave the ground. We're going as fast as a train—as fast as a plane! "Wheeeeee!" I scream as we become a rockct ship streaking through the night sky.

"Wheee, indeed." I think she's smiling but it's hard to hear. The wind is snatching her voice away.

My hands are getting cold and I tuck them in against her back and hunch forward.

"Chilly, huh? I'll get you a jacket for tomorrow. We're almost there," she calls.

And then she's cursing and reaching one hand around to hold me.

"Don't fall asleep," she tells me.

Why would I fall asleep? Don't be silly. I'm not tired at all.

There's a big city in front of us, and in the light, I can see that her hair is the loveliest color.

"Your hair! I want hair like that!"

"Do you?" She thinks about it as we pull into the city. "That's not a bad idea. All right."

She starts looking about. "Okay. There's a discount store. What color do you want your hair to be? Purple like mine?"

Oh, what an exciting question! I can't decide. There are too many choices!

"They make a really good blue. Want blue hair, lady? Like, really bright neon blue?"

"Oh yes! Let's do that!"

So we go to the store and she buys a bottle of shampoo and a child's winter coat that she expects me to wear. Well, actually it feels quite nice.

And then we ride on a motorcycle—it's like flying!—to a motel.

"Stay right here by the bike while I get us a room," she says. She's so serious, I love her!

I'm looking at the empty swimming pool when I hear someone curse behind me. It's a woman with the prettiest hair.

She looks even madder when she sees me. "I told you to stay by the bike!"

"What bike?" I ask. I see no bike anywhere, although I'd like to see one. I love to ride my bike. And not just to school. I ride it everywhere.

"I mean the motorcycle. Jeez. Come on. I got us a room."

Oh, how nice! I follow her. She seems to have her long hair woven into the fringe on her jacket. It looks strange. Perhaps it's the style now. It's so hard to keep up with these things.

The room smells funny, but I don't mind. I've never been picky. The woman holds up a bottle and says "Are you ready to have bright blue hair?"

I cheer in delight. Can it be? Will I really have bright blue hair? How wonderful!

The woman starts to curse again. She's trying to take off her jacket, but it won't come off.

"What the hell—what have you done?"

"Me? What are you talking about?"

"Well, undo it!"

"Undo what, dear?"

"Look at my jacket. What did you do to my hair?"

I laugh, pleased with her pretending game. "Oh, how funny that is! You're all woven together!"

"I know that! Undo it!"

"How do I do that, sweetheart? I must say, I think you should know how to get it undone. You're the one who did it."

After a bit she pulls out a large knife and cuts some of her hair. My, what an impetuous woman! She's delightful.

"All right. Time for a disguise."

"What, dear?"

"Would you like blue hair, lady? Like, electric blue?"

"How fun!"

She's washing my hair in the sink and I look up at her. "What's your name, dear?" I ask.

"Wanda," she says shortly.

"Wanda. That's a lovely name. I've never known a Wanda before. And look at your hair. It's such a pretty color! Why is half of it short and half of it long? Is that the new style?"

"All right. Time to rinse now. Sit up."

I enjoy the warm water running on my head and then a rough towel. It feels funny. Like I'm being licked by a giant mama cat! I try to tell the woman, but she can't hear me through the towel.

And then I'm looking in a mirror.

"Oh!" I shriek. "I'm so gorgeous!" My hair is like a peacock! I'm a fairy! I'm a princess!"

I can't control my happiness. I start to shout and run in the ugly room to let my excitement out.

"Hush!" says the woman. "Don't draw attention to us!"

But I can't stop my dance of happiness. And then I see my reflection in the night-dark window—and my hair is utterly blue! I'm magnificent!

"Do you want some dinner," the woman asks, and I think she sounds desperate. She must be hungry.

"Dinner? That's the best idea ever!"

She dresses me in the warmest jacket (it's my size and I love her for it) and then we get onto a motorcycle!

It's like flying, and it's over too soon. We pull up to a diner and we sit at a booth. She orders for me. Soup and a grilled cheese sandwich. My favorite!

While we're eating, she pulls out a deck of cards and holds it to her ear.

"This is it," she says to the deck of cards. "If you don't call me back in the next twenty minutes, I'm ditching this nutbag right here. I have had absolutely enough of this. Twenty minutes, man— I'm not kidding. Then I'm calling the cops and telling them to pick her up at this diner and you'll lose your shot. Two hours with this kind of crazy is two hours too many, and I'm not doing this alone."

She puts the deck of cards down and eats her cheeseburger, but she keeps looking at the cards.

"Do you want to play?" I ask her politely.

"Play?" Eating doesn't seem to have made her any happier. I don't know why. My food is perfectly prepared and I'm in a wonderful mood.

"I can play hearts. Or gin rummy. I'm great at gin rummy." She's looking at me as if I'm crazy. It makes me grin. "Or we could ask those men over there if they'd like to join us for bridge. You could meet a nice young man."

"I'm not in the 'nice young man' game, grandma. I could go for a nice young lady, though."

"Well, certainly. Anyone can play bridge if they learn the rules."

"Right." She's still looking at the cards, and then at her watch.

Then, as if she's come to a big decision, she asks me, "Do you want some pie? And maybe a nice cup of coffee?"

I clap my hands in delight and she calls the waitress over.

"Do you want to play with us?" I ask her. "We're looking for a nice young lady."

Purple hair cuts me off. "Can we have a slice of cherry pie and a cup of coffee? And I've got to run to the ATM. I just realized I'm out of cash. But I'll leave you my grandmother as collateral, okay?"

They both laugh as if that was a wonderful joke. I laugh too.

And then she's gone, and I have pie and coffee and it tastes so incredibly good that I lick the plate. I know that's impolite, but no one is watching.

And then two nice policemen are there and they ask me, "Are you Madeline Carteret Root?"

"Why, yes I am! How nice to meet you!"

One of them starts talking on a radio. The other looks at a piece of paper he's holding and then at me. "Ma'am, what happened to your hair?"

"My hair?" I look at my reflection in the side of the napkin dispenser. "Oh! Look at me! How gorgeous I am!"

NINETEEN

CYN

IT WAS EVERY DESPERATE NIGHTMARE I'D EVER HAD, ROLLED into one brief moment. I watched Maddy disappear on the back of a motorcycle, going the wrong way up the off-ramp. She was hooting and waving her hands in the air. Her obvious joy cast my blind horror into sharp relief.

"Maddy!" I screamed, but it was no good. She was gone.

My panic fizzed up and overwhelmed me. I needed a car. Immediately. "Will's keys! Where are the keys to his van?!"

Rhys had holstered his now-useless pistol. He stepped up beside me and tried to restrain me, but I was fully insane with desperation. I pushed him off. There had to be a way—there was always a way. "Let go! We've got to find her!"

"Not us," he said firmly. "Not you. Not this time."

"What? Get out of my way! I have to go after her!"

Agent Ashwood appeared on my other side. The two of them flanked me, and I felt the impotent frustration of being so small in a world of tall people. "The police directing traffic at the top of the ramp say the bike has gone cross-country. We can't track them on the roads." Ashwood's voice was calm, and as I squirmed to get past him, he, too, reached an arm out to stop me. They'd boxed me in, and inside I was howling. "It won't do any good to try to follow them, Ms. Quimby."

My frustration made my knees shake. Sudden tears blurred my vision. No!

"But look," Ashwood said, turning me gently and pointing up the access road. "That's the police precinct. Right there. Look who's coming."

Cops on huge motorcycles were zooming down the road toward us. I watched open-jawed as two of them peeled off to follow the rifle-shooting pickup truck cross-country and the other three snaked up the off-ramp, weaving between the stopped cars heading down. The police at the top of the ramp directing traffic were pointing the motorcyclists on. They moved out of sight, heading for the field on the other side and following Maddy's trail.

"See?" Rhys said in my ear. "We can leave it to them."

Tears blurred my eyes. I was torn between hope and panic and gratitude and the feeling that I might fly into a million pieces at any moment. "Well, can we drive around some? And look for them?" I looked with desperation to Rhys, and he shook his head.

"You have another responsibility now."

"Maddy *is* my responsibility," I tried, but he shook his head again, kind but firm.

"Not anymore. Let the police handle it. Cyn. Look at me." He tugged at my chin lightly to stop me from darting my eyes about in search of some miracle. "Cyn, darling, you have to help us build the legal case so we can prosecute the people who abducted you."

"What?" I was confused and angry. What did a legal case matter when Maddy was lost with a purple-haired biker?

"You need to let me take you to the hospital."

"The hospital?!" I broke away from his arm. "I'm fine!"

Ashwood stepped away to talk to the police chief, and Rhys continued to speak to me in a soothing tone. Distantly, I accepted that he was handling me. He was treating me like any hysterical person at the scene of some FBI-type situation. Rhys had probably been trained to do exactly this. He was using a voice that I was sure could gentle wild horses—and, damn it, I realized it was working to calm me down. The horrible fight-or-flight feeling inside my skin was receding slowly, leaving an adrenaline soap scum in its wake.

"Today, you were sedated when they abducted you. We don't know with what. That chemical is still in your system. We need you to be tested so we can present that as evidence in the court case. You get a blood test now, and that is going to get at least one of these bastards put behind bars for many, many years."

"Oh, Jesus." I deflated. I'd forgotten that I'd been unconscious at the start of this impossible sequence of kidnappings. Ashwood returned and led us to a waiting police cruiser.

"This officer is going to drive us to the local hospital," he said.

I found myself in the back seat wedged between both of them, their broad shoulders overlapping me and pressing me back into the seat. Did they think I was going to jump out and run away?

The confinement made me crazy for a moment. Then, I took a deep and deliberate breath. Could I live in the Maddy Mantra now? Even now? *Be in the now. Don't worry about what has passed. Be grateful for what you can appreciate in this moment.*

I realized that it was warm in the car. Even pleasant. Two large men were protecting me, and I was safe and still. It occurred to me that it was very unlikely that anyone would succeed in kidnapping me again, and although I was still worried about Maddy, I was gradually relaxing for the first time in—well, in hours.

Be in the now. A hard lesson to learn.

"Miss Quimby," Agent Ashwood said, "There's another reason to have a doctor examine you, but you won't like it."

His tone was enough to set off my "danger" radar. But they'd definitely rescued me, and I gave him as grateful a smile as I could. "I don't like any of this. What is it?"

"Because you were unconscious, I want you to be given a rape kit and examined for signs of sexual violence."

No. Nope. There went the Maddy Mantra, right out the window. That was territory I wasn't even willing to acknowledge was possible on any plane of existence. He and I were going to have to agree to disagree. "I think I'd know if I'd been raped, Agent Ashwood!"

"No, baby. You might not," Rhys said on my other side. "Let the doctor examine you and make sure. There are steps you can take to protect yourself."

"I can't get pregnant. I've had my birth control injection like always."

"That's not the only thing to be concerned about."

"Oh, Lord God almighty!" I dropped my head into my hands. But there was no peace to be found there. They were talking about sexually transmitted diseases, and I'd be an idiot to ignore those implications. What would my mother say?

And that reminded me of another worried mother—or, in this case, daughter. "Belinda!" I cried. "I have to call Maddy's daughter! She needs to know what's going on!"

Rhys and Ashwood exchanged glances. "What time is it where she is?" Ashwood asked me.

"They're eleven hours ahead of us." I looked at my watch. How could it be not quite five yet? We'd been through hell and disaster, and only about three hours had passed. Surely something was wrong with the space-time continuum.

"So it's not yet four in the morning there. Why don't we give her until 8 a.m. and then call her? We'll probably have more information by then. Can you wait a few hours, Ms. Quimby?"

I collapsed against the seat, suddenly exhausted. "You might as well call me Cyn, Agent Ashwood."

"Cyn, then. And you call me Dash. Since we can't be on your case anyway."

"What?!" As much as I'd resented them corralling me into this car instead of going after Maddy personally, I realized how critical their support had become. Who else can a girl call from the trunk of a kidnapper's car? The thought of losing them was terrifying to me.

"Since Agent Jones is dating you, the FBI will assign another team to investigate this case. Don't worry," Dash said, seeing the panic in my eyes, "we'll stick with you until you're comfortable with them."

"And I'll stick with you after that too." Rhys took my hand, and I clutched it gratefully. Now, I discovered, I couldn't wedge myself in quite closely enough behind his shoulder to settle my anxiety.

"But only in a personal capacity," Dash reminded Rhys. "You're not to work the case in any respect."

"I'll run everything past you to make sure I do the right thing."

"Well." Dash surprised me with a genteel leer. "Not everything, I hope."

"Oh, jeez," I said, hanging my head in mortification.

THE BEST THING I COULD SAY ABOUT MY HOSPITAL VISIT IS THAT the medical care there was efficient, kind, and quick. I gave them both urine and blood samples so they could identify the kind of sedative I'd been doped with, and the exam and rape kit confirmed my belief that I hadn't been assaulted. They gave me prophylactic medicines just in case.

During the exam, I was able to maintain an emotional distance from the situation that allowed me to get some perspective on the startling violence that had befallen Maddy and me. We'd been through something that most people correctly assume would never happen to them . . .

And we'd survived it. So far. I felt a flicker of pride. I'd endured some pretty serious threats, and I was still on my feet. And I had to believe that Maddy was too—otherwise, the guilt and sorrow would crush me.

"Maddy won't have to go through with this when you find her, will she?" I asked Rhys when I met them in the waiting room.

He looked uncomfortable. "Well, yeah. She should be tested. Is it going to freak her out?"

Dash joined us and they walked me to the exit. "No." I was suddenly almost too tired to walk. "Nothing freaks her out. She'll be fine. I'll be a wreck on her behalf, but she'll be fine."

Outside, a plain, moderately ugly beige sedan sat at the curb. "The State Police is loaning us a ride to get you home," Dash said, "since our helicopter is going to be out of commission for a while. Hop in."

They tucked me into the back and recommended that I try to get some sleep. Dash drove, and Rhys kept an eye on me from the shotgun seat. It was the first silence I'd heard in hours. Instead of relaxing me, it clarified an emptiness at the pit of my stomach.

"How long has it been?" I asked.

I didn't need to specify my question, and neither of them had to consult a watch. "About ninety minutes," Rhys said.

"Nothing?"

"Not yet."

I blinked back tears, glad that we'd passed beyond streetlights so he couldn't see that despite my best "brave little trooper" façade, I was beginning to cry quietly.

We drove in silence, and then I was hit with the shivers. "Is there any heat in this car?" I asked.

Rhys looked back again. "Why don't you pull over, Dash? I'll ride in the back with Cyn. She's having a delayed reaction."

By the time his big, warm body climbed in next to mine, I was shuddering with the cold. He pulled me across his lap and wrapped me up. The heat from his body was blissful and I probably should have calmed down because of it, but somehow the contrast with the ice in my veins simply made me start to cry in earnest.

"Doesn't look like you're obeying seat belt rules," Dash commented dryly.

"Better not get in an accident, then," Rhys replied. He tucked as much of me as he could under his coat and cradled me against his warmth while I shivered and sobbed and clung to him.

And then he woke me, a smile in his voice. I was confused—had I fallen asleep?—and he held out his phone so I could see the message glowing there in the darkness.

Madeline Carteret Root found in
York, PA. Healthy and happy. More
info to follow.

"From the Pennsylvania police. She's found, Cyn. Maddy's been found and she's fine."

"Oh, thank God!" I thought I'd cried enough, but apparently there was more moisture in me. "Can we go get her?"

"I'll turn around at the next exit," Dash said, changing lanes to take the next off-ramp.

"Hang on," Rhys said. He showed me the next message.

Miss Maddy invited to spend the night
in the police chief's guest room. We
will give her an honor escort home
tomorrow. She's really something. We
will hate to give her up!

The next message was a photograph of Maddy wearing a huge grin and a policeman's hat, surrounded by smiling policemen.

"She's made yet more conquests. Cyn, let her have a good night's sleep. You'll see her tomorrow. Okay?" I nodded. "Home, please, Dash."

"Yes, sir!"

I studied the photo with deep gratitude. It wasn't just that Maddy was my responsibility, and that Belinda had trusted me to keep her safe. I was also absolutely devoted to that sweet old lady, and so relieved that she was alive and, quite clearly, happy.

"Rhys," I asked, drawing his attention back to the photo, "is this a trick of the light? Does Maddy's hair look blue?"

He examined it. "Definitely. Electric blue. Color-saturated. What the hell has our girl been up to?" He smiled down at me. A bubble of happiness was welling up in me, forcing an answering smile onto my lips.

More texts and conversations followed. The purple-haired biker had vanished. Maddy had been seen by a doctor and was pronounced quite remarkably healthy. As I predicted, she had no objections to any of the tests, and was apparently deeply fond of the policewoman who stayed with her throughout the entire process.

"They know she has dementia, right?"

"They know."

"And they know she's an escape artist?"

"Ah, but is she?" Rhys said thoughtfully. "It looks like many of her escapes might have been botched abductions."

The very idea scared me. I sat up from my cozy position tucked against his chest. "They have to watch her! What if they come back?"

Rhys soothed me. "They know what's going on. They'll take good care of her. She'll be back tomorrow, happy as a clam, and not remembering anything useful at all."

"Damn it," Dash added from the front seat.

"I should call Belinda."

"Maddy's safe, and there's nothing her daughter can do from the other side of the planet. Let's call her tomorrow and brief her in full once Maddy's home. We can spare her some unnecessary anxiety. Can you wait?"

The idea of calling to explain our endless afternoon made me dizzy with weakness. I agreed to keep Belinda in the dark for a while longer.

We pulled up at an apartment building close to Belinda's place. "What are we doing here?"

Dash put the car in park and looked back at me. "Oh. I'm sorry. Did you want to go back to your place all alone after the day you've had? Wouldn't you rather stay with a friend?" He grinned at me.

Rhys snorted. "Dash Ashwood, FBI matchmaker. This is my apartment, Cyn. Would you like us to take you home? Not that you wouldn't be welcome to stay with me."

I felt paralyzed. "I have to make a choice?"

"Nope. Not now. Come in. I'll make you some dinner and then I'll run you home after you've eaten."

"Sure you will," grinned Dash.

"Oh, shut up." Rhys got out of the car, leaving me for a moment alone with the lean, wonderful Agent Ashwood.

"Thank you, Dash. Thank you for everything."

He held my hand briefly from the front seat. "It's going to be okay, Cyn. I'll see you tomorrow with the new team, and we'll put our heads together and figure some stuff out."

Impulsively, I leaned over and kissed his cheek. "Thank you. Good night."

The next moments were blurry, and my life proceeded in a strobe light series of images, which was all I could process. I was in a brightly lit lobby. I was standing next to Rhys in an elevator, his warmth still holding me close to his side like a magnet. I was in a hallway, standing while he unlocked a door. I was in a living room littered with moving boxes. Stacks of unhung paintings leaned against the walls.

"Sorry. I haven't really finished moving in yet," he apologized, but I didn't mind at all. The lack of strong personality actually made me more peaceful in my shattered state.

He took my hand and led me into the bedroom. It seemed suddenly far too intimate to be in his bedroom, but he forestalled objections I wasn't even sure how to form, much less voice.

"You'll stay here tonight with me, won't you?"

I was incapable of answering. I didn't want to leave him, but I didn't have the emotional or physical strength for anything more. Somehow, he understood.

"Nothing is going to happen in here tonight," he said. He opened a drawer and removed a clean T-shirt. Handing it to me, he went on, "It's not that I don't want something to happen. But you really need a good night's sleep. And because you've been sedated, legally you're not capable of making any significant decisions anyway. There is no way you can give consent tonight, and I wouldn't believe it if you did. So get that frown off your face."

"It's not that I don't want to," I blustered, but he cut me off.

"I know. You've had a hell of a day. Here's the bathroom. You can take a hot shower and put on the T-shirt. It'll look like a dress on you and I'll feel absurdly proud to see you wearing it. I'll run down to the deli in the lobby and grab us some dinner. You'll be okay alone for a bit?"

I nodded.

"Then after you eat, you'll crawl into that bed and I'll crawl into that bed, and you'll let me hold you so I can get over the scare I had when you were abducted, and we'll both go to sleep. And then tomorrow we'll get Maddy back and figure out who all these people are who are after her. I mean, I know she's charming, but this seems excessive!"

He grinned at me and the last of my concerns faded away. "I like this plan," I admitted.

"Good. Take your shower. I'll be back in ten or fifteen minutes."

He brought me tomato soup and grilled cheese. It was the perfect choice. I managed to eat quite a bit of the meal before jaw-popping yawns overwhelmed me.

Rhys was looking at me. "What?"

"I love seeing you in my T-shirt, and I'm going to love holding you in my bed, but I'm asking you to let me have one more gift, please."

He looked silly and slightly abashed and adorable. I smiled at him. "What?"

He stood, and before I knew it, he'd slipped one arm around my shoulders and the other under my knees. He picked me up as easily and casually as if it was something he did every day. "Let me carry you to bed."

"Oh my!"

"We're going to say it's because you're so tired. It's not at all so I can get my arms around you."

"Oh, I'm so tired." I looped my arms around his neck and admired how beautiful he was. "I'm not too heavy?"

He chuffed his amusement. "Right," he said, meaning he wasn't even considering my question. "Now." He let my feet slide down until I was standing, and then he pulled back the sheets. The bed was made with military precision. Clearly, this was the FBI agent in him and not the artist. "Slide in."

I did, muttering a coo of appreciation. Simply being horizontal was delicious. The fact that his bed was large and firm and soft all at the same time was an added bonus.

To my confusion, he pulled the covers up to my chin. "I'm going to grab a shower. You go to sleep. I'll join you in a bit. You won't mind if I gather you up when I come to bed, will you?"

His position, leaning over me as I lay in his bed, set off desire like bells ringing in my system, and I smiled at him.

"None of that, now," he admonished me. He kissed my forehead and backed off. "I'm trying my best to be a gentleman." He turned out the light.

"Thank you, gentleman."

I watched the closed door to his bathroom and heard the shower start, but that's all that I remembered until much later, when I was gently rolled over until my head rested on a broad chest and two arms looped around me. I sighed without really waking up. I was safe now.

TWENTY
RHYS

THE SOFT EMAIL CHIME DIDN'T DISTURB CYN'S SLEEP, BUT SHE woke slowly after I uttered a surprised chuckle of amusement when I opened the attachment. The York police chief had sent me a photo of Maddy with a child in her lap, both of them roaring with laughter. "Jeannette wants to know," read the accompanying message, "if we can take Miss Maddy to our favorite restaurant for pancakes. Agreeable? It will put off our arrival time in Arlington, VA until 11 a.m. Please let me know soonest."

Madcap Maddy. Charming the world wherever she went.

Cyn was buried in the blankets, curled up in a ball. She hadn't moved in hours. The sight of her asleep in my bed, in my T-shirt, inspired a powerful possessiveness in me. *Mine.*

I felt a strong urge to protect her and keep her safe. The girl had had a hard, high-adrenaline day. She deserved her rest. At least, that was the civilized face I was putting on the grunting of the caveman within, who was thinking seriously about clubbing anyone who even looked at her wrong.

My altruism, however, was sorely tested as she woke up, because she uncurled in a blissful stretch that pressed every inch of that gorgeous body against me. *Down, boy.*

I thought her face was perfection until she opened those eyes, and then I was lost.

"Hey." She smiled sleepily.

"Hey, yourself." I rolled to face her, curling up to hide the growing interest in my groin. I held up my phone to show her Maddy's photo.

Her face lit up, and my heart lifted. "Oh, Maddy!" Her hands pulled the phone from mine and she pinched the photo to zoom in on Maddy's laughing face. "She looks happy, doesn't she? And look at that blue hair."

"She's got an invitation for pancakes. Are you okay with that? It will mean she doesn't get back until around 11."

"Absolutely. That's great. My God. Is that the time? I've been asleep for eleven hours?"

"You conked out after eight last night, and it's almost seven now. So, yeah."

"Holy smokes. I have really got to pee."

She scrambled out of bed, and while I mourned the loss of her warmth at my side, I did enjoy the view as she left me.

I emailed the police chief with Cyn's permission to take Maddy to breakfast, and I called Dash. He was already in the office, of course. He told me that Agents Elaine Proctor and Jim Biays had been assigned to the case. I didn't know Proctor, but I'd played basketball in the Bureau's gym with Biays; he was a good guy. We agreed that we'd all meet at Maddy's before her arrival, so Cyn and Maddy could meet their new protective detail and so we could put our heads together over strategy.

"We're all meeting at your place at 10:30," I called to the closed bathroom door.

She pulled it open. "I used your toothbrush. I know that's gross."

I was trying so hard to give her the kind of warm, no-pressure support she needed—to keep everything PG. But she was standing there with my T-shirt falling to her knees and her hair adorably tousled, and her statement was irresistible. I stretched and leered at her. "Pixie, you have permission to put anything of mine that you want in your mouth."

She blushed, but she also grinned. Hm. My hopes and my cock grew. I patted the bed next to me and pushed over. She sat at my hip, folding her legs under her. "Maddy's having pancakes," I said. "Want me to take you out for breakfast?" *I can be a gentleman. I don't have a big, hard erection for you, ma'am—really, I don't.*

"Well," she said, chewing her lip, "we've got three hours, don't we?"

"Three and a half."

"So . . . weren't we wondering how we could have our next date before Belinda got back to give me a day off?"

Fitness experts will tell you it takes abdominal muscles to sit up from a prone position. I'm here to say it was all cock that pulled me up so I was face to face with her. "Do you think three and a half hours is going to be enough time?"

I held my hand to her cheek, and she leaned her head into it. Closing her eyes, she exhaled and whispered her truth. "I'm nervous."

I pulled back. "Nervous?" I noted absently that my protectiveness was capable of overriding my lust. Curious. "We don't have to do a single thing. Come on. Let's get panca—" The word wasn't fully out of my mouth before her lips were on mine.

"No," she said through her kiss. "I don't want to miss this. I'm nervous, but—" And then she stopped talking. Her tongue was in my mouth, and adrenaline shot through me. Every muscle in my body woke up, and I dragged her across me. Caveman ascendant— and growling. So much for being a gentleman. I turned as I pulled her to me so that she was under me at last, her hands scratching at my scalp and her breasts pressing against my chest.

If my soul were a cat, it'd be a tiger. And it was purring. Huge, powerful, dominated by want, and purring.

But I could rise above the beast. I could control the caveman.

This wouldn't be just a quick fuck, and I wanted her to know it. "Cyn," I said, breaking from her mouth. "I can stop whenever you want. We don't do anything you don't want to do. Just tell me."

"I want it all," she said, pulling my mouth back to hers. "I'm not very experienced . . . but I want to be. So show me, Rhys. Show me what making love is all about."

My heart was already pounding, but her simple declaration put it into overdrive. She was a match and I was a pile of bone-dry kindling. We were going to make one hell of a fire.

"I'd love to help you explore." I grinned at her. She shivered in excitement. "You put yourself in my hands, then?"

Those incredible green-blue eyes were locked on me. "Absolutely. Teach me. I promise, I'm a good student."

Ahhh. The woman was making my mouth water with words alone. Let the lessons begin.

"Turn over," I said, easing her to her stomach. She made a sound of protest but allowed me to rearrange her. "I've only got three and a half hours, and I'm going to need them all," I explained as I straddled her luscious ass. She laughed as I ran my hand down her delicate spine.

"Three and a half hours? Is this like the Kama Sutra? I'm not *that* good at sex, Rhys."

"I am," I said with boastful confidence. "But that's not what I mean. I mean I need that time to learn your body. And I'm a good student too." I was stroking her back gently.

"I assure you, I have all the requisite parts."

I gave her a light swat on her rump, enjoying her startled reaction. "I'm mapping your nervous system, and that takes a long time." I settled in, looking forward to exploring at length a theory I've held for a while. "You might learn something about your body too. You see, some nerve endings are awake and interested right away." I put firm fingers to the nape of her neck and massaged the strong, long muscles there. She groaned in delight. Her response quickened my pulse. I felt powerful and strong, and a bit like a mad scientist whose lifetime of experimentation was coming to fruition.

"But other nerve endings take longer to come online." I slid my hand to her waist and squeezed gently. She tilted her head on the pillow to peer back at me. She smiled and my balls drew up, tight and excited. "It's important to check all the nerve endings often as we go along. So I can tell what is and isn't working. That is, to figure out what's not working *yet*."

I tugged up the hem of her T-shirt—my T-shirt—and she obligingly lifted her hips so I could bunch the material around her waist.

No panties. So good. "Christ, you've got a pretty ass," I breathed, running my hands over the firm globes, feeling with almost violent satisfaction the secretive skin that only the very luckiest could ever stroke.

"Not too small?" she squeaked.

"Everything about you is small," I told her. "Small and perfect. Let's see how the nerve endings are doing here." I swatted her again—not hard, just with a flat hand to make more of a sound than a sting.

She jumped again. "Rhys! Are you going to keep spanking me in order to judge how turned on I am?" she protested. Her laughter was masking nerves and, I thought, a pretty strong measure of excitement too. The more I turned her on, the more I was turned on myself.

"Maybe. Mostly I like the look of my handprint coming up pink on this gorgeous ass." I kissed her where I'd smacked her, and then kept things in balance by also kissing the other cheek. "That felt like a slap to you now, but pretty soon, that's going to feel like a thrill. Like pure pleasure."

She turned her face into the pillow to hide her blush. Voice muffled by the pillow, she asked me, "You're not a sadist, are you, Rhys?"

"Guess you should have figured that out before you asked me to show you everything, huh?"

I was teasing her and I figured she knew it, but just in case, I leaned over her. Putting my chest against her back, I whispered in her ear. "Nothing. Nothing happens here that you don't like. All you have to do is tell me. Right?"

"Right," she gasped.

I'd never pressured a lover in my life and had made similar statements before. But this was the first time, I realized, that I'd have stopped on a dime without frustration because of that need to protect her. Even from myself.

Protectiveness stronger than lust, and the lust was pretty powerful. Hm. This girl was sinking deep into my soul, and I needed to make sure she understood she had the power here.

"If you say 'no'—just the word 'no,' I'll stop. I promise."

"No safe word?" she giggled nervously.

"We won't need a safe word. 'No' is good enough."

"Okay."

"Okay, then. Quit distracting me. I was heading for those legs."

Warming to my task, I kept up a running commentary, combining the elements I've always thought made for the best sexual experiences: engaging brain and body at the same time.

I told her how beautiful she was. I opined on the quicksilver nervous system. I caressed and kissed and petted and lightly slapped parts of her body that surprised her. A kiss on the back of the knee? Not so surprising. A light swat on her instep? Startling.

I bit at the tender strap of her Achilles tendon. I scratched at the backs of her thighs. I kissed inward along the crease of one beautiful ass cheek, where it met her thigh, until my nose brushed against the other cheek . . . and then, when my ears told me she was holding her breath in anticipation of what I'd do next, I stopped.

"Let's check on those nerves in the back again."

She uttered a mewl of frustration that filled me with satisfaction.

This time, I bit at her waist, where my hands had squeezed before. She uttered a gasp, and I laughed. "See? These nerves are more awake now. That's good. Now I know something about your synaptic responses."

"Synaptic responses?" she repeated incredulously. "Like—my nerve synapses? Are you kidding me?"

I used my big hands on her rib cage to slide the T-shirt up. "Lift up. This comes off now."

Now she was lying before me, facedown and nude. I inhaled the scent of her warm skin. Her entire naked back was displayed to my fascinated gaze like a work of art. No Ingres odalisque ever looked so creamy—so desirable.

I kissed her spine from where it emerged from her tailbone all the way up to her neck. I let her feel my chest behind her—my weight, my strength. At the top of her backbone, I bit lightly at the long, graceful tendons of her neck. She moaned.

"See? These nerve endings are still lively and quick. And others have joined in. I'm mapping you now."

She bent her head into the pillows, baring the nape of her neck —an unconscious gesture of submission that made the tiger in me growl with lust. "Don't you need to map anything on the front of me?" she asked, a hint of begging in her tone.

I ran my hands up her sides until I met her arms, which I pressed gently upward until her hands were over her head. Then, to surprise her and to satisfy me, I grabbed her hips and flipped her over. She gasped. Her nipples were hard points, her skin pebbled in gooseflesh.

"Yeah," I breathed in pleasure. "Yeah, I do."

My thumbs met over the velvet of her stomach and I marveled at how she could be so slight and yet affect me in such a big way. I ran my hands over her ribs as slowly as I could make myself go, and she arched her back to fit her breasts into my hands.

"Christ, you're so pretty." It came out of me like a prayer, and then I was kissing and licking those rose points.

She twisted under me and her hands came down and into my hair, holding my mouth closer to her. I indulged myself by sucking a nipple into my mouth with greater pressure than I'd yet used, and then flicked the tip firmly with my tongue.

That earned me the reward of an excited cry, and so I did it again. Her body jerked.

"That jump you just did—like electricity. That's your entire nervous system reacting to the stimulus. Here. I'll do it again over here."

I sucked on her other nipple, cupping the curve of her breast in my hand, and she jerked against me.

"We know the point of origin, don't we?" Her stunning eyes were half closed and shining. She was panting lightly. "The impulse starts here." I licked the ruby tip lightly, admiring how it gleamed in the light, the wetness from my mouth picking up the morning sun's highlights. "But where does it go? Where does that nerve ending finish?"

"Rhys . . ."

"Yeah? Want to tell me? Or shall I find out?"

She closed her eyes and shivered. "Find out."

I grinned. "You know I can."

"I know it," she admitted.

"Okay. Let's map it." I craned my head and captured her mouth in a soft, wet, long kiss. I savored her taste. I learned her contours. I feasted on her lips. I was determined to remain in control, but my cock was screaming for attention and my muscles were tight as steel. And when I thought I was coming close to giving in and fucking her until I banged her into the headboard, I broke the kiss.

"I'm betting that ended up in the same place. Let's see. Where do those nerves go? Was it to your fingertips?"

I pulled back and she pouted. Taking both of her wrists, I

pulled her hands up to meet my mouth, her arms stretched straight in a line between us. I licked her palms, nibbled at the web of her thumb, sucked lightly at her fingertips. I turned her hands over so I could kiss her delicate wrists, and then I bit at her forearms. Keeping her arms straight, I leaned in and sucked at the skin at the bends of her elbows.

I moved on, nibbling at her upper arms, and as she tried to hold my head, I pulled her arms upwards so she couldn't hold me, and I kissed each armpit.

"Rhys!" She giggled and writhed. "That's gross!"

"Gross? Hang on." I did it again, first one armpit and then the other. "Yep. I thought so. These nerve endings have arrived at the party too. Where do you feel it, Cyn, when I do this?"

I bit lightly at the edge of her muscle where it disappeared into her arm. A ripple went through her, lifting her ribcage almost off the bed.

"Quit biting my armpits!" she gasped.

"Why? Turn you on too much?"

"Stop teasing me," she protested.

"Oh, I'm definitely not going to stop teasing you. Just for that, I should flip you over and check your back muscles again."

"Don't you dare! Rhys, I'm aching. I feel so empty. Can't you just—?"

"Just what? Do you want to explain to me where those nerve impulses are ending up?"

"Oh God."

Her desire, warring with her shyness, sent a thrill through me. I wanted to be inside her, but teasing her was turning out to be as much fun. We'd play a little longer. "So let's keep going."

"*Oh God.*"

"Yeah. So we know what happens if I suckle at your luscious breasts." I paused long enough to lick those taut nipples, so I could see them wet from my mouth again. "But let's examine the nervous system in the belly."

"Oh God!"

She'd gone from a breath to a gasp to a cry as her tensions mounted. I grinned, loving her responses and thinking about how I could delay her satisfaction (and mine) with some more teasing. I spent my time kissing over her belly, adding in the startling effect of suddenly blowing a raspberry below her dip of a belly button. She rose halfway off the bed and I put a hand on her breastbone and pushed her back down again.

"Lie still, please, while I'm mapping you."

She had her hands on my head and maybe didn't even realize that she was urging my head down. I imprinted her skin with the victory in my grin. She needed me and I was going to give her exactly what she—and I—so desperately wanted.

But not quite yet.

I reached the fringe of her curling, dark hair and I stopped.

"You'd like my head to go lower, wouldn't you? You'd like my tongue, and you'd settle for my finger, I imagine. But I'm not done mapping you."

"Rhys . . ."

"I need to chart the nerves in your legs."

"Oh Christ, Rhys. Not my legs. I can't stand it."

"Sure you can." But a voice in my head metaphorically tapped my shoulder. I stopped and looked up at her. "Are you saying no, Cyn? Should I stop?"

"Rhys!" she cried in objection. "Whatever the hell you're doing, do *not* stop now!"

"Okay, then." I moved off her, and she was reduced to making noises of frustration.

I knelt on the floor and tugged her down so I could focus my attentions on her feet. I launched a new assault, teasing her anew and watching her reaction to each kiss, each nibble, each lick, each bite. Her skin was rosy and flushed, her eyes were closed, and my cock twitched when I saw that her two hands were cupping her breasts, her fingers tweaking the crests.

I moved up slowly, licking along the shinbone and then breathing on the dampness to make her shiver. I bit her kneecaps, lifting them to my mouth with a hand behind each knee. I bit the muscles of her thighs. And then once I reached the top, I leaned back far enough to suddenly and firmly separate her legs.

"There," I said in victory. "That's where all these nerves are leading. I'm right, aren't I?"

She bit her lip and watched me in rapt fascination.

I shifted, lying between her legs so I could examine her very, very closely. She was luscious. Her folds were an intense blush pink and gleaming gently with wetness. "God, your scent is amazing. I have to taste you."

I nuzzled her, tasting and licking and exploring with fingers and tongue, and she writhed against me. Her thighs came up and her legs wrapped around my back. I gripped her hips tightly to hold her in place and then licked firmly and deliberately up her sweetness until I at last landed on her clitoris.

Her hands fisted in my hair and she offered soft moans, pushing her pelvis into my mouth.

"Rhys," she gasped. "Help me—"

My cock was hot steel, and I was almost desperate to get it into her squeezing grip, but I could still hold back a little longer. "I've got you," I murmured, and then applied my tongue ruthlessly, opening her slick wetness with my fingers and slipping them inside her.

"Oh my guh—" She was panting like a runner.

So I treated her clit the way I wanted to grip my cock. I leaned into her without mercy, rubbing that high-alert nubbin of nerve endings as she gasped and climbed and—finally—shattered, crying out and all but bucking me off with her response.

I hid my grin of satisfaction in the taut tendon between her core and her thigh, but she may have felt it just the same. Her hands slowly unlocked from their death grip on my head.

"Holy shit," she breathed.

"Good?" I shouldn't have needed it, but I was greedy for her praise.

"Holy shit," she repeated. Then she took her hands from her eyes and peered down at me. "I've never done that before."

I was surprised. "What? Never come before?"

She blushed—her entire body was mottled and rosy, and yet I could still see the beautiful flush of laughing embarrassment pass over her face—and clarified. "No. I've never had an orgasm that I didn't create myself."

Oooh. "I wouldn't mind seeing you do that someday."

She blushed even harder, and I took pity on her. "Nothing from the ex?"

She shook her head. "Uh-uh."

"So, never had a vaginal orgasm, then?"

"Well, I've heard of them . . ."

"Want one?"

"What?"

I grinned at her, cocky. "Oh, yeah. I can hold off that long at least."

"You make it sound like it's easy."

I rose and fished for a condom in my nightstand. "Darling. I've got your entire nervous system tuned up. This is what you were made for."

"Rhys . . ."

I ripped off my T-shirt and shorts.

"Wow," she said. "Let's do that again more slowly. Later."

I laughed and knelt between her thighs again, concentrating hard so I didn't come just from rolling on the rubber. Finally, I was sheathed—the light pressure a mockery of the squeeze I was now desperate for—and I caught her eye.

"Ready?"

"Fuck me, please—and hurry up about it!"

I laughed, the sound possibly more like a gasp than I'd care to admit. Just as I was tugging her down the bed to fit her body up against mine, I stopped.

"So tell me. Are you still nervous?"

"Goddamn it, Rhys! Fuck me, will you please?"

"Oh, well. I'll take that as consent, ma'am. Okay. As you prefer."

She was so small I could move her where I wanted her, and at last had the head of my cock snugged up against her.

"You're so big. Go slow at first," she breathed.

"Slow as I can," I promised.

I leaned into her. Her heat and wetness were incredible. Every moment took me deeper and deeper into the vise-like grip I was aching for. "You okay?"

"Oh, yeah. Go. Go on. More."

"More." She and I were both down to grunting single syllable words.

And then I was fully in her, my aching balls brushing against her ass. "That's me," I gasped. "That's all of me."

She blinked at me—a slow blink that somehow expressed her passion and desire. And then she nudged at me with her hips and I was overwhelmed by the desire to claim her as mine forever.

"Again," she said. My good girl.

The withdrawal was torture and the return was paradise—this time smoother and easier.

"Yes," she breathed.

"Yes," I echoed.

Again and again, we pulled away from each other and came back together. And I knew the moment when, as our tempo increased, she felt something new.

Her eyes flew open. "Ah!" she said in surprise.

"Got it?" I asked, watching her carefully.

"Oh jeez," she replied, and I was as proud of that answer as of anything else in the world. "Do that again."

I stroked into her and she was clearly jolted.

"Again!" she demanded. I loved that she was getting bossy.

"Hang on." I pulled out of her and she cursed me.

"Damn it! What are you doing?"

"Flip over. Hands and knees." I moved her to the edge of the bed where I could bend my knees to fit into her.

"Seriously?" But once again, she allowed me to arrange our positions. Soon I was standing behind her, the tip of my cock in her.

"Okay," I panted. "Now you're in control. It's up to you. Hard or soft, fast or slow. You do it. Just lean your hips into me."

She leaned back into me and her heat and wetness squeezed around me. I put my hands on her hips to stop her from rocking too far forward, but that was my only attempt at control. I let her lead completely . . .

. . . except for one swat on her ass. Not for pain—just for the crack of noise, to see her jump, to enjoy the print of my hand coming up pink on her creamy skin.

"Oh, yeah," I grunted. "All those nerve endings are definitely online."

"Test successful," she agreed, panting as she thrust back against me. "Stop talking."

"You're driving," I confirmed.

And drive she did. From quick gasps to fast pants, from a tentative shifting of her body to a brutal slamming back onto me, Cyn pushed my cock repeatedly against the spot deep inside her responsible for sending silvery electrical sparks all along her nervous system.

Soon her movements were almost a stutter as opposed to a stroke. She was barely withdrawing an inch before slamming back into me, and I had my teeth clenched in an effort to avoid coming. She was so hot and responsive and bent before me and I was —I was—

Thank God—she screamed, shivering, and her arms gave out. Her head fell down to the bed and I took her from behind in one more deep stroke, and then I was jetting out pure fire and glory, a yell of relief wrenched from me . . .

. . . and then I was down on the mattress beside her, spooning her, our legs in a tangle and half hanging off the bed.

I found her hand. She clasped my fingers as our breathing slowly returned to normal.

TWENTY-ONE
CYN

A WOMAN LIKE ME—ONE WHO GREW UP IN THE RELATIVE SOCIAL isolation of continually being ahead of her peers in school, and thus perpetually regarded as a child by her classmates—developed her own concepts of romantic love, which were rarely tested and never refined through typical social interaction.

For my entire life I was ahead of everyone else in book learning, but woefully behind the learning curve in relationships.

Sappy movies and sweet love stories didn't have much in common with the grubby couples I saw making out in corners of my high school (or later, in dorm rooms). Adolescent couplings seemed to me to be hasty, stress-filled, and based entirely on one's social standing in the class microsociety. Jocks and prom queens, potheads with stoner chicks. Never the twain shall meet.

Physical love seemed scary. Worse, it seemed awkward. I wasn't sure I was so interested. On the other hand, an intellectual compatibility, I decided, was far more desirable. That would stand the test of time. That would keep a person happy whether their skin was dewy and fresh or wrinkled and thin.

And my marriage to Don had borne that out. Our sex life was

formulaic. I was as content to rest in his arms after sex as I was to carry him, grunting, in the cradle of my body.

So, yes. I thought the smart person would choose to engage the brain, not the body.

I'd been astonished to discover a different reality after being mapped by Rhys. My morning was illuminated by the startling discovery that all those awkward adolescent fumblings I'd observed were leading to something quite earthshaking. After all my foolish assumptions, I realized that I was very interested in sex with Rhys. Possibly even greedy for more. And this definitely distracted me.

I was still getting used to these new understandings when we met the two new FBI agents back at Maddy and Belinda's condo. But all lustful thoughts were driven out of my head when Maddy bounded from the shotgun seat of a Pennsylvania State Police car and I'd shrieked with joy and relief. She wrapped me in an excited hug, and I cried to have her alive and safe, and surrounded by officers of the law to ward off any attempts to abduct her. Together we admired her brilliantly blue hair.

"How did this happen?" I asked her, still not ready to let her go.

"I don't know—I woke up and it was like this this morning! Isn't it heavenly?"

We thanked the large retinue of law enforcement vehicles that had accompanied her. They'd gathered steam as they rolled from Pennsylvania, and by the time she arrived home, Maddy was escorted by many of the Maryland troopers from yesterday's extended car chase as well as the Pennsylvania troopers and a few Arlington County police who came to see what the fuss was about. Several of the represented precincts offered to adopt Madcap Maddy as their mascot, and they only left once she'd promised to keep in touch.

Once we were all safe upstairs, I paid careful attention to all that was discussed . . .

But as if Maddy's security was only of passing interest, my libido woke up again and I could feel the ghost of a powerful sensation.

As crude as it was to say it (to even think it), if I concentrated, I could still feel Rhys's cock buried deep in me, hitting on a trigger that I never knew was there. I was having orgasmic aftershocks for hours after being with him. At times it was a challenge to remain straight-faced and serious during the entirely focused discussions taking place around me.

It had taken me a long time to discover the truth that all those teenagers around me had learned so much earlier, but I was in the know now.

Sex was glorious.

And sex with Rhys had made me stronger. More confident. Unwilling to settle for less.

Therefore, not only did I want more of it, but I also thought that a person like Don would never be able to have as much control over me ever again . . . because I merited better treatment than that. I wanted better.

And I wanted it now. With a gorgeous blond hunk who lit up my brain as much as he delighted my body.

Rhys was clearly reading some of what was going on behind my eyes, and I reveled at him shifting his positions occasionally to hide the evidence that he was at least somewhat hard through most of the conversations we had with the other FBI agents.

I did that to him. It was me.

I loved it.

But finally, he shook his head at me with a smile and looked pointedly at Maddy—and I got the message. We weren't here to play footsie. We were putting together the strategy that would keep her (and me) safe.

It was time for me to focus. All right. I could do that.

Mostly.

Agent Elise Proctor was the new senior agent in charge. She

looked like a Russian prima ballerina, with white-blond hair and the most beautiful posture I'd ever seen outside an animated movie. But like an actual ballerina, there was steel below her grace, and I never doubted her natural authority.

Her partner, Agent Jim Biays, looked like any anonymous DC bureaucrat in a suit and tie, but his speech was pure Brooklyn. He'd greeted Rhys as a friend. They'd played basketball together in the gym and even in the short time that Rhys had been posted to DC, they'd clearly formed a friendship.

Maddy was delighted with both of them, of course. She showed absolutely no evidence of trauma, and had, as predicted, forgotten her adventures on the motorcycle. She'd startled Proctor and Biays by suddenly sniffing her own hand and then announcing with delight that she smelled like maple syrup and butter.

"I think," she said to us all, "that I'm a particularly tasty breakfast! Smell how good!"

I took her to wash her hands. When we returned, the four FBI agents were grouped in the living room. I wouldn't say any of them were relaxed, but at least Dash and Agent Proctor were sitting down.

Maddy regarded them as if we were having a particularly delightful party. Then she turned to me.

"Cyn, dear, I think I should have a gun."

Try as I might, I never could predict what Maddy was going to say next. "What? Why?"

"Well, everyone here has a gun. I should have one too. I'm underdressed without one."

Dash and Rhys turned to Proctor and Biays with expressions that could only be defined as a shout-without-words "See? I told you!" The two newcomers to our group shifted nervously, but Rhys laughed out loud and moved to take Maddy's hand, his other hand closed protectively over his holster.

"Madcap," he teased her.

Sometimes she knew people, sometimes she didn't. This

happened to be a time of clarity. "Peanut Butter Cup!" she cried. "Hello, my tasty fellow! Used any of those condoms lately?"

Rhys looked startled—he must've expected her to go for his gun again and wasn't prepared for a different attack—and I knew I was blushing. Maddy read my color and chortled in delight. "Oh, I see! Good for you!"

Perhaps my embarrassment was so great that I only imagined the others squirming in discomfort. Dash distracted Maddy's attention by standing and gathering the group's attention.

"And that's why Rhys and I are only here in an advisory capacity."

Maddy turned to me. "Is there going to be dancing at this party?"

"Dancing?"

"Well, there are three men here, and three women." Maddy gestured to the FBI agents. "You and the Peanut Butter Cup will do very well together, although he's so tall. And those two people can dance together." She smiled at Proctor and Biays. "Dancing would help them to remember how to smile." They were caught in poses of astonishment and tried to cover, too late, with beaming fake smiles. "Which leaves this handsome creature for me."

Maddy held out her hand to Dash, who took it and then, to Maddy's obvious delight, bowed over it with distinguished formality, clicking his heels together like a Prussian diplomat. "Miss Madeline, it would be my absolute pleasure. Do you rumba?"

"Oh, I love to rumba!"

"We must get some music. In the meantime, won't you sit here?" If I hadn't been so gone on Rhys, Dash would have finally and permanently captured my heart with that particular move. What a charmer.

He seated Maddy with great care and she beamed at him. Then he turned to address the deck of cards—no, I mean the cell phone —on the coffee table. "Dr. Root, can you still hear us?"

Ah. Belinda had returned the call at last. I was filled with remorse and relief and guilt and hope, all in a rush that heated my skin. I'd left her a long message about what had happened, and followed it up with an email, but it wasn't the same as hearing her voice. I bit back the urgent desire to beg her for forgiveness, for something I had no way to control. I knew it made no sense, but the emotion spoke in a language all its own.

Belinda was talking. "Yes, it's quite a good connection. Will you go over the physician's reports again for both my mother and Cyn?"

Agent Proctor nodded at Agent Biays, who gathered up some papers and spoke. "Both were dosed with a short-acting benzodiazepine. Neither has shown any evidence of negative effects. Neither showed any signs of sexual or physical abuse. Both were treated prophylactically just in case. Miss Maddy"—he sent her a smile—"is in excellent health and high spirits. Ms. Quimby"—I got the nod this time—"had an appropriate and expected reaction to the stress and trauma." That must mean I soaked Rhys's shirt with my tears on the ride home. "She, too, is in excellent health."

"Well, that's good to know," I said dryly.

"Thank God," Belinda said. "Cyn, I'm so very sorry this happened to you."

My eyes filled with tears. I craved confession but didn't feel I deserved absolution. "Please don't apologize. I'm the one who's sorry. I don't know how I could have been so careless."

The resulting protest was vigorous and reassuring, but it didn't do much to lessen my belief that I'd somehow exposed Maddy to tremendous danger. Then Maddy shut us all up when she spoke with a casual calmness.

"It was in the coffee," she offered. "Don't you remember, Cyn? You and I shared a cup after lunch."

We must have looked like a family of startled meerkats, upright and blinking at her, because she laughed merrily. "Do you people think I have no memory at all?"

"Yes, that must be right," I said, remembering as if it was a dream. "You ordered a cup and then liked it so much you persuaded me to share it with you. And I guess that would explain why Grumpy Bear said I wasn't supposed to be there."

This set off a great deal of discussion, including Rhys's chilling query: "If he didn't think Cyn would be rendered unconscious, what did he think he was going to do with her?"

I wished he hadn't asked. It was bad enough having been drugged and kidnapped. I didn't want to imagine what would have happened if I hadn't been drugged in the first place.

Finally Belinda shouted them down. "Can we go over the chronology, please?" she insisted.

Agent Proctor took over from Biays. She sat forward and consulted her notes, and Maddy and I both sat straighter from watching her upright carriage.

"Best estimates are that the subjects—I'm sorry, I mean Miss Maddy and Ms. Quimby—"

"Please, Agent Proctor. Just call me Cyn."

"Hello, Cyn!" Maddy chirped, delighted to see me. I smiled back. I was truly delighted to see her as well. I nodded to Agent Proctor to continue.

"Maddy and Cyn were apparently drugged at the Morris Street Café in Arlington at about 1 p.m." She stopped and tapped on her tablet, muttering to herself. "Sedative might have been in the coffee they shared." She went on. "It's theorized that the subjects were abducted by—do we have to use this name?" She broke off to look up imploringly. I bit back a smile. Maddy's nicknames had a way of sticking, as a new team from the FBI was about to discover.

"Grumpy Bear," said Dash with great assertiveness.

"Hello, Rumba!" Maddy called to Dash, who bowed to her with a brilliant smile.

"Grumpy Bear," Proctor repeated resignedly. "Grumpy Bear and possibly associates—"

Biays beside her murmured, "Snoozy Bear, Sneezy Bear, and Doc," but Agent Proctor shushed him.

"Grumpy Bear and possible associates drug Maddy and Cyn and put them in the trunk of a white 2017 Ford Taurus, West Virginia plates KKM-209. The car was reported stolen from Keyser, West Virginia four days ago."

"How do you know that so specifically?" Belinda asked.

"Because we found the car abandoned on the Route 270 entrance ramp from the scenic overlook south of Frederick. Its right rear tire was shredded, and the rim was crumpled. The trunk had been pried open and will no longer shut."

"Mac," Maddy said with satisfaction. "Remember, Cyn? He whacked merry hell out of that tire with his crowbar."

Again, we regarded Maddy with astonishment. "I remember, Maddy," I said. "That was back when I thought he was a Good Samaritan. How quickly things change, hm?"

Maddy, who I felt certain didn't know what I meant, agreed with me nonetheless, out of general principles of kindness.

Agent Proctor resumed her report.

"Subjects—I mean Miss Maddy and Cyn—were rescued by a MacMillan Shipman who broke them out of the trunk of the Taurus and put them in his 2020 blue Honda Odyssey van. He then informed them that he, too, was kidnapping them."

"Jesus Christ," said Belinda.

"There's more there," Biays interrupted. He turned to me. "What did MacMillan say to you, Ms. Cyn?"

"Just Cyn, please. He said he wanted to ask Maddy a few questions and take us on a trip."

"To Chincoteague!" Maddy added. She was having quite a good day. "I love Chincoteague!"

Peanut Butter Cup leaned in. "I'm sorry; you all seem to know what that is. What's Chincoteague?"

"Barrier island on the Virginia shore," replied Rumba. "There's a famous children's book called *Misty of Chincoteague*. I guess you don't have any sisters who went through a horse phase, huh, Agent Jones?"

Rhys shook his head with a grin, and I felt a pang deep in my core, he was so beautiful. Agent Proctor unbent from her rigid formality enough to admit, "I sure did! I loved that book!" She and I exchanged nods. I'd been through all those books in my childhood.

"Hang on," said Belinda. "Chincoteague?" She sounded thoughtful. "Cyn, in my office. The letter from the lawyer about someone leaving Mother some property in Chincoteague. A fishing shack, I believe."

I was already on my way, my hackles rising as I went. Even before I located the cream envelope from a law firm in Maryland, I knew that a missing piece was about to click into place. I couldn't wait and was reading the letter by the time I came back into the living room.

"Someone named H. de Salles Shipman. Shipman like in MacMillan Shipman?" I handed the letter to Rumba—I mean Dash—who wouldn't take it and instead directed me to the senior agent in charge. "Sorry. Agent Proctor, here's the letter."

Biays was already doing research on his phone and read us what he found. "H. de Salles Shipman, wealthy investor, died two months ago at the age of—hey. He was ninety-nine."

Rumba was also typing. And then he was cursing. "Shit. H. de Salles Shipman changed his name in 1966 when he got out of prison. Before that, he was Hector Battelle."

"Oh! Hector!" Maddy straightened in her seat, her eyes sparkling, and her hands held before her like a child about to get a treat.

But the four people with guns under their jackets weren't happy about the connection. It was more like they were fixated. "The jewel thief? That Hector Battelle?" Rhys said, astonished. "A jewel thief left a fishing shack to Maddy? Why?"

"Don't be silly. He's nothing so common as a jewel thief."

Maddy dismissed her Peanut Butter Cup with a coy look. "Hector is a cat burglar. The best in the business!"

All gazes swiveled to her. There was absolute silence.

Then Belinda spoke from the phone speaker. "Mother! What are you talking about?"

"Oh, hello, Belinda, dear! When will you be back? You know your father wants you home by ten."

"Mother! What do you know about cat burglars?"

"Cat burglars? Now, Belinda, don't try to distract me! Your father said ten o'clock, so you be home by ten o'clock!"

"Miss Maddy." Agent Proctor was trying to recapture the conversation. Maddy looked at her and straightened again, unconsciously mimicking the way the senior agent sat.

"Yes? Are you a dancer, dear? You sit like a dancer."

"Miss Maddy, did you know Hector Battelle?"

"Who? Look how beautifully that jacket fits you. You must have the most marvelous tailor. Doesn't she?" She turned and found the rest of us looking at her. Then all the eyes but Maddy's swiveled to me.

"Can you get her back?" Proctor asked.

I shrugged but sat up straighter too—the woman really did have the most beautiful posture. "The first thing to distract her will do it. But we can maybe bring the subject up again in a bit. It's hard to tell what she will and won't remember."

"Who are you talking about, dear?" Maddy asked me.

"A friend of mine," I explained with a smile. "I don't think you know her."

"I'd like to meet her, though. I'm sure I'd love any friend of yours."

There was a kindness, a loveliness of spirit to Maddy that transcended everything around her and filled me with a glow of happiness. It was hard to stay frustrated with someone who so sincerely wanted to like everyone around her.

"All right," said the dancer. I mean, Agent Proctor. "Jim, we need more information on Shipman." She turned to Rumba next to her, who nodded. "And Dash and Rhys, I know you're not on the case. But could you see if the lawyer for Shipman's estate would talk to us? We'll get a court order if we need to, but let's first see if he'll cooperate."

"Shipman is MacMillan's last name," Rhys pointed out. "I guess we know how he and Will are involved in this."

"Look!" Maddy whispered to me, "it's the Peanut Butter Cup!" As if I wasn't already having enough trouble with her nicknames.

"I get the feeling there's a lot we don't know," Proctor said. "Let's work on getting some answers."

"Before you go tearing off," said Belinda through the deck of cards on the coffee table, "would you finish yesterday's chronology? Just so I'll know too?"

"Yes, you're right. I'm sorry, Dr. Root. Let's review before we begin the next phase in the investigation. So we have a dead car by the side of the road, but no Grumpy Bear in sight. Maybe he hitched a ride, maybe he took off cross-country on foot."

"Or maybe he had an accomplice," Rumba pointed out.

"Right. So Grumpy Bear is our first person of interest, and he's at large. Next is Mac Shipman, who is also in the wind. His car, too, was dead at the side of the road."

"Because the Oatmeal Man drove it off the road." Rumba was nodding and consulting his own notes.

"At the very least, we can identify that man as Barry Gambert, of Winchester, VA. We don't have to call him the Oatmeal Man." Proctor's voice dripped with contempt. Maddy nodded firmly in agreement.

"Yes," she said, "the Oatmeal Man is a loathsome individual."

"Gambert takes Maddy and Mac in his car and leaves Cyn by the side of the road. Cyn runs into Mac's brother, William Shipman."

"He almost ran into me, actually." I hadn't had time to review my less-than-important details, but I offered them in this conversation for the sake of completeness. "I'd found the phone—I'd dropped it when the Oatmeal Man forced Mac's van off the road—when another van screeched to a halt and Will jumped out, shouting about that's his brother's van and where is his brother and is he okay."

"And then you got in his van and made him follow Barry."

"Right. And when I was calling Rhys and Dash, he tried to take the phone and tell me he was kidnapping me, but he was a total wimp and I made him drive faster."

Just thinking back on how angry I'd been made me flush with rage. Rhys and Dash were both grinning, probably because I was becoming an unflattering shade of red.

"And just as we caught up, along came Timmo."

"Who is Timmo?" Maddy asked with great interest. She was following the story as if it was a particularly fascinating soap opera. Perhaps it was. "What?" Maddy asked to all the watching eyes.

"Okay," said Proctor. "Here comes another West Virginia mountain man who shoots out his own windshield and then forces Barry's car off the road."

"I think he shot into the engine," I offered.

"Apparently not, because both cars are gone—although we found evidence of a crash. So the theory is that both persons of interest drove away under their own power."

"So Timmo and Barry fight while Cyn steals Maddy back." Peanut Butter Cup looked at me with mingled approval and anxiety. "And then Timmo and Barry both leave under their own steam. So where's Mac?"

"An excellent question," Proctor responded. "Unknown. And then Cyn, Maddy, and Will are collected at the roadblock in Reisterstown, where Will is arrested."

"And a third member of the West Virginia contingent wants his brother back and shoots at us." That was Rumba, adding his note. Maddy, drawn by Dash's handsome face, beamed at him, and he smiled back at her.

"Not at us," clarified Rhys. "That guy's a great shot. He wasn't trying to hurt anyone." His voice rang with authority. It was clearly important to him to point out that the man who shot the helicopter hadn't intended to harm anyone.

"I hear your response was equally skillful," said Proctor, and Rhys flushed. "And then Maddy was abducted by a biker woman with purple hair."

They were all looking hopefully at Maddy again. "What?" she asked.

Then Agent Biays said a naughty word.

"Language," chided Agent Proctor.

"Sorry," he replied, but it was clear that his was a pro forma apology. "I'm reading the back records on Hector Battelle. He went to prison in 1952 for theft . . . and they never found his loot. He was finally tracked down after a 1951 theft in New York City when he stole the jewels of visiting British royalty from the fourteenth floor of the Waldorf Astoria, including something called the Jaipur Princess."

"What's the Jaipur Princess?" I asked.

"A flawless emerald. Huge. Over seven hundred carats."

A gemstone of that size was far outside of my field of reference. My sister made her husband buy her a two-carat diamond engagement ring, and it was the biggest thing I'd ever seen. "How big is seven hundred carats?"

"Well, it's too big to fit in my bellybutton," Maddy laughed. "I know. We tried."

We all stared at her in silence. "It's really a very ugly stone," she offered, trying to be helpful. "It's not even a good green. It's muddy. You know. Kind of cloudy."

"Nobody say a word," I breathed. Maddy was remembering something important. We could find out what it was if we could keep her from being distracted.

Then Agent Biays did something and his phone uttered a pretty chime.

"Oh! How did you get your cards to make that noise?" Maddy wheeled to track down the sound and I exhaled my frustration. She was gone. I knew it.

"What about the emerald?" Biays asked her hopefully.

"What emerald? Silly man. What are you talking about?"

TWENTY-TWO
CYN

"I'm sorry!" howled Agent Biays. "I was turning on the recorder in my phone so we wouldn't miss anything!"

A storm of discussion erupted, creating chaos in the living room. Maddy applauded and laughed at the resulting noise, and Rhys reached over and gently tagged Agent Biays on the shoulder with a loose fist, a gesture of solidarity between two junior agents who still didn't know enough not to screw up the small stuff. They exchanged winces of shame and frustration.

Eventually Agent Proctor brought us back to some kind of order.

"All right. Calm down. There's a lot we're missing, but Miss Maddy seems to have information. Whether or not she can access it is a different question. But at least we can surmise why so many different people have attempted to abduct her."

The quartet of FBI agents was nodding. "The missing jewels," said Agent Biays.

"The missing jewels," agreed Agent Proctor.

"The missing jewels," echoed Maddy. But since she had nothing more to add beyond a sweet smile, I assumed she was joining in because she was so pleased with everyone in the room.

Agent Proctor held her comment briefly in the hope that Maddy would have something more to add, but Maddy was in her own happy place. "Look at her feet," Maddy whispered to me. "Aren't they so lovely?"

We all looked at Agent Proctor's feet—the senior agent was as curious as we were about her own foot placement. She'd hooked one ankle behind the other so her feet were lying alongside each other in perfect parallel. They were, indeed, lovely. Effortlessly graceful. Every single person who was currently sitting unconsciously attempted to duplicate the pose, to see if we could. Maddy beamed at all of us.

Agent Proctor shook off her bemusement first. "Let's focus, please. Dr. Root, I'd like to call you back in a half an hour, maybe forty-five minutes. We've got research to do on this situation, but I want you to know that your mother is safe. There are four FBI agents in this room, and we're dedicated to her safety first and foremost."

"Thank you, Agent Proctor. I'll wait for your call."

After disconnecting, Proctor made her assignments. "Jim, what's the estimated value of the jewels that were never recovered?"

That slowed down Agent Biays. While he was doing his research, she turned to the rest of us.

"Dash, I know Rhys's personal involvement means he can't be on this case. But while you're here, can I use you?"

Dash frowned. "I'll let Owen know first. What do you need?"

"We have mug shots for Barry Gambert and Will Shipman. Would you go downstairs to the lobby and see if anyone at the desk recognizes them?"

"I'm on it. Rhys, you sit there and look pretty. If she needs anything"—he gestured with his chin at me—"you can help. Otherwise, you're only backup here." Rhys nodded obediently; I had a twinge in a tender place to see a glimpse of the little boy inside the large man. Dash pulled out his phone as he left, no doubt calling Rhys's high-level father to keep him up to speed.

Agent Proctor turned to me, and I had to pull my eyes from Rhys. "Cyn, I know it's unlikely, but is there any chance that Maddy could be in possession of these jewels now?"

I looked at Maddy, who looked back at me placidly. Nothing ventured, after all. "Maddy, do you have the Jaipur Princess?"

She laughed merrily. "Oh, sweetheart. You know Hector has it. Along with the Merlin Twins."

Ahh—we were back in Maddy's memory. Having learned this lesson already, Rhys and Agent Biays both froze. Agent Proctor's eyebrows disappeared into her hairline. She darted her eyes to me insistently. It was up to me to navigate the foggy wilds of Maddy's dementia in pursuit of the investigation. I blanked for a moment and then realized I should keep it simple. "What are the Merlin Twins, Maddy?"

She dimpled at me and put a slim, wrinkled finger to her lips. "You know we don't talk about them, my dear! Never, ever!" She looked sly and very happy.

"Do you know where he hid them?"

"Of course!" She laughed and I worked to keep her looking at me, so she wouldn't be distracted by anything that might catch her eye anew.

"Will you tell me?"

"No, no! It's a secret." Her smug look was clearly meant to fool me. "I could show you, though."

"Can't you tell me?"

"Oh, tosh, you darling fairytale creature. Let's go to Chincoteague. You'll love it there. I promise!"

"Well . . . " I exchanged a glance with the rapt FBI agents gathered around us. Finally, Agent Proctor shrugged. No advice for me. I thought for a moment. "Shall we look through your jewelry box, Maddy? Just for fun?"

"Oh, yes! Let's! I'll show you my charm bracelet. Az is working on it. I have all sorts of wonderful charms on it!"

I walked with Maddy back to her room, but I could still hear Agent Biays.

"Holy shit," he said.

"Language, Jim," murmured Agent Proctor, but he was unrepentant. He wasn't the only one swearing, but he was apparently the only one she felt she could correct.

"The Merlin Twins are earrings—a flawless matched pair of diamonds from the Merlin mines in South Africa. They were stolen in 1951 and never recovered. Estimated value in 1951 was $2.6 million."

There was a pregnant moment of silence behind me in the living room, broken when Agent Proctor said, "I'd call that motive."

As fraught and interesting as the research was in the living room, I was actually grateful for a few moments of peace in Maddy's bedroom, by now as familiar to me as my own. Maddy and I spent a pleasurable fifteen minutes pawing through her jewelry box, which was—as I knew—unremarkable and contained no secret cache of jewel thief loot. Just to be thorough, she and I went through her drawers and her closet, which she greatly enjoyed.

She was getting tired, though, and I was glad we were in the relative quiet of her room. She laid down willingly for her nap. "Hasn't this been the most wonderful day, darling?"

I remembered how the day began—waking in Rhys's arms and then being shattered by the power of an orgasm that went way beyond any physical response I've ever had—and I could only agree with her. I experienced an aftershock from the memory, which I did my best to suppress from her quick eye.

Then there had been the overwhelming relief at Maddy's return, and the offers by police from Pennsylvania as well as Maryland that they were to be considered at Maddy's service, should she need anything—an offer that made me tear up at the kindness.

I flashed back to the hard task of explaining to Belinda what had happened to her mother in my care and thought about all the support that four FBI agents had given me.

Not to mention the discovery that Maddy's past wasn't quite as simple and normal as one might have suspected. After all, how many of us can claim to have tried mounting a seven-hundred-carat emerald in their navel?

"An absolutely amazing day, Madcap Maddy. You're exactly right. Have a nice rest."

"See you when I wake up, sweetheart!"

I stood at the doorway for a while, watching her sink into uncomplicated sleep, and wished I could stop the mad spinning of my brain so easily. Maddy was such a delight. Maddening, but darling too. The Maddy Mantra—*be in the now*—apparently made for easy and deep sleep.

Dash had returned from the lobby, and the two teams were in full consultation in the living room. Rhys smiled at me as I came back in, and even though we were in the thick of a very serious series of events that most definitely should have dampened my newly awakened libido, I blushed once again. I was suddenly over-whelmed by the knowledge of how beautiful his naked body was, and what he could do with his thick, hard penis . . . which caused me to stumble as I attempted to navigate the perils of open, smooth, wall-to-wall carpeting. Rhys watched my flush with a smile and a raised eyebrow.

"Cyn, no sweet spot, I'm guessing?"

Agent Proctor's question jerked me out of my reverie, and I gaped for a moment at her. *Wait. What was she asking me?*

"No gemstones hidden in a drawer? No Jaipur Princess or Merlin Twins?"

"Oh. No. Nothing."

Rhys's face was stern, like an Easter Island sculpture. But if eyes could giggle, his were laughing behind serious granite.

"Too much to hope for," Proctor said.

I wasn't completely hopeless, though. I did have something of use to offer beyond lustful imaginings. "But someone's been through her things." It wasn't obvious, but I cared for Maddy's clothes as I cared for the woman, and her bureau and closet were both slightly out of place.

"All right. Let's bring in Dr. Root before we share what we know." Agent Proctor had Biays call Belinda again and put her on speakerphone, while I found a seat far from Rhys and attempted to clear my lust away and un-blush my face.

"Dr. Root, Cyn thinks someone's been through your mother's things," Proctor said.

"I wouldn't doubt it," said Dash. "I showed their photos to the people at the front desk, and they both agree that Barry and Will have been in the building. Will didn't make it past security, but Barry seems to have been squatting in the apartment next door. He told the front desk he was subletting while the owners were in Jamaica."

"The Thompsons?" I said, startled from my rich fantasies. "There's no one in that apartment at the moment. They're on vacation."

"Huh," said Dash, stepping to the sliding balcony doors. Beyond him the day was gray and blustery. The wind had picked up. "Does Maddy ever eat breakfast out here?" he asked me.

"Sure," I said. "She loves to eat on the balcony on sunny mornings."

"Does she ever have oatmeal?" He looked at me, and the sudden burst of fear made me recoil with a wince.

"Oh, Jesus," Belinda's voice came over the phone. "I found her out there crying a few days ago. She asked if I'd seen the man. God —I failed her. I thought she was delusional. And he must have been right there."

Her cry was straight from the heart, and I recognized the feeling like an old friend. We shared this one: shame that we'd let Maddy suffer without believing or even understanding her.

"We both did," I said. "Was he really bothering her across the balconies?" Hot tears prickled at my eyes. I was horrified that someone could have been scaring Maddy while I was a few feet away, ignoring her fear. Was I really so oblivious? Rhys's arm came around me—he'd moved to my side without me even noticing—and he made soothing noises in my ear.

"The Oatmeal Man," Dash agreed. "And it'd be easy to climb from balcony to balcony. I wouldn't be surprised if the whole place had been searched—and thoroughly. There were plumbers here last week who sound like our bearded West Virginia team."

"We didn't have any plumbers in," Belinda protested. Goosebumps crept over my skin.

"Doesn't mean they didn't show up," Agent Proctor said.

"Well, they clearly didn't find what they were looking for," Biays said, "because they came after Maddy after searching this place."

"Maddy knew," I whispered. "She knew he was bad, and we didn't get it. And when she saw him at the grocery store—" The event with Rhys's gun took on an entirely new cast. Suddenly I was proud of Maddy, who shot at the man who was tormenting her. She met him with fury instead of tears. She stood up instead of curling up.

I straightened under Rhys's arm, actively hating my own weakness. Suddenly, my entire relationship with my ex-husband was laid bare to me. I'd been paralyzed by fear that a loathsome man would leave me . . . and then he left me.

I should have found a gun and aerated his jacket. I should have showed a little spine. Perhaps the Maddy Mantra had room for more than just "be in the now." Perhaps there was a measure of "don't mess with me" too.

Maddy was my hero. And I wouldn't forget the lesson.

Unaware of the earthquake running through my already-overstressed nervous system, Agent Proctor continued gathering the reins of the investigation into her competent hands. She turned to her partner. "What did you find out, Jim?"

"There's no way to know how much Hector Battelle got away with. He was apparently a fearless climber and could get in through second-story windows, third stories, fourth stories. The investigators in the 1951 Waldorf Astoria case decided he may have climbed down the outside of the building from the roof. Looks like he was one of those guys who's missing the fear receptor in his brain."

"Like that Free Climb guy," Dash nodded. "Rare, but impressive."

"This guy was actually a junior lawyer at a DC law firm in the '40s and '50s, but that was apparently too boring for him, so he added cat burglary to his law practice."

I could offer a tiny piece for this jigsaw puzzle. "Maddy was a legal secretary in DC before she married Azariah."

Agent Proctor pointed at me in approval. "Who wants to bet that Maddy and Hector worked at the same firm? Put that on the list of questions we can research, Jim."

"Right. So you wanted to know: Just how much did this guy steal? During the time when Battelle was thought to be active, there was a rash of second-story jewelry heists from Atlanta to Boston, but it's hard to know which ones were him and which were other people."

"Anybody hurt?" Rhys still had his arm around me, and I basked in his warmth.

"Never. It's part of how some robberies were eliminated from his possible targets. He seems to have been quite a gentleman."

"A gentleman cat burglar. Haven't I seen this movie?" Agent Proctor wore a wry smile.

"Screenwriters have to get their ideas from somewhere," Biays offered. "Real life is sometimes crazier than fiction. So this guy gets sentenced to fourteen years. It'd have been longer if they could have proved all the jobs he'd pulled. And while he was in slam, he begins to study investing."

"Because of course he was disbarred as a lawyer." Rhys again.

"Right. Can't have a criminal record and still practice law. Something to keep in mind, Agent Jones." Biays's voice was teasing, and Rhys snorted. This was clearly one friend getting back at the other for junior partner screw-ups. "By the time he gets out in 1966, Hector Battelle is pretty good at the market. No fear receptor, right? He's bold and smart. So he changes his name and somehow—gee, like magic—he manages to cobble together a stake for his first foray on Wall Street. I wonder how."

Collectively, we all rolled our eyes. No one had ever found the jewels he stole. How hard would it have been to fence a random ruby or two to bankroll a big business adventure?

"And he turns out to be pretty good at it. By the time he died a few months ago, the guy was almost a hundred years old. And Forbes estimated his net worth at $43 million."

I was uttering a soundless whistle when Dash proved that I hadn't seen the whole picture. He added, "That was $43 million *not* counting the jewels."

"Not counting the jewels," Biays agreed.

Agent Proctor's phone rang, and she stepped away to take the call.

"What else did you find, Jim?" Rhys asked.

"He marries a Fiona Patterson in"—he consulted his notes—"1983."

"How old?" Dash asked.

"How old was Battelle? He was, let's see . . . sixty-one."

"And I'll bet she was a sweet young thing. Maybe there's hope for me too. I just have to earn a few million." Dash grinned.

"I happen to know an old lady who might have a real trunk full of jewels," Rhys offered, and Dash chucked him on the arm.

"Focus, gentlemen." In Agent Proctor's absence, Belinda clearly felt justified in pulling the boys back to attention, even if she had to do it by phone from Indonesia. "Agent Biays? What else?"

"Um, well, Hector's son MacMillan was born in '84—that's Miss Maddy's friend Mac. And then Mac's brother Will was born in '86. The lawyer managing the Shipman estate is demanding a court order before he'll let us see the will—or, in this guy's case, the estate trust. People with that much money don't have anything as simple as a will."

"I'll get on the subpoena." Dash said. Then Agent Proctor returned.

"I've been on the phone with the sheriff in Chincoteague. Shipman did, in fact, own a house there—the house that he apparently left to Miss Maddy. The sheriff said a neighbor had already called in a disturbance a few days ago. Seems the house has been ransacked, and there's a large hole in the backyard, like someone's been playing with explosives."

"Or using a seismic reader to search for underground chambers." Dash nodded.

"Right. And the resulting hole is filled with water already. The island is about two feet above the water table. The 'buried treasure' myth isn't looking very likely here."

Agent Proctor glanced out the window at the scudding clouds. "He offered me some advice, though. He says the island is in the path of Superstorm Etta, which unfortunately will be hitting around high tide tonight at 9:14. They're expecting major devastation."

She looked at us. "We either go right now, or we run the risk that the shack won't be there after tonight." She looked at the phone and spoke directly to Maddy's daughter, on the other side of the planet. "And I think we have to take Maddy with us."

There was an agonized silence from the phone.

"Cyn," Belinda said, "will you go with her?"

"Of course!" I was grateful and proud that Belinda had decided to trust me a second time with her mother. And I was determined to be worthy of that trust. "They couldn't keep me away."

"All right, Agent Proctor." Belinda was giving her permission, but she had conditions. "All of you have to go." She cut through the resulting protests her words caused. "Maddy trusts Rhys and Dash, and so does Cyn. If you need to take my mother with you, then she's going to go with people who know and love her, and that she knows and loves. All four of you agents can take my mother, and not one agent less. I don't care if it's a conflict of interest. Too many people are after my mother. I want her kept safe."

Her demands were met with silence and furled brows. "They're thinking," I called out, since Belinda couldn't see the reaction her words were having.

"I've got to call HQ," Agent Proctor said, as Dash said, "I'll call Owen," and Rhys said, "I'd better talk to my father."

"Okay," said Belinda. "You make your calls. If all of you go, then Maddy can go. But you take care of her—and of Cyn. Nobody gets hurt, understand me?"

It was the world-famous epidemiologist who gave the words their undeniable authority, but it was the fearful daughter who added the tremor of anxiety under the pronouncement.

"You have my word," replied Agent Proctor staunchly. Then she disconnected the call and turned to us.

TWENTY-THREE

RHYS

I LIKED ELAINE PROCTOR. SHE WAS A HARD-ASS, A SMART woman, and a good agent. And although it wasn't something I would usually notice, she apparently had very flexible ankles.

More to the point, I liked the way she was organizing us now.

"All right. If we're heading to the eastern shore, we'll need to be ready. Cyn, how much longer will Maddy sleep?"

Cyn had stepped lightly from the shelter of my arm. I missed her warmth beside me and fought against the instinct to follow where she led. I wanted to put my body between her and any danger, even when no danger was evident.

She looked at her watch. "Another half hour. Maybe forty-five minutes."

"Very good. I'll get the lawyer to messenger the Chincoteague house keys to you here. He's local. It won't take long. I'm going back to the Bureau to get a van, and I have storm-ready clothes in my locker. Jim, can you be back here in forty-five minutes, ready to both defend Miss Maddy and also weather a storm?"

He nodded.

"Dash?"

"I'll ride back to headquarters with you, Elaine. I'd like to get a shotgun too."

Her efficiency impressed me. We were being shuffled up and dealt like a firm, swift hand of poker. It inspired confidence. She turned to me.

"Agent Jones, you're back on the team. Don't make me regret it." I nodded. This wasn't going to be another error for me. Emotion wasn't going to upend law enforcement this time—even if I was eager to do what I could to protect the two women who had somehow come to own my heart in a shockingly short time.

Agent Proctor wasn't done with me yet. She went on, "We could wake up Maddy and bring her and Cyn with us to headquarters for protection while we prepared, but since you're already storm-ready in jeans and sneakers, will you stay here to guard them?" I nodded. I wasn't leaving either of them alone again until this was settled.

"Want me to call in backup until we return?"

"I've got it," I said.

"Are you armed?"

"My Glock," which rode under my arm as always, "and a Walther in an ankle holster."

"Good. Cyn, you and Maddy will need decent shoes and good rain gear. Grab wool sweaters for when it gets cold. Pack an overnight bag for each of you. It's going to be a very long day, and we'll try to find some place out of the path of the storm to sleep if we can't get you back here by tonight." She looked around her, clearly searching to make sure she hadn't forgotten anything. Then she nodded. "Everyone back here at 1:00. We'll plan on getting to Chincoteague by 4:00 by virtue of ruthlessly violating the speed limit. That will give us five hours to search and get the hell out before the peak of the storm."

Yes, I definitely liked her.

There was a flurry of activity at the door, and then they were gone. I turned and looked at Cyn. She and I were alone in the suddenly silent apartment.

All she had to do was look at me and I started thinking about how her skin felt in my hands. The supple warmth of her belly against mine. The tangle of her tongue slipping into my mouth.

"No, no, no," I chanted.

She feigned surprise and innocence. "What?"

"Don't look at me like that."

"Like what?"

I cleared my throat and, thanks to rigid determination, did not beat on my chest like a silverback gorilla declaring his dominance. "Like we didn't roll out of bed a few hours ago. You stay over there."

She blushed—I was really getting addicted to that rosy shade washing over her cheeks—and offered her rationale. "Well, we *do* have forty-five minutes alone."

No, no, no. I was maintaining that chant quite firmly in my mind. The problem was: That wasn't the only thing that was firm. "We're not alone," I reminded her. "Maddy is sleeping right down that hall. Also . . ." I had to look away from her pout. Those pursed lips were definitely distracting me.

"Also," I went on, "the minute I hear that elevator door open, everything in me is going to be immediately distracted. Let's keep in mind that many, many separate people tried to kidnap you and Maddy twenty-four hours ago."

Her face fell and the sunrise blush faded from her heartbreaker of a face. "You're right. Okay."

"And we have good reason to suspect that the Oatmeal Man, at least, has been in this apartment."

She startled visibly and looked around with renewed suspicion and alarm. She was looking a lot less interested in exploring our forty-five minutes, which made me simultaneously relieved and regretful.

"So I need to keep my mind on the job."

"Fair enough." She leaned against the front door and crossed her arms over her chest. Alarmed or not, she still had it in her to give me a fiercely saucy attitude that thrilled me. "You and I understand that. How do we explain it to your groin?"

Now I was blushing. "Shut up. Only two of the three brains in this room can be reasoned with. Ignore the other one."

She'd gotten her smirk back. I liked that more than the fear. "So what *are* we going to do for forty-five minutes?"

I straightened and put my shoulders back. This was the physical equivalent of changing the subject. Time to close off emotion and apply a quasi-military discipline. Everyone gets a job, and then everyone does their job. And my thick, throbbing cock could get over it. "We're going to prep for a storm. Do we have enough food to make sandwiches or something for the ride down? No one is going to want to stop. And if we're delayed, it'd be smart to have some dinner too."

She pushed off the wall. "I can make a pasta salad, and you can put together sandwiches."

She headed for the kitchen with a purpose. Everyone liked having a mission in times of stress. I checked the doors and windows to make sure they were locked, and peeked in on Maddy, who was still sleeping. I liked a mission too.

"Let's fill thermoses with water and coffee," I said, joining her in the kitchen.

"And tea. Maddy likes a cup of tea."

"There isn't much Maddy doesn't like," I commented and caught her grin.

"That's true. She's awesome. And having something hot to drink in a storm—that's a good idea."

If we touched each other more than was absolutely necessary while we put the food together, at least I was also focused on the environs around the condo. She ran her hands across my waist as she crossed to the stove while I was spreading mayo on an entire loaf of bread, but she did not grope my ass. My hand went from her shoulder to the nape of her neck briefly when I reached for the baggies in the pantry closet, but I did not follow up that closeness by leaning down to kiss her velvet-soft mouth.

I was turned on—but none of that kept me from good situational awareness. My training was paying off, and I was alert to possible threats. Mostly, I was determined not to let my compromised nature put Cyn or Maddy at risk, no matter how much I'd have liked to bend Cyn over the breakfast island and make her moan.

Yeah. *Focus.*

We'd filled several tote bags and a cooler with enough supplies for an army, and Cyn had packed an overnight bag for her and Maddy, when the front desk—which had been alerted to our need for heightened security and observation—called up from the lobby. They let us know that a messenger had dropped off the keys to the Chincoteague house, and that Agents Proctor and Ashwood had pulled into the parking garage under the building and were on their way up.

I indulged in a reward, snagging Cyn as she went past and taking just a sip from her lips. She inhaled me, and the fire flared up between us again without warning. I wrapped her around me. Her moan inspired nerve impulses that ran not just into my groin, but also into my scalp and down to the soles of my feet. *Careful, there*, I thought. *Things could get out of hand with this woman pretty quickly*.

"Ahem," said the little old lady at the kitchen door.

We broke apart, embarrassed and laughing.

"You two remind me of Azariah and me when we were first dating," Maddy said. "How pretty you both are! What pink cheeks! Aren't you darling?"

By the time all three of my fellow agents were once again crowding the living room, Cyn had gotten Maddy and herself ready for our journey, with warm sweaters, rain jackets, and hats as well as sturdy shoes. Maddy, of course, was delighted with the plans.

"To Chincoteague? Yes, that's wonderful! It's perfect for you there, Cyn, darling. And for you too, Peanut Butter Cup. Oh, how fun this is!" Maddy was always in the present tense.

For her sake, we maintained an air of calm as we left the apartment and took the elevator to the parking garage. But knowing Barry Gambert, at least, had figured out how to gain access to the parking facility, all four agents were still on high alert while we smiled and laughed with Maddy.

Our abundance of caution might have been overkill, but not one of us minded. We made it into the van without incident. With Elaine Proctor at the wheel and the phone number for every police department between Arlington and Chincoteague on speed dial, we flew down the road. Dash had pointedly seated himself next to me in the van, keeping me separated from Cyn. He did it with a significant look, telling me to keep my mind on the job, and I appreciated his oversight.

However, our link didn't require physical closeness. She and I exchanged glances, and once she reached her hand back between the seats and I held her fingers, hidden by my knee from Dash's eagle eye. Not that we fooled him. I think he was trying to keep the venture on a professional footing.

I was trying too. There's nothing like a tinge of adrenaline to keep me aware of every car that passed us—not that many did, at the speeds Proctor was driving. Still, between the four of us, there probably wasn't much that the FBI didn't notice on the two-hundred-mile drive.

We discussed strategy as a group. Sometimes Maddy participated with intelligence (including one thoughtful dissertation on how to extract information from someone with dementia—a strange addition to a strange conversation) and sometimes it went over her head, which she never minded.

Cyn's opinion was that we'd have our best luck questioning Maddy if we could keep her in a very stable environment, in some place where distractions were kept to a minimum. Biays said he thought the long drive to Chincoteague, past winter-bare fields and long pastoral stretches of nothing much, would be an ideal time. But Maddy immediately proved him wrong by noticing a billboard for a local car dealership, which reminded her very clearly of her deceased husband's Chevy Bel Air, purchased when they were first married.

We were going to have to come up with something more controlled.

The weather was holding. Superstorm Etta was as yet far enough offshore that we were experiencing smaller rain squalls and wind, but so far, the nightmare storm hadn't materialized. When it wasn't raining, sunlight broke through fast-rushing clouds and lit the passing scenery with an almost Hollywood-like drama.

We came across the long causeway to Chincoteague Island at low tide, but the storm had pushed a pillow of water ahead of itself, and the ripples of waves in the wetlands were coming close to the road. The wildness around us was gorgeous. It was a view of nature that stood in contrast to the impressive column of cars coming the other way, as less-hardy island residents opted to make for higher ground while the getting was good. We were definitely driving into the path of danger. But on the positive side, our journey was uneventful, and we saw no signs of Maddy's many abductors.

Agent Proctor placed a call as we got closer, and the island sheriff, Lenny Selmer, met us on the island side of the causeway. Dressed in a large, yellow rain slicker, he leaned into the driver's side window and laid an elbow on the sill. Looking at us, he raised an eyebrow.

"Afternoon, folks. FBI, huh?" Maddy waved at him from the middle seat and he waved back. "You're about the only people coming on the island today." We'd amused him. Sheriff Selmer was a large, phlegmatic man with an impressive belly and a sharp eye. "I'll take you to the Shipman house and send a patrol car by a few times this afternoon. See if you need anything. Wish I could do more to help the FBI, but it's going to get a mite airish in a bit, as you know, and my team has its hands full."

A mite airish. I liked the guy.

We were lucky that he led us to Maddy's new property, because she didn't recognize it at all.

"You're sure this is the Shipman place?" Proctor asked from the driver's window.

"Sure enough," the sheriff replied. "Been coming to the island for, oh, must be twenty, thirty years, now—him and those kids of his. Nice enough fellah. Heard he died a bit ago. Shame. Caretaker's already come out to board up them windows, so you won't have a view, but you can go out the doors to the porches if you want to admire the scenery."

We were facing a modern, pretty vacation home, large and roomy. Big sheets of plywood had been fastened over what I assumed were large plate-glass windows, and the house was ringed in decks and low balconies set to provide the prettiest view of the surrounding wetlands. This was not the fishing shack that the lawyer's letter to Dr. Root had implied.

It was my luscious architectural historian who figured it out. "This is all new construction," she said. "See? It's up on pilings and tied to bedrock far below the soil line. This house is designed for a massive storm."

"Yep," the sheriff agreed. "The new places are a might sturdier than the local houses. 'Course, they're a lot harder to rebuild when the ocean comes crashing through, but that's the choice you make!" This, too, gave him a great deal of amusement.

Cyn pointed out that the original shack was off to the side and almost tucked under the stilt house, where it was largely blocked from view. "It looks like an addition, but that's the original place, and all this is the new part. They made it into a garage. We should be able to get into the fishing shack from inside the house. Let's go in."

Sheriff Selmer waved as he drove back to his "a mite airish" evening. We were on our own. I hoped we could persuade Maddy to share what she knew before the entire ocean came crashing through the property.

The house was handsomely designed, with a bedroom wing opening into a large great room and an open-plan kitchen. From inside, there was still enough light creeping around the edges to confirm that the plywood was covering entire walls of glass. Doors to the various porches must have had thicker glass. Most of them weren't boarded over. It provided more natural light, which was nice. The electricity was still on, but I assumed it'd be the first thing to go once the storm hit.

Near the kitchen area, a door opened to a short staircase down. Cyn was right. The original fishing shack was intact. But it didn't look anything like the way Maddy would have remembered it. Now it was a storage area, and part had been walled off as a garage, with space for a boat on a trailer. We escorted her down the stairs hopefully, but Maddy looked at it without any interest or recognition at all.

I exchanged glances with Dash and then with Cyn. Maddy hadn't had any brilliant flashes of memory. Being physically in the location hadn't proven to be the key to unlocking her information.

"Maddy," Cyn asked. "You said you could show me Hector's hiding place once we got to Chincoteague. Will you show me?"

"Don't be silly. This isn't Chincoteague—although it's very nice."

We all thought about that for a bit.

"What if I take her for a walk along the road? If we go past that little dock and into the wetlands?" Cyn asked. "The rain is holding off, and the landscape looks unchanged. It might jar her memory."

"Uh, no," I said flatly. "Neither you nor she leaves this house without one of us. Preferably two of us. How many people are trying to get to Maddy?"

My rhetorical question instigated an impromptu counting game.

"Grumpy Bear and Timmo," said Proctor.

"And Big Rifle," added Biays.

"No," Cyn put in. "We don't know about Timmo."

"What? We're assuming he just likes to run into people on the road?" Proctor wasn't having it. "For purposes of estimating the need for protection, I think we count Timmo."

"Okay. That's three. Then there's Barry—that's four." Biays was counting on his fingers.

"Mac and Will," Cyn joined in.

"Can you count Will, though?" asked Dash. "He's in custody."

"That's true." We all turned for a ruling from Proctor, the senior agent in charge.

"Five and six," she said decisively. "They both want Maddy. It's fair to count both."

"And Barry," finished Biays. Cyn shuddered, and Maddy frowned.

"The damned Oatmeal Man," she said.

"No, you've counted Barry twice." That set off another round of counting. Eventually they agreed. "So, six." Agent Proctor said, resorting to a second hand.

"And Wanda," Maddy added.

"Who the hell is Wanda?" Biays asked, confused.

"The lesbian biker. With the purple hair," Maddy added helpfully.

"Wait. Her name is Wanda?"

"Wait. She's a lesbian?" Agents Proctor and Biays were already scrabbling for their notes.

But Maddy had spotted a chart of the island on the wall. "Look! That's Chincoteague! Where's . . . there! There's where Hector has his place! Oh, it's lovely there!"

"Want to take a walk with me, Maddy?" I said. "And Dash and Cyn can follow along behind us."

"That would be lovely! Let's go!" Maddy hustled up the stairs, leaving trained FBI agents a third of her age panting in her wake.

Outside, the wind was fresh and not too painfully powerful yet. There wasn't another person in sight. "Isn't it wild and gorgeous!" Maddy was thrilled with her view.

So that she wasn't tossed away by a gust, I tucked her hand into my elbow, and we began a slow stroll past the dock and through waving marsh grasses, down a gravel road that bent to invisibility at the next curve.

"Isn't this paradise, Peanut Butter Cup?" Maddy was completely happy, her startlingly blue hair whipping in the wind.

Despite the looming storm, the scene was reasonably monochromatic. Tall marsh grasses, the tasseled fronds often higher than my head, bent in the wind in mesmerizing waves. The air smelled of salt and damp earth. It was oddly tranquil for such a rain-soaked afternoon. If we didn't startle an egret on the wing, I might have a chance to get her to remain undistracted.

"Hector loves it here," I tried.

"Oh, he's happiest here. He's like a different man. So free and unbuttoned. Not like at work, where he has to be so careful."

Feeling my way, I murmured anything I thought might encourage her. "No one can know."

"Oh, certainly not. It'd ruin my reputation."

"You're an unmarried lady, of course." The professor—her husband, Azariah—was years in the future at this point.

"And he's a married man."

That surprised me. What period of time was she remembering? Hadn't Biays said Hector didn't marry until after he got out of prison? To a young woman, once he was an older, richer man?

"Fiona?" I said, hoping I wouldn't distract Maddy with a name that came from a different era.

"Fiona!" She laughed scornfully. "Certainly not. I mean that piece of trash, Louise. From West Virginia."

Ding. West Virginia. Like the license plates of the bearded mountain men. Another piece of the puzzle.

"Right. Louise. She can never know about you."

"No one can know about me. Or about the jobs Hector pulls."

I felt like I was trying to paint moving water. A single slip and the whole thing would fail. "Oh, right. The jobs. Those are so tricky."

"Tricky. But you know how he loves the thrill. And, of course, I do too."

"You're not called Madcap Maddy for nothing."

"That's right! Although he calls me Mac. My initials, you know."

"Yes, that's right."

"He says I'm his darling. We're so in love. I love to come here on the bus. It's so secret! No one will ever find us here!"

"It's a great place to be in love." I cast my mind briefly back to Cyn, walking arm in arm with Dash behind us. What was he telling her?

Trying to imagine what they might be saying, I almost missed the earthquake Maddy created in front of me.

"And of course, he's so much more successful when I'm helping him. Our takes have gotten better than ever."

I almost came to a halt, which might have broken her from her memories. She'd definitely said "our" takes. Maddy didn't just know the jewel thief. Maddy was an accomplice. Why had I ever assumed anything else? Maddy wasn't one to sit on the sidelines, and in her ninety-three years, she'd had some experiences. I bit back a laugh and re-focused. This was fragile ground. I kept going and thought about my response.

"Hard to believe you can climb like he does."

"Don't be silly!" She offered a trill of laughter that was caught up like a loose scarf in the fresh wind. "You know perfectly well that I don't climb! All *I* do is break my ankle."

This made sense to her, but it left me utterly confused. Stupidly, I repeated her words. "You break your ankle?" and then cursed myself for a possible distraction. But the magic of the wetlands' beauty held.

248

"Of course! I pretend to break my ankle on the sidewalk or the garden path or wherever, so everyone is looking at me when Hector climbs in the window. Oh, how we laugh afterwards!"

Her girlish laughter masked my astonishment. Hector Battelle had been one of the East Coast's most successful cat burglars . . . because he had sweet Maddy as an accomplice.

Madcap Maddy indeed.

"And then you bring the jewels here."

"Oh, some of them," she said breezily. "Look at those clouds! My goodness. It's like angry cotton wool rolling across the sky! Isn't it wonderful?"

The gusts were picking up. Despite Maddy's delight, she was beginning to shiver in the late afternoon wind. It was time to go back.

I turned her and attempted to continue our conversation, but she spotted Cyn behind us, and wanted to run to her and take her hand and laugh at the wind.

Our chat was done, and I still didn't know where they'd hidden the Jaipur Princess, the Merlin Twins, or any of the other gems she'd helped Hector steal, but I'd learned a lot. I nodded to Dash and Cyn and we made our way back to the house.

Maddy was gone again, lost in her happy, foggy world. And still she smiled.

The storm had picked up again and the gusts were getting stronger. I thought about scooping her up like a child, but she was almost skipping at my side, happy as could be.

Dash was watching out for Cyn, who wasn't much larger than Maddy. I was grateful to my partner when he put his arm around my girl to make sure no particularly vigorous gust blew her off her feet.

Maddy uttered a gleeful chortle at the wind. Perhaps she thought she was walking through a fantasy of air, with the waving marsh grasses pressed almost flat and then springing upward. Blue water in the channels flashed in the fleeting orange sunset, and clouds sent shadows scudding over the earth. She looked like something from a myth, her wizened, beautiful old face turned up gladly to the storm, and her electric blue hair whipping about her cheeks.

Maddy lived her life as if it was exhilarating. She was inspiring, and I took a moment to inhale, pulling deep on the scents of salt and ozone and wildness. She was right. It was crazy and wild and untamed and invigorating.

Then I did at last scoop her up—she hooted in delight and looped her arms around my neck—and I carried her up the stairs and into the house.

The sudden quietness was a blessing, and the warm air was a kind embrace. Both of my girls were inside and safe, and I felt a wave of relief.

Cyn smiled at me and then turned to Maddy. They laughed together as Cyn untangled the blue hair and helped Maddy out of her coat and hat. "Want a cup of tea, Maddy?"

"I'd be delighted!"

Cyn had the most beautiful smile, but Maddy's was a close second.

"Anyone else want tea or coffee? Won't take a moment," Cyn offered, but the rest of us declined.

Seeing them safe and engaged in their tea-making, I pulled the other agents to me to share what I'd learned.

"She didn't tell me the hiding place. But Maddy was definitely an accomplice to the thefts." I grinned. "Think the statute of limitations has run out on those crimes?"

"I'd like to see that firecracker in jail." Biays laughed. "She'd have the hardest con wrapped around her little finger within minutes."

"It'd be a complete takeover," Proctor agreed. "Best we keep her out of the federal system. What else did you get?"

I walked them through my conversation with her as I kept half an eye on the pair in the kitchen area. When Maddy wandered over to the stairway to the original fishing shack, I straightened.

"She's going down," I whispered to my fellow agents. "Maybe we should go with her."

Proctor put her hand on my arm and shook her head. "Don't disturb her. Let her go back in her memory. Let's see if she remembers the hiding place. We'll give her a few minutes."

Maddy was starting down the stairs and Cyn, ever attuned to her charge, called out to stop her. "Wait, Maddy. I can go with you."

She looked up and Proctor shook her head, the unspoken "let her go ahead" traveling across the room in a glance.

Maddy didn't want any help. "Don't be silly. I'm fine on my own."

"We've checked down there," Proctor said aloud for Maddy's benefit. "I can see her and most of the room from here. It might spark an idea. I'll watch over her."

TWENTY-FOUR
MADDY

THE SCENT COMING UP THE STAIRS IS FAMILIAR. IT SMELLS LIKE salt and memories.

Down I go. The room is dark. All the windows are boarded over. There's a lot of wind blowing outside. It makes this large shed seem very cozy.

The party upstairs is clearly merry. They're all laughing and talking, and it makes me happy to hear them. I see a wooden mantelpiece over a fireplace. It looks old, but familiar. I'm looking at it—do I recognize the old wrought iron log-holder?—when something behind me moves.

I turn. Part of this shed is a garage, and there's a nice, old Boston whaler in a trailer against the far wall. That's a good boat for these shallow waters. Easy to drive.

The door to the boat's cabin is sliding open. A man is coming out. Such a surprise! Like a rabbit from a magician's hat!

No, it's two men. One is that nice Mac fellow from the hospital. How nice to see a friend here in this dark place!

"Hello!" I call, but he holds his finger over his lips and beckons me forward. He wants to keep this a secret, and that is exciting. I can be quiet!

I sneak over to the boat and he introduces me to his brother, Will.

"How do you do?" I say with my best manners. More people for the party!

Will doesn't look as happy as his brother. "Do you remember me, Miss Maddy?" he whispers.

"No, dear. Should I?"

He shakes his head sadly. Mac is smiling at me.

"I think he named me for you."

I smile at him. "Who did?"

"My father. I think he gave me the name MacMillan so he could call me Mac."

"Oh! People call me Mac too! Those are my initials, you know!"

He looks wistful. "I know. And I think that no matter how much he loved my mother, you were always his first love."

What a sweet story! I don't know who he's talking about, but he seems sad and thoughtful, and I don't want to disturb him. "That's nice, dear."

He's still talking. "So he left you the most important place of all. At least to him. The house in Darien and the New York condo went to my mother. But he left you this house."

I look around. "This house? It seems quite dark and small."

"Well, the windows are boarded up. And there's an upstairs now."

He gestures up the stairs. I can hear people up there talking. A party. Let's go!

He stops me with a hand on my arm. He's holding me too tightly, and his brother makes a sound of protest.

What does this sad fellow want?

"Tell me, Miss Maddy. Tell me where my father hid his jewels."

Gracious. Such a question! What could he possibly mean? I must say, it does sound interesting.

"She doesn't know, Mac," the brother says. "Let's get out of here."

"She knows," Mac says, and he shakes me. I don't like that, and I try to pull my hand away. "Tell me where his hiding place is."

"Where whose hiding place is, you unpleasant thug?" I believe in speaking truth. Yes, even to the angry!

"My father, Miss Maddy! Hector Shipman!"

"Take your hands off me. Who is Hector Shipman?" I'm quite outraged.

"Keep quiet," he hisses, but the silence upstairs is suddenly very loud indeed.

"Mac," says his brother unhappily.

"Take out your gun," Mac says insistently.

"Mac."

"Do it now!" And then they're both holding black, ugly pistols. One is pointed at the floor and one is pointed at me. Both of the men beside me are tight with tension.

"We're coming up," calls Mac, "and we're both armed. Don't shoot or I'll have to hurt Miss Maddy."

There's a female squeak of fear from upstairs but no other sound. Then a strong woman's voice speaks.

"Come up very slowly. One at a time."

"Get behind me," mutters Mac to his brother. "Come on." He tugs me forward, and I have to trot to keep up with him.

"You don't have to pull, young man. I'm coming. Don't be rude."

"Sorry, ma'am." His words are polite, but he keeps tugging on my arm just the same.

We come to the top of the stairs and he nudges me past the open door.

We are making our entrance at a debutante ball. Everyone is staring at me, so I stand up straight and offer them my most regal smile. "Good evening," I say. "How nice of you to invite me!"

TWENTY-FIVE
CYN

WHEN I HEARD MADDY'S VOICE DOWNSTAIRS, RAISED IN ANGER, a haze fell over me.

Someone was downstairs with her. How was that possible?

It was like the moment when you realize you hadn't ever actually woken up from the nightmare, and this was a continuation of something terrible that you simply couldn't control.

No. I wanted to reject this reality. I wanted to get back to the reality where we were all doing expected things. And smiling.

I had had enough of fear and confusion and anger.

Rhys and his agents had turned, eyeing the doorway to the fishing shack with intense focus. Proctor hissed at them and the three men separated from her, each moving to different corners of the room.

Maddy appeared at the head of the stairs, her thin, frail arm clutched in Mac's white-knuckled hand. My heart threatened to explode in my chest.

"Maddy!" I squeaked.

She gave me a brilliant smile. "Cyn, darling! I'm so glad you're at the ball too!"

"Come over here, Maddy," I called, but Mac refused to let go of her.

"Stay right here, Miss Maddy." She eyed his hand on her arm with scorn but attempted to hide her annoyance under a polite veneer. She smiled and nodded to me with an air of apology that broke my heart. "I'll be with you in a moment, Cyn, dear. Look at you—aren't you darling? You look just like a pixie!"

"Mr. Shipman, I'm guessing." Agent Proctor drew his attention away from Maddy and me. I saw with a wash of inevitability that her gun was out. All four of the agents were holding their guns. "And your brother, I see." From my angle in the kitchen, I couldn't see anyone else, but I assumed Will was lurking on the stairs behind his brother, and a sudden burst of infuriated hatred straightened me up and burned away the unreality. Will—always a coward. Hiding from my rage.

Agent Proctor was still speaking to Will. "Either you made bail, Will, or we're going to send you away for a prison break as well as abduction."

Will scuttled out of the stairway and hunkered more closely behind his brother. He was even paler than usual. Mac spoke for him. "Our lawyer bailed him out. He's golfing buddies with the judge."

"Not for much longer," Dash growled with a fierce grin, but Agent Proctor regained control of the dialogue.

"And how did you get in this house? The place was locked up, and we searched the interior when we arrived."

"First, I've had a key to this house since I was in college," Mac said with scorn in his voice. "And second, if you're going to search a house, don't forget to look in the boat in the basement."

Proctor shot an evil look at Biays. He remained fully focused on Mac and Will, but a flush of red crept up his neck.

"Everyone has a very ugly gun," Maddy observed. "This ball has the strangest party favors."

She looked to me. I was stupidly holding a tea bag in my hand, frozen in place. "I suppose I should have a gun too," Maddy said, "to be a part of the group. But I don't want one. I'd like a cup of tea instead. And I'd like to sit down."

I started forward, but suddenly Rhys was by my side. He pulled me back and stepped in front of me. I had a moment to consider that he didn't seem even slightly compromised by our relationship. It was like standing behind a robot. His focus on Mac and Will was total, and I knew better than to push him by trying to reach Maddy again. But perhaps Will could be persuaded to let her go.

"There's a cup of tea for her on the counter," I called from behind a large column of muscle. "Can she have that?"

"Nobody moves," said Mac.

"Oh, tosh. It's just a cup of tea," Maddy said. "You're far too bossy, I must say. If you keep that up, this won't be a very nice date." To my astonishment, she twisted her arm and then was free. She reached for her tea and Rhys reached for her. But Mac had one arm wrapped around her waist and dragged her back against him. It had happened before I'd finished with my hopeful, horrified gasp.

Somehow, Maddy ended up with the tea.

"Don't move!" Mac shouted.

Maddy, cradling her teacup in delight, leaned back against him and apparently enjoyed his warmth. She sipped her tea and chided him. "Oh, you silly. How can we dance if we don't move?"

"All right," Agent Proctor said. "Everyone stay calm. Mac, you don't strike me as a violent type. What do you say we all put our guns away? We can talk more comfortably that way."

Mac was silent behind his Maddy-protection, and I could barely look at him for hating him so intensely. He was thinking, indecision on his face, so Agent Proctor kept talking.

"You can keep Maddy with you. You can even let her sit down. I'm Elaine. I'm going to put my gun away. See?" Very slowly, she put her gun back under her jacket. "We're all going to put our guns away. Aren't we?"

Rhys, Dash, and Agent Biays had spread across the room and were in separate corners. They matched her move and Rhys backed me away from the kitchen counter. His hands remained open and ready, but I rested my hands lightly on his broad back, and he eased his weight back, as if he was glad to feel me behind him.

Agent Proctor dropped her voice to a conversational tone. "Now you, Mac. I know your arm is getting tired. You and Will put your guns down too. Go ahead. So we can talk."

Beside his brother, Will the Impossible Wimp was uneasy. "Come on, Mac. We can lay them on the counter here. Let's be calm."

"Shut up," Mac said crossly, but then he moved Maddy back until he and she were behind the kitchen island, in the semi-protected space that Rhys and I had vacated. Will scuttled along behind them, doing what he could to keep anyone else between himself and the bullets. What a loathsome creature.

Finally, Mac lowered his gun and put it on the counter in front of him.

"Oh, good!" Maddy said. "Now we can dance!" She turned in his arms and tried to take his hand—while I offered a silent prayer for her rescue—but Mac pushed her back and grabbed his gun again. So everyone else also pulled out their guns once more.

I couldn't help the squeak that slipped out of me at the rapid return to implied violence, and that drew Maddy's attention.

"Cyn! How are you, dear? Come out from behind that big, handsome, blond man. We're going to do some dancing. I think someone mentioned a rumba?"

She threw a flirtatious smile over her shoulder to Mac, but he was focused on the weaponry pointing at him and ignored her. Dash called out softly to Maddy.

"I'd love a rumba with you, Miss Maddy. You come over here if you get the chance."

Mac's gun swiveled to point at him.

"Knock that off," said Agent Proctor. "We were making progress. No one is going to take Maddy from you, Mac. Come on. Put the guns down. Everyone."

Following her lead, all the guns were lowered.

"Maddy, please stay still." Because Agent Proctor asked nicely, it got through to Maddy, whose feet were still moving in dance steps. But finally, she stilled.

"We need some music anyway," she said. "Is there a radio?"

"Let's talk instead," Proctor replied. "Mac, I gather you're looking for your father's jewels. Are you why the house has been ransacked?"

I took a moment to see the empty vacation home as she'd seen it. And now that she'd pointed it out, I saw that she was right. The house was more than just untidy. Pictures had been taken off the wall and all the cupboards and closets were open.

"It's a mess in here," Maddy said. "I can help clean up!" Mac tightened his grip on her waist and his brother put up his hands to stop the growing pressure on Maddy's middle.

"Maybe I could hold her, Mac," his brother said. "It looks like you're holding her kind of tight."

Will had surprised me. He didn't quite oppose his brother, but he did attempt to advocate for Maddy, and I decided I perhaps didn't revile him as much as I'd previously thought.

"She's fine," Mac said shortly. "You bet I went through the house. Those jewels should be mine. Mine and Will's."

"So let me understand you. Your father died with a massive fortune, and you still don't have enough money?" Agent Proctor was attempting to be nonjudgmental and evenhanded, but we could all hear the slightly scornful tone in her words.

"Enough money." Mac gave back all her scorn and then some. "You know how much that man left us? One million dollars each. That's it. A trust for my mom and some property. All the rest went to charity. It was the old man's way of shitting on his children once again for not being self-starters." He sounded positively furious, and his arm around Maddy was cutting off her air. She writhed against him, her hands fruitlessly attempting to pluck his arm away.

"Mac," his brother said. "You're hurting her. Let me hold her. I promise I won't let her go. Come on, man."

He talked his brother into passing Maddy to him.

"Oh, you don't feel so overheated." Maddy breathed deeply at last and smiled at Will, who looked ashamed. "I can tell this one is a better dancer. He doesn't hold so tight."

"Will." Agent Proctor got the attention of the cowardly brother with her "All Must Obey" voice. "Let Maddy go right now."

Mac reached for Maddy immediately, but his brother straightened against Maddy and refused to release her. "My brother and I just want to know where the hiding place is. Then everyone gets let go, and no one gets hurt."

"Until this point," Agent Proctor told Will, "you could be considered an accessory at best. I've heard you try to keep your brother calm, and I'll tell the judge you've been trying to defuse the situation. But if you don't let her go right now, then you're in this to your neck."

She fixed him with a stern eye, but he proved to be stronger than I'd have guessed. Will shook his head. "I know. I'm already in this to my neck. Miss Maddy stays here with us."

"Your choice," Agent Proctor said. Mac, still at Maddy's side, relaxed a fraction and Proctor returned her attention to him. "So your father is worth—what was it, Jim?" She turned to Agent Biays in his corner. "Thirty million?"

"Forty-three," spat Mac before Biays could respond. "And he leaves thirty-nine million to all kinds of worthless goddamned charities."

"Hang on." Agent Proctor was working something out, and I found myself doing the math with her. "He left you a million and

Will a million, plus thirty-nine million to charities. So where'd the other two million go?"

"I told you," said Mac. "He left each of his children a million."

She turned her head as if hoping that would shake free some clarity. "He had two children. You and Will."

"He had four kids," Mac corrected her.

This was greeted with confusion.

"Well, who are the other two?"

The door to the porch behind me opened, letting in darkness, a huge gust of wind, and a large bearded man who slipped an arm around me and pulled me back against him, away from Rhys.

"That would be where we come in," he said, putting a gun to my temple.

All the other guns in the room came back up again.

TWENTY-SIX

CYN

THE ARM CLENCHED AROUND MY RIBS WAS DRAGGING ME farther and farther from Rhys, who'd spun around as I was taken. His face was stone. He wasn't looking at me. The gun he held was as steady as a rock and aimed about a foot over my head.

"Grumpy Bear!" squealed Maddy happily.

"Who?" the man who held me grunted.

"That's you," I gasped. "Could you ease up a little? I'm having trouble breathing."

Rhys actually growled, although I don't think he realized he was doing it. The fierce intensity of his stare was terrifying—and it also filled me with hope. No one was going to be able to defy him. I could see it from looking at him. Why Grumpy Bear didn't lay down his weapon immediately was beyond me.

"You're too fucking small. You city women gotta eat more," Grumpy Bear said. Grudgingly, he eased his grip across my ribs and the pressure let up. He dragged me over to another door and kicked it with his foot. "Jim!" he hollered. "Get in here!"

He refocused on the quartet of FBI agents aiming at him and took in Will and Mac, holding Maddy. They were also aiming at him. He pulled me tighter again and I felt ice against my temple. I closed my eyes. It was definitely the barrel of his pistol. "Nobody moves," he barked.

The door behind us opened, and I could feel that someone had entered.

"Fuck," said Agent Proctor. "Are you telling me that no one checked the porches when we arrived?"

"I checked them," Dash said. "There was no one there."

"We came over the side," the new arrival said smugly. His low voice seemed to be coming from around the ceiling.

"And through the marshes," Grumpy Bear admitted with a gruff measure of pride. "We've been bowhunting on this land for decades. Nobody knows it like we do."

"So," said Dash. He was strangely relaxed in the face of what I thought of as a disaster. He seemed to have gotten exceedingly calm and friendly as conditions escalated. Was this insanity? Or skill? "We've got two of the three of the West Virginia team right here. Do we have to guess where the third one is?"

The man holding me must have gestured to the newcomer. "Go get Timmo. He's on the winter porch."

"The winter porch," Agent Biays repeated, his voice showing a hint of a la-di-dah attitude.

"Shut the fuck up," Grumpy Bear said. "That's what they called it. I didn't name it."

Biays held up a hand in appeasement, but no one moved. The newcomer stepped forward and into my peripheral view. The voice didn't lie. The guy was huge. It was the man I thought of as Big Rifle, the one who'd shot through the engine cowling of the FBI's helicopter in Reisterstown.

"Shove over, there," he said to Dash. "Let me by."

Dash shook his head with the most pleasant smile, which made Grumpy Bear press his gun more closely to my head. My ear was practically on my shoulder and Rhys's growl got louder.

"You stay there," Dash said. "I'll be glad to let Timmo in."

"Slowly," said Grumpy Bear.

Dash exchanged looks with Agent Proctor and Biays and eased the door open.

Timmo was on the other side, his back to the door, watching the growing storm with wide eyes. When the light from inside fell on him, he turned with a happy smile.

"Look, you guys! It's really blowing a fuck-ton out here!" He came into the room, a rifle held over one arm, and looked at the assembled masses. "Oh. Fuck."

"Get over here, Timmo!" Big Rifle called, but Grumpy Bear stopped him, no doubt seeing the tactical advantages in spreading his troops out as far across the room as possible, to match the wide field of fire the FBI had established.

"You stay right there, Timmo. We got some talking to do."

"Yes, we do," Agent Proctor agreed. "Perhaps we could start with introductions. Should we keep calling you Grumpy Bear?"

I could hear the sneer in his voice. "You better not."

"All right. What's your name? I'm Elaine."

Her attempt to ease the tension was appreciated, but Grumpy Bear didn't seem much appeased. My head was still canted way over to the side, and I was grabbing at his wrist to try to relieve the pressure on my ribs. I'd have as much luck pulling on a tree stump. However, he did offer up a grudging "Elmer."

"That's your name? Elmer?"

"That's right."

"And I'm guessing Timmo is your—what? Your brother?"

"Brother," Elmer allowed. The sketchiest version of civility was helping. His gun was no longer pressed into my head, and I risked looking away from Rhys.

"That leaves us with this gentleman." Proctor looked at Big Rifle.

"Jim," Elmer said, and Agent Biays grunted.

"What?" Biays said.

"What what?" Elmer replied.

"Did you call me?"

Elmer was scornful again. "Is your name Jim?"

"Uh—yeah."

"Oh." Elmer sounded deflated. He rallied. "Well, not anymore, it's not. *This* is Jim."

Agent Proctor soothed them both. "You can be FBI Jim," she said to her partner, "and you can be Big Jim," to the giant. "How's that? Is that okay?"

Both men nodded. Big Jim added a grin. "Big Jim," he said happily. "That's about right."

"All right. That's Dash over there with Timmo, and Rhys is in front of you. You're holding Cynthia. And I guess you already know Mac and Will?"

Elmer grunted, his attention on the preppy brothers.

"And me!" Maddy chirped happily.

Agent Proctor even offered a laugh. "Everybody knows you, Madcap Maddy!"

"And I know everybody!" Maddy was the only one having any fun at all.

Somehow the FBI agent had managed to reduce the tension a bit. She took advantage of the calming atmosphere to buy my muscles a little relief. "Elmer, would you consider letting Cyn straighten up? She looks like her neck is cramping, and I bet she's having a hard time drawing a deep breath."

Rhys had never looked away from what I assumed were Elmer's eyes, and I was slightly discomfited to realize that Rhys was wearing an unconscious smile, as if he was thinking violent thoughts. Elmer backed me up another few steps, but then his arm got looser around me and the press of the gun against my head withdrew slowly until I could straighten up.

Rhys flicked a look at me and I tried to reassure him with a smile, but his gaze barely touched on my face before it was back on Elmer.

My improved position was a relief. With increased air and blood flow, I also discovered a flicker of anger at my captor. Fear, definitely. I was terrified. But I was also beginning to think I'd been pushed too far. In keeping with my new resolve to not be so easily used by the Dons of the world, I thought that perhaps I had the presence of mind to give a little back, if I saw an opportunity. After all, the Maddy Mantra now included "Don't mess with me."

Agent Proctor was still using smooth FBI negotiating tactics on the assembled gun-toters. She turned next to Will, choosing him, perhaps, because he seemed the least happy about holding a gun. "Will, can you tell me what's going on?"

Will ducked his head. "We all want the jewels."

"The jewels!" Timmo hollered happily. "The motherfucking jewels!"

"Oh, Timmo. Your language!" Maddy said reprovingly, and Timmo hung his head, a red flush appearing high on his cheekbones above a rich, bushy black beard.

"Sorry, ma'am." She beamed at him, and his smile bloomed across his face again.

"And you all know each other," Agent Proctor went on.

Will shook his head, but he meant that he agreed. "These are my nephews."

To my astonishment, he gestured to Elmer, Big Jim, and Timmo, the youngest of whom must have been fifteen years older than Will.

"Your nephews? Do you mean your uncles?" Agent Proctor was as confused as I was.

"Not our uncles," Mac broke in with venom. "Our damned nephews. My father had two kids when he went into prison."

"He was incarcerated in 1952—like seventy years ago," said FBI Jim.

"Right. My half-brother Heck is almost eighty. He has three sons, so I have three nephews." Mac used his pistol to gesture at the West Virginia trio. "Elmer, Jim, and Timmo."

"Uh-huh," said Agent Proctor. "And so we're clear, who's the fourth child? Heck's brother or sister? Someone related to the Oatmeal Man, I'm guessing?"

"Who the fuck is the Oatmeal Man?" Mac, Elmer, and Big Jim offered some version of the same question.

"Sorry. I mean Barry—uh—Gamberetti?" She looked to Rhys for assistance. Rhys grunted out "Gambert" without ever taking his eyes off Elmer, who tightened his grip on me again, possibly (and intelligently) beginning to feel more uneasy under the unwavering stare. Elmer again edged me away from Rhys and closer to the less-threatening Agent Biays.

"Barry Gambert. I don't know who that is," Mac said. He looked to Elmer. I could feel when Elmer shook his head. He didn't know either.

"He forced you off the road," Dash said to Will. Dash remained as calm as if he were at a cocktail party, even as a certain alertness sparkled around him.

"Oh. That guy. I've never seen him before. He was crazy."

"And you, Timmo? The guy you forced off the road and fought with. Did you know him?" Agent Proctor's tone was instinctively kinder to Timmo, who looked confused most of the time.

"That guy who had Elmer? He didn't have him. I looked in his car and everything."

"You ran him off the road because you thought he had Elmer? Not because he had Maddy?"

Timmo looked at Maddy—the two of them exchanged delighted greetings—and then Timmo was brought back to the topic at hand. "Nobody could find Elmer. His car was all tipped on its side and the tire was like when you skin a deer. Jeez. You should have seen it. It was a mess. And he was gone and wouldn't answer his phone, and Jim said I was supposed to chase him down and get him back, so I did, but then it was some other guy who shot at me, so I had to hit him. You know?"

He looked around at all the fascinated faces following his

recitation. "I hit him real hard," he added. "He went *down*." He gave us a happy smile.

Agent Proctor was stumped. "I admit. I'm confused. I can't remember where we are."

"Chincoteague!" offered Maddy with a wave. Will had his arm across her shoulders in friendly fashion, but like his brother, he hadn't lowered his gun.

"Thank you, Maddy," Proctor replied dryly. "Okay. I've got it. Who was Hector's fourth child? Will, can you tell us?"

He answered. "My half-sister Vicky. She's—what, seventy-seven now, Mac?"

Mac nodded. Surprisingly, so did Maddy. "Her real name is Victory," Maddy offered. "She was born in 1945. Height of the fighting in Europe. Hector wanted to give her a real patriotic name. It's pretty, isn't it?"

As a group, we were all nonplussed by this addition. You never knew when Maddy was going to join right into a conversation.

"Is that right?" Mac asked Elmer.

Elmer shrugged. "I've never heard of her called anything other than Vicky. I guess it could be."

Agent Proctor gaveled the meeting back to order. "So Mac and his brother have keys to this place, and Elmer and his brothers know where to go for bowhunting. You all visited here regularly. Am I right?"

"Sometimes together," said Will in an offended tone. All the various offspring of jewel-thief-turned-millionaire-investor Hector Battelle nodded in agreement at this. "Dad's idea to get us all here at the same time. And that was really horrible."

"Fucking right," Big Jim intoned. "Pussies."

"Rednecks," Mac spat back.

Pistols came up higher, and Agent Proctor raised her hands to calm the situation. The howling wind only added to the tension.

"So we know most of the players. The only ones we're missing are Barry the Oatmeal Man and Wanda the lesbian biker."

Timmo looked particularly interested in that. "Yeah?"

"Not to make things complicated," said FBI Jim, "but we still don't know who made the crater in the back yard."

"Looks like explosives," said Big Jim.

"That's what we think too," FBI Jim nodded. "Someone was doing seismic testing, looking for underground chambers. That wasn't you guys?"

"Nope."

"And it wasn't you guys?" Agent Proctor turned to Mac and Will.

"No. We did the ransacking, but not the crater."

"So who blew up the hole?"

That's when the front door flew open, revealing the Oatmeal Man, who was sporting a massive black eye—Timmo's hit, no doubt. Behind him, with short, raspberry-pink hair tossed by the wind, was Wanda.

Just to keep things action-packed, he was carrying what looked like some kind of automatic weapon with a long clip sticking out of the bottom. Great.

"The crater is mine," he said, striding in. "Whole fucking island is nothing but wetlands. Buried treasure, my ass."

Now all the guns were on Barry, and Wanda looked entirely annoyed about it.

"Barry, what the hell," she said shortly.

"Shut up."

"Kiss my ass. Look at all these guns. I did not sign up for this."

"I said shut up, Wanda."

"FBI," Agent Proctor said helpfully. "You're under arrest."

"Oh, Wanda! Hello, darling! Look at your hair. It's the prettiest color!"

"Hey, Maddy," Wanda said with a suddenly brilliant smile. "I'm going to get the hell out of here. I think I can make it across that causeway before it floods. You want to ride with me?"

"You know I do!"

Maddy stepped away from Will, but Mac grabbed her again. All the guns swiveled to him. "Nope. You stay right here, old lady, until you tell me what I need to know."

Wanda took in the situation with a raised eyebrow and made her decision. "Sorry about that, Maddy. I gotta ride."

To the envious gaze of everyone else in the room, Wanda simply turned on her heels and walked out of the house. Barry cursed her and Maddy cried, "Next time, darling!" and then Wanda was gone. Barry slammed the door against the rising wind.

"Okay," said Agent Proctor, "that was Wanda."

We all nodded.

"We'll get her later for abduction. Barry," she went on, "I wonder if you'd mind answering a few questions."

Of all the people in the room, Barry looked the most unstable. And so, I assumed he was the most dangerous.

"Bitch," he said shortly. He turned to Maddy.

"Come on, granny. You come over here or I'm going to start shooting."

"Pictures?" Maddy cooed. "Oh, let me run a comb through my hair, will you? Isn't it the most gorgeous blue?" She fluttered and dimpled at him, and he looked completely confounded.

"Barry," Agent Proctor called, "how long have you been working for Vicky?"

It was a lucky shot. "I don't work for that cunt."

"Now, I don't like that word, young man. Not one bit."

Maddy's admonishment further unbalanced Barry. "I'm partners with Bob Yancy."

"Vicky's husband," Elmer added. His arm had relaxed as he focused on Barry. I was waiting for my chance.

"That's right." Barry swung his machine gun to point at Elmer —and so, unfortunately, also at me. There went my opportunity. Every one of Elmer's muscles clamped down again, limiting my breath and blood flow. Rhys became even more still.

"That's right. Vicky is nothing to me. And while Yancy's serving time, I'm in charge," Barry boasted.

Agent Proctor got Barry's attention again. Rhys's tension eased as the machine gun was pointed away from me. "And what's he in prison for?"

"Same as always. He's a con man. A fucking idiot of a con man."

"And you're his hired muscle."

Barry bridled. "I'm his partner," he said again. "So that cunt Vicky—" He cut a look at Maddy, almost shame-faced, and she frowned at him. He drew himself up. "That cunt said she'd give me half if I got the jewels for her. But what I want to know is, why the hell would I give her anything? Seems like if I find them, those jewels are one hundred percent mine. Right?"

This time his gaze at Maddy was full of insanity. "And now you're going to tell me where those jewels are hidden."

Maddy's face was as dark as the storm. "You Oatmeal Man!" she said with loathing. She made a grab for Will's pistol and almost got it. Mac pulled her arm back at the last moment.

Everyone in the room froze—which is why we could hear the call from outside over the wind.

"Hey, Elmer! The time has come, brah!"

"Now, who the fuck is *that*?" asked Agent Proctor. Control mixed with irritation in her voice. Even the senior agent in charge was frustrated by this ever-increasing cast of characters.

Elmer raised his gun hand slightly. He sounded embarrassed when he answered.

"Sorry. That one's mine."

"Hey! I know you hear me in there, man!" The voice was getting stronger. "I can see you in the door. You're meat, man. You're dead meat."

Elmer ducked against the wall, drawing me with him. He nodded to Big Jim, who took the other side from the porch door and its glass panel.

"Explain," barked Agent Proctor as all the FBI agents once again reassessed their positions based on the newest threat.

"Dad and me, we kinda need those jewels because—" Elmer was trying to watch through the porch door as he kept an eye on everyone else inside the room.

"Crystal meth," offered Timmo helpfully.

"Hillbilly heroin," sneered Mac. "Why aren't I surprised?"

"Shut up, you prick," Elmer said, briefly waving his gun at Mac and Maddy.

"So who's that out there?" Proctor asked. "A supplier? A junkie?"

"Uh, no. That's the Wheeling Mafia."

"Excuse me?" Her expression crystalized how far out of left field things had suddenly gone. "What the hell is the *Wheeling Mafia?*"

"Me and Dad, well . . . we got in with the big drug pipeline into West Virginia. Crystal meth is okay, but you can really make money with crack."

She sighed and shook her head. "And how much do you owe them?"

Elmer was abashed. "Four million, give or take."

Mac snorted in derision at his half-brother. No, at his half-nephew. "So Daddy's million was never going to cover that." Scorn dripped from his voice.

"Shut your damned pie hole, Mac."

"Shut *your* pie hole, Elmer!"

"Both of you shut the fuck up!" Apparently Barry didn't want to be ignored any longer.

And then all hell broke loose.

TWENTY-SEVEN

RHYS

I HAD NEVER EXPLAINED TO ANYONE—NOT EVEN TO MY FATHER —that it wasn't just a cloak of calmness that fell over me when I took part in a shooting competition. I also discovered that time slowed down to entirely manageable levels. I had hours to make every decision, to correct every angle, to calculate wind drift, trajectory, the ideal pressure on the trigger to keep the shot true.

The pulse of my heart ticked along steadily, slowly—patiently.

When I'd shot the child pornographer's pistol out of his hand, when I'd stopped a scared young man from firing on police officers, even when I'd shot the dirty white Stetson off Big Jim's head—in each instance, time had gotten plastic and flexible.

But nothing had shut down my emotions like it did when I had such a personal stake in the outcome. I entered a sort of machine state of hyper-alertness, providing me with ample opportunity to witness, assess, judge, act.

Having Maddy—or even more so, Cyn—in the line of fire left me in an almost dissociative state. It was as if all emotion had left me from the moment Mac's gun made its way up the stairs, attached to a man who worried me simply because he was so unsure of himself.

Events unfolded with almost painful slowness. Elaine Proctor had been masterful, defusing tensions and uncovering needed information and motivations.

But except for Cyn's one attempt to go to Maddy (when I'd pulled her back behind me), I was focused almost exclusively on the weaponry in the room, and everyone holding them.

Proctor and I had a conversation entirely by eyeball. By the time the shooting started, I'd clinically assessed the greatest threats in the room as being Barry (who I held to be on the dangerous edge of true insanity) and Big Jim (who I knew well was a crack shot). Despite my almost physical ache to secure Cyn's safety, I told Proctor I was going for those two first.

She had both Will and Mac in her line of fire. Maddy was between them. Proctor would need to be a very good shot, and that assumed that Maddy would stay still.

Biays was on the other side of Elmer, who was holding Cyn with a degree of carelessness that was causing a screaming part of my brain to be pushed closer to primitive violence. Looking away from Cyn was painful for me, but my analysis made it clear that Biays had the better angle on Grumpy Bear. I caught Biays's eye and made sure he knew his job. He nodded fractionally at me.

Farthest away from me was Dash, the partner I relied on. Experience was coming off him in waves. I knew his deceptively calm and friendly attitude was a cloak over razor-sharp reflexes, but I was wound so tightly that his looseness was hard to factor into my plans. Biays and I were junior partners who would do our best, and I assumed Proctor wouldn't have gotten the job if she couldn't have handled it. But it was Dash I looked to for the solidarity of a powerful team. He offered me the ghost of a cheeky grin as he nodded to Will and Mac, and to Timmo.

I shook my head in warning. Yes, both Will and Timmo seemed like low-level threats, but both were armed, and both had shown themselves to be loyal to their brothers. If bullets started flying, both could be trouble. Dash gave me an insouciant shrug that made me want to bitch-slap him. As if reading my mind, his smile grew.

And then the Wheeling Mafia arrived.

The motherfucking Wheeling Mafia. Who were they? How many more people—how many more weapons—were going to mess this situation up? Had someone placed an ad somewhere?

There was no doubt in my mind that the Wheeling Mafia could take a ticket and wait their turn. Barry Gambert remained the biggest threat, for his instability as well as for the gun he dared to hold on the woman I was pretty sure I was in love with. I was watching the Oatmeal Man and saw his rising frustrations as Elmer and Mac engaged in decades-old bickering . . .

And I saw Barry snap. I saw the moment it happened, and I saw his finger tighten on the trigger. He began to fire his MAC-10, and he was aiming at Elmer and Cyn.

My bullet went through his brain. He hit the ground in a sprawl. Proctor's bullet thudded in behind mine.

Time had slowed again. Every gunshot was a separate, distinct percussion beat ticking away in my ears. As I turned from Barry to Big Jim, I saw Elmer release Cyn entirely and fire at Will, who was astonished to be caught in Elmer's sights. Elmer's first bullet pushed meatily through Will's shoulder.

I saw that Cyn, released, had curled up in a ball at Elmer's feet, out of the line of fire. And I saw that on the way down, she'd landed a determined fist right into his testicles. In the fraction of my brain where emotion had been walled off, a voice screamed in pride at my warrior girl, who'd disabled an attacker with nothing more than a wicked hard hit to the balls.

Elmer felt it too. His second shot went wide as he doubled over shrieking. His bullet creased Dash's skull, leaving a crisp gash and showing a white hint of bone before the blood poured out.

Big Jim had stupidly taken the time to scream his rage to the roof. Now he was swinging to me at last, apparently seeing me as the most dangerous threat. I admired his assessment as I took careful aim and clipped him in the biceps. He howled and dropped his gun.

Fire was spraying through the windows. The Wheeling Mafia didn't want to miss their chance at the mayhem and were getting in on the battle. Dash, blood pouring down his head, was aiming at the starbursts erupting outside through the wind and darkness. I swiveled and joined him in shooting at our unknown assailants.

Behind me someone thumped to the ground. Proctor barked, "Drop it," with undeniable alpha authority.

I heard the cursing when a bullet—mine or Dash's—hit a member of the Wheeling Mafia, and I knew when they gave up. In a sudden flash of lightning, I saw one man helping another across the marshes to a flat-bottom fishing boat, a ridiculous craft to take out in more than a light breeze and pure insanity in a vicious superstorm. It was bobbing on the wild waves at the dock. The two men limped toward it with determination.

"Fuck," Dash said admiringly. "They think they're going to make it through a hurricane in that thing? Crazy loco."

By his voice, I could tell he had more warmth in him than I did. I was still in robot mode.

All the threats inside and outside the room had been neutralized. I had fired seven times (including five shots at the Wheeling Mafia) and had hit my target three times. As far as I could tell, twenty-seven shots had been fired in all, each one still ringing in my head like a terrible symphony. The silence pressed painfully on my ears.

I was having a hard time unlocking my emotions, but once I'd confirmed that all the weapons were in the hands of friendlies, my eyes sought out Cyn.

She and Maddy were on the floor. I could see no blood or sign of injury in either of them. Cyn was hugging Maddy and crying, and Maddy was petting her. Timmo was curled around Maddy. He'd opted to drop his rifle and put his body between her and any bullets. He'd tried to protect Maddy.

With that realization, I began to thaw, knowing the shakes were coming next.

I knelt down next to Cyn, and she jumped when I put a hand on her warm, fragile, beautiful shoulder. "Are you okay?"

She refused to let go of Maddy, but she nodded to me, her eyes too full of tears to see me. "I'll be right back," I said, suppressing my urge to hold her and never let her go.

Will was frantically trying to deal with the spurting wound in Mac's shoulder. He'd managed to get bloodier than his brother, and his panic was beginning to freak out Mac.

Proctor had gathered up all the weapons in the room and was already on the phone. I knew without listening that she was calling the sheriff for backup.

Elmer was lying on the floor, dazed. I looked to Biays, sitting next to him and cradling his own wrist.

"I couldn't get a shot without hitting you, so I smacked him with the butt of my gun. He hit his head as he fell, and I think I broke my wrist."

He was so rueful that an unwilling chuckle bubbled out of me. It felt very strange, indeed.

"You're okay, though?" I asked him.

"Just embarrassed."

I shook my head, still too numb to be able to put my thoughts into words.

Barry's body had fallen against the door, blood and brains fanned out behind him. Proctor had already collected his MAC-10. I turned away to the last threat.

Big Jim was sitting stoically on the floor, holding his now-bloody hand against the wound I'd shot in his arm.

"Been meaning to tell you," he said. "You owe me a hat."

"I owe you a hat," I repeated stupidly.

"My Stetson. You shot it off and I lost it. I liked that hat."

"Sorry." I sat down next to him, the strength suddenly running out of my legs. "How you doing?"

"You could have killed me," he acknowledged.

"You too," I said, moving his hand to check that I hadn't hit an artery. The graze was deep and was going to hurt, but if he was treated promptly, he wouldn't die. "You should still be able to shoot once this is healed. It's going to take a while, though."

He nodded stoically. The man was tough. "Where'd you train?" he asked me. "You in the service?"

"Nah. FBI Academy. You?"

"Army," he said proudly. "Expert marksman."

"Shit," I said, my admiration sincere. "I never made it past sharpshooter."

"Well, fuck. Sharpshooter's good enough."

Proctor appeared. She'd found towels and dish cloths to form impromptu bandages that she was distributing. "You okay?" she asked me.

I nodded. Now that she was taking care of Big Jim, I was able to turn and reach out blindly . . .

. . . and when Cyn's hand met mine, I found my strength again and pulled her into me as if my life depended on it.

I held her as the shakes swept through me.

TIME SPED UP AFTER THAT. MAYBE IT WAS MAKING UP FOR TIME delayed during the gun battle. The sheriff appeared, mightily pleased with the chaos he found.

"Well," he said, as the storm crashed through various broken windows. "So far, we've still got an island clinic with some medics who can help those who need it."

He looked at Will, Big Jim, and Elmer. Elmer had woken up and almost immediately vomited in the bucket Agent Proctor had thoughtfully placed next to him. Concussion, we all agreed. Biays needed an X-ray and a cast on that wrist, and Dash grinned, white

CYN & THE PEANUT BUTTER CUP

teeth gleaming in a red face, when even the unflappable sheriff blanched at the sight of him.

"What the fuck happened to you? You look like Carrie at the prom."

"Bullet creased my scalp." Skull was still showing through when he pulled away his towel bandage to show off the graze from Elmer's bullet. "You know they bleed a ton. I'm fine."

"Boy, you need stitches."

"And a good barber," Dash agreed happily. Possibly showing signs of post-traumatic euphoria. He was glad to be alive. I knew how he felt.

"And I got holding cells for the others." Timmo and Will were unharmed and unhappy about the thought of prison. Too bad. "But I'll need some help watching them, and those in the clinic. As you might imagine, we're spread a tad thin tonight." The storm had reached a shrieking stage, and the house was shaking on its stilts. It was, as the sheriff no doubt would have said, "a mite airish."

Agent Proctor nodded. "I'll watch our prisoners in your holding cells, and Agents Biays and Ashwood can keep an eye on those three at the clinic once they're treated themselves. No one's going to be able to get very far tonight anyway."

It was unclear if she meant that the agents wouldn't get very far (which was probably true), that the prisoners in the clinic wouldn't get far (which was definitely true—getting shot isn't like on TV shows; you don't bounce back from it during the commercial break), or the fact that the storm was raging so fiercely it was unlikely anyone would be able to get anywhere soon.

"Want me to help?" I asked.

"I want you to take care of Maddy and Cyn. There are bedrooms back there that aren't part of the crime scene. Can the three of you stay out of this area until the forensic crews can gather the necessary evidence for the court case?"

I nodded with certain relief. I hadn't had my fill of holding Cyn yet, and she hadn't held Maddy enough yet. Staying holed up in the house to ride out the storm sounded about right to me. As for restricting ourselves to the bedroom wing, no one wanted to remain in the great room anyway. Shot-out windows letting in the storm were only the beginning of why we'd want to remain in another part of the house.

Working together, we secured the room as best we could, including taping up where bullets had passed through plate glass and plywood, and securing doors against the howling wind.

"We're going to need your van," the sheriff observed when the great room was taped up. "Can't fit everybody in my cruiser."

"That's fine," Proctor said. "We'll be back for you three tomorrow, Rhys." I nodded. "You'll be okay?"

"We'll be fine." I knew it was true as I said it. We'd made it through our own personal storm, and Mother Nature wasn't going to upstage that.

Ducking against the rain, we moved the three injured prisoners to the van. Elmer could stagger along with some help, and fortunately Big Jim (who really was too big to carry) was tough enough to make his way shakily on his own two feet. Will insisted that his shoulder wound was so horrific that he needed to be carried on a stretcher we made of a blanket. He soon regretted it, as we weren't quite as careful as we could have been as we negotiated doorways and stairs.

The wind was blowing so fiercely that I worried about them on the road to town.

The sheriff helped me load Barry's body unceremoniously into his trunk. "You shut that door to the old part of the house, now—that garage," he shouted. "Those stilts are tied to the bedrock. The house can weather the blow, but the original fishing shack isn't likely to make it through this."

"Thanks," I called. "I'll do that."

"You're probably going to lose power too. See if you can find some candles or something. Flashlight is even better. Can't burn down your house with a flashlight."

"Good advice. Thanks for all your help."

"Looks like you guys did fine without me!"

I waved, squinting in the driving rain, to Dash, who rode shotgun in the van as Proctor followed the Sheriff (with Timmo, Will, and FBI Jim) down the long drive. He grinned back to me and gave me a thumbs-up.

When I turned back to the house, Cyn was silhouetted in the light streaming from the door, her arm around Maddy. I felt a wash of gratitude and weariness.

"Let's get inside," I called, and we struggled between us to close the door against the wind.

In the resulting calm, Cyn looked at me.

"Well," she said simply.

"Well," I agreed. Then, wet as I was from the fierce rain, I swept her into a hug with Maddy snuggled between us. Cyn and I were both crying. Maddy was laughing.

"What an exciting party!" she giggled happily. "The best I've ever been to!"

Cyn wiped her eyes and broke away. "First we find a towel for Rhys and call Belinda to let her know everything is all right. Then we need some supper," she said wisely.

"Lovely! What are we having, dear?"

I took one last look around the old fishing shack before locking the door at the top of the stairs. Wherever the hiding place was, it was probably going to be lost tonight. *Goodbye, stupidly named gemstones. You've caused a lot more trouble than you're worth.*

We took all the food we'd brought with us into a pair of connecting bedrooms. Cyn put Maddy on the phone first to talk with Belinda. She knew that hearing her mother's voice would soothe Belinda's fears more rapidly than anything we could say. But Cyn finished up the call with a rough outline of the details. She decided to save the more sensational bits for when Belinda could hear the details in person. Belinda told us she'd changed all her plans and would he home in two days. Maddy and Cyn agreed this was wonderful news. They both expressed a desire to "hug Belinda until she was blue in the face"—Maddy's phrase.

I helped Cyn unpack the food we'd put together—could it possibly have been just a few hours earlier?—and the power stayed on long enough to have light on while the three of us worked together to make a bed for Maddy. Cyn had come across flashlights and plenty of batteries, so we were able to leave a light glowing in Maddy's room in case (or when) the power went out.

Getting Maddy to bed turned out to be an unexpectedly intimate moment. I had a vision of Cyn and me putting our children to bed, and it filled me with warmth and hope and joy.

Maddy thanked us for a wonderful evening and gave us a sweet and sleepy smile. I couldn't resist kissing her thin and papery cheek after Cyn did. "Good night, Peanut Butter Cup. You take good care of my girl tonight!" she whispered.

"Promise," I said.

Then it was just Cyn and me in the outer bedroom. She looked at me, fatigue in every line.

"I know we're alone, but . . ."

I had the strength to chuckle. "I got it. Too damned tired."

"Too damned tired," she agreed. "Should we get more sheets and make up this bed?"

The house was rocking in the wind, and the sound of the storm was massive. "I'm tapped out. Let's lie down with the bed like this. Is that okay?"

She nodded. We kicked off our shoes, and I sank onto the bed as if it was a cloud in heaven. Felt as good too. I propped pillows behind my head and patted the mattress at my hip.

"That's a perfect plan," she said, curling up against me.

"Oh, that feels better."

"Mm."

We lay in silence for a while, letting the day wash over us. And then she was the one trembling.

"It's the shakes," I whispered as I pulled her into me. "Happens after an adrenaline dump. Let them come. They'll pass."

And they did.

The entire house was rattling around me, but I was completely at peace. "I've been thinking," I said.

"Yeah?" Her face was hidden in my neck, but her voice told me she wasn't sleepy yet.

"I really, really don't like shooting people. I'm not sure I want to be an FBI agent." I hadn't thought about it consciously, but as the words came out of me, I knew they were true. I felt a rush of relief at the statement.

She uncurled and looked at me. "Dash and your father think you should quit."

Of all the things I'd heard today—and I'd heard a lot—this was the most confusing. "What? What did you say?"

"That's what he was talking to me about when he and I followed you and Maddy on your walk. They both think you're a great agent, but they don't think you're happy."

"They don't think I'm a great agent," I protested, but she cut me off.

"They both think you could have a brilliant career. But Dash says they've both watched you wall off so much of who you are to be in the FBI. It makes them sad."

"He didn't say that."

"No, of course not. He's a guy. But I can hear what he's saying, and he's saying that it makes them sad. For you. I think it's what you were talking about—that you can't be an agent and an artist because of the emotion. And your emotions are such a huge part of who you are. Or who you should be."

I had to chew on that for a while. "Really."

"Really."

"My father thinks that too?"

"That's what Dash said."

"Huh."

"Yeah. Dash says he wouldn't even have known that side of you if he hadn't seen you in the art room at the Boys' Club."

"Huh."

"Again, yeah."

I still couldn't wrap my head around it. She cut through the wheels whirling in my brain.

"So, you don't want to be an FBI agent, and your father and Dash would encourage you to quit. You've in no way failed. You need to be an artist and you can pay the bills by being a lawyer. In some capacity or other. Maybe part-time at the Boys and Girls Club, or something that leaves time for art. You need to have emotions. To make stupid jokes and go to work still drunk from the night before, and maybe even get speeding tickets, and now you can. What's the problem? Why are you stewing over this?"

Well, when you put it that way.

My only reasonable response was to kiss her.

A lot.

We made out for a while and I wondered if it was absolutely too soon to tell her I was in love with her, or if it was ridiculously, absolutely too soon.

We reached the point where if we'd gone on any longer, we'd end up making love on an unmade bed in a raging storm with a demented and happy old lady one room over, and neither of us wanted that. Regretfully, I pulled back.

She curled up on my chest. "I want to make a change too."

"Yeah? What's that?" I ran my fingers through her hair for the pleasure of feeling the silk against my fingers.

"I don't want to be an architectural historian anymore." She sat up and smiled at me. "Good thing, huh? Because I never really became one!"

I smiled at the lightness she was exuding. "So, what then?"

"I liked teaching the kids about their dream houses. I'm

thinking—why not architecture school? My original school debts are paid off. A million years ago, before Maddy and I were kidnapped—yesterday!—my lawyer called. He thinks I'll be getting my share of Don's inheritance. It gives me a lot of freedom to make some choices of my own. Think I'd be a good architect?"

"You'd be brilliant. You can design our first home."

It slipped out before I had a chance to think about it.

"Shit." I followed my statement with a graceful profanity. "Sorry. Too soon. Ignore me. Shell shock. Temporary insanity."

She stopped my rambling with her lips. "Can I design our first house? Really?"

I lost the ability to breathe. "You're not freaked?"

She smiled and shook her head. "Not freaked. What are you saying, though?"

I felt shy. "What are *you* saying?"

"Are you saying . . . you want us to move in together?"

"Well, yeah. But also . . ."

"Also?"

I longed for the icy cool of a firefight. My heart was pounding louder than the storm. It took more courage than I thought I had to say the words. "Also . . . I'm in love with you. I know it's too soon, but—"

"I'm in love with you too, Rhys."

"Really?"

"Really."

"Holy shit. We're in love?" I couldn't believe it. I was going to explode from happiness.

"We're in love!" She said it in wonder, and then I was kissing her again. This was a different kiss. There was heat—and god knows, there was tongue. But there was also reverence and wonder.

"You don't love me," I decided when the kiss ended. "You're having a reaction to the gun fight."

"I see," she said as she curled into me. "And you don't love me, either. You're just pumped from the adrenaline."

"Well, no," I pointed out. "I'm quite sane. It's you that's crazy."

"Crazy about you."

We carried on with nonsense and teasing, slowly growing into the new reality where we were together, until finally we slept.

TWENTY-EIGHT
MADDY

THE WALL OF WINDOWS IN FRONT OF ME IS BOARDED UP, BUT I can see golden sunlight pouring in around the edges, warm as love itself. I can't wait to see what the day will bring!

In the next room, an adorable pixie of a woman is sleeping in the arms of a golden man. They're curled together in a picture of love and security and warmth. I fill my eyes with the sight of them and my heart swells with happiness. How lovely they are!

The door is stiff, but I manage to tug it open to the dazzling, clear day.

The air is washed clean and the sky is brilliant blue, sunrise colors fading on the horizon in the brightness of a brand new and glorious day. The marsh grasses wave their tasseled heads, and the canals are rippled with blue waters. The earth is damp and gives off the smell of rain and wet leaves.

I dance along the walkway, delighting in the sun on my shoulders. There never was a prettier day and never have I been happier!

As I move farther from the house, I see boards and window frames and scattered detritus lying in the soggy grass. A Boston whaler is resting on its side, broken at the keel. Something big has been destroyed in the storm.

I sit on the dock for a moment. The sun is warm, but it's still too chilly to dangle my feet in the canal. But summer will come soon enough. Hector and I will put the boat in the water, and we will go to a sand bar that no other human has touched, and we will make love and laugh and drink beer and watch for dolphins and sea turtles, and it will be perfect once more.

But not in this cooler weather. Not just yet. I turn to my task, happy to know what to do.

The old cabinet is roped to the bulkhead. Hector keeps his fishing supplies here. Crabbing nets and lead sinkers and sun-faded cushions for the boat. All the bits and bobs that accumulate. The cabinet is so useful that it gets unstrapped every time the bulkhead has to be rebuilt—the pull of the water is endless, and the bulk-head must be realigned every decade or so.

But when the bulkhead is back, the cabinet is replaced. It's too useful to be cast away. Old and tatty, but weathered and well-suited for its job.

And in the bottom of the cabinet, washed up like shells at low tide, are a series of tins. They're rusted—they show the evidence of plenty of storms washing over and into the cabinet—but they all still have nice, tight lids.

One that holds fishhooks.

One that holds nails and screws and bits of string.

One that holds three pitted and corroded clamps.

And one that holds Hector's jewels.

I pull it from the bottom of the cabinet, from where it's laid in plain sight and safe from observation since he put it here.

I remember to walk off the dock and back onto the grass. Once, I pulled the lid off with such a tug that a positive shower of diamonds flew out and fell into the water. How Hector laughed!

"An oyster will pick up one of those diamonds and make the

most magnificent pearl out of it, and I shall open the oyster and take the pearl and make you a ring fit for your beautiful hand, Mac, darling. And you'll look at it and know I love you, no matter what happens next. I love you, Mac."

He kisses me and wraps me in his arms, and I know that our love is worth every risk, every dare, every danger.

I'm holding a tin in my hands. It's Hector's jewels. I open the box and push past the ugly, oversized Jaipur Princess. Tawdry, cloudy bauble.

Underneath, next to the lovely Merlin Twins, I fish out six stones. They're much smaller, but they sparkle in the morning light. I slip them—three diamonds, two emeralds, and a luxuriously dark and velvety ruby—into my pocket.

No one will miss them. Not once they've gotten the Jaipur Princess back, and the Merlin Twins, and all the other stones. These are the gifts Hector left to me, and I shall leave them to the people I love.

Two diamonds will go into Belinda's jewelry box. She'll never think they're from me, and that secret makes me want to giggle. One day she'll find them and will wonder where they came from.

I dance back to the stilt house and slip quietly in through the door. I tuck one diamond and one emerald into the pocket of the pixie's coat where it hangs on a hook, and one emerald and the flawless ruby into the Peanut Butter Cup's jacket. He can make her an engagement ring out of the ruby, and she'll wear it on her left hand. Every boater knows that left is port is red, and right is starboard is green. So he can make her a companion ring out of the emerald for her right hand—a starboard ring and a port ring—so she'll always know which direction they should go. And he will follow, trusting in her to know the way home.

Then I make my way back to the bedroom where they're sleeping. I nestle the tin of Hector's gemstones on his chest, where her hands and his will find it together.

They stir and look at the tin with puzzled expressions.

"There's a flat-bottom fishing boat floating in the canal," I tell them. "Let's get it and go for a ride!"

———————

EPILOGUE

I HOPE YOU ENJOYED *CYN & THE PEANUT BUTTER CUP*.

For the FREE epilogue (*Cyn Puts the Righteous Smack-Down on Her Ex-Husband*), sign up for Bliss & Giggles, my newsletter at https://www.pruwarren.com/

When you do, there will be an automatic reply (really fast; if you don't see it in a minute or so, check your spam folder). Once you confirm, you'll get the email with the epilogue download link.

Once you have it, you can unsubscribe to the newsletter; I won't be offended...but why not stick around? We'll have fun!

SNEAK PEEK OF DASH & THE MOONGLOW MYSTIC

I fell in love with Dash. Can you blame me?

So I wrote him his own story. Turn the page for a sneak peek!

DASH & THE MOONGLOW MYSTIC

Chapter One

Dash

I felt the Moonglow Mystic like electricity on my skin before I ever saw her.

I stood in the registration line at a luxury dude ranch, my "wife" at my side. (Rose Bennet had been my partner at the FBI for all of five weeks.) Rose bit a thumbnail and murmured to me, her low voice hidden under the hum of new guests recently released after a two-hour drive through the utter emptiness of Wyoming.

"Maybe I should change my name to Roz. Roz inspires respect, right?" she asked.

A buzz on my skin caught my attention. I sharpened my surveillance. The main lodge had a low ceiling, a stone fireplace (unlit on this summer afternoon), and antler chandeliers. Western chic, if you liked that sort of thing.

"Your name doesn't give authority. The toughest agent I know is named Percy. Do you feel that?"

She looked up. "Feel what?"

I plastered a smile on my face while eyeing the room. My skin was definitely tingling, and I could almost hear a faint hum, a tiny vibration through my bones.

And then I saw the woman.

She was across the lobby. Caucasian, early thirties, above-average height. Slim build, long silver hair. Eyes . . . blue. Violet, really. Those unusual eyes were fixed on me.

She didn't look away. I didn't either.

It's simple human psychology. If you're staring at someone and they catch you at it, you drop your eyes. You turn away. Maybe you flush or squirm or offer an abashed grin.

That's not what she did—and caught by her gaze, I didn't turn away either. The murmur of other guests continued but was suddenly far away. And I could still feel the electricity dancing on my skin.

"What? Do I feel what? Dash?" Rose tracked my stare and found the silver woman on the other side of the lobby. "Do you know her?"

I shook my head and fought to regain my focus. I pulled my gaze away. Looking at Rose, I clarified. "You don't feel . . . something? Electricity? Or something?"

She shook her head, her brunette bob swinging with the movement. I showed her my forearm, the hair standing on end. My skin was pebbled with goose bumps.

Rose looked at her own arm. She wasn't having the same reaction. "Huh," I said. Brilliant assessment from an experienced FBI agent.

I looked up again. The woman still stared at me. But whispers had started in the line for check-in.

"Who's that?"

"Is that one of the new ones?"

"Isn't she lovely! I want her to tell my fortune!"

The woman behind me gasped. It was Kimber. We'd met her on the bus ride from the airport. "That's her! That's the one who helped me!"

She shared her story with the fascinated guests—how, upon meeting Kimber a year ago, the Moonglow Mystic had diagnosed Kimber's cancer. "She was the receptionist at my vet's office in San Diego. She reached out and took my hand and told me. And she was right! My oncologist said we'd caught it really, really early. I owe her my life!"

The crowd *ooh*ed in appreciation, but the woman—the Moonglow Mystic—ignored the growing tide of curiosity. She kept her eyes on me. Was she judging me?

"Do you still feel it?" Rose wore her we're-so-happy-to-be-here smile, but her interest had been piqued, and she scanned the room.

"Like an iron filing next to a magnet. I feel . . ." The comparison died on my lips. I was going to say I felt like the tide pulled by the moon. Too close to the mindset that would allow a so-called moon goddess to con me. "Someone switched on a field generator —a powerful magnet," I said. "You don't feel it? Here—stand in front of me."

But no matter where she stood, Rose couldn't feel the electricity.

"I suppose it could be under the floor. Or in the attic. Shift around."

No luck.

I kept my eye on the silver-haired woman, and she watched me in turn. Then she pivoted on her heel and vanished through the double doors at the back of the lobby.

The buzzing on my skin faded.

I was confused until I remembered these "psychics" were con artists. That cleared my head. A con man's tricks could be extremely sophisticated. Had someone learned how to focus the effect of a large electromagnet so I was the only one feeling a strange pull toward the woman on the other side of the room?

Sure. That would explain my sensations. As soon as I figured it out, I felt better.

I turned back, refusing to shake my head in disbelief. It

wouldn't do to appear immediately suspicious when surrounded by guests who were—according to all indications—eager to be conned by "prophets" and "mystics."

The fact that the entire ranch had been rented out for "Prophecy Week" hadn't been lost on my bosses at the FBI. "You're going to look for evidence of a counterfeiting operation, Dash," Owen had said to me. "We have reason to suspect Wolf Koenig is running the operation, and he's the son of the ranch owners. It's dumb luck you'll be there while six charlatans are fleecing some wealthy believers. As far as Prophecy Week goes, if you don't witness a crime, don't worry about it. The fake bills are why we're helping the Secret Service—not the con men."

Fair enough. I'd keep my focus on the mission and ignore the con. But that was no reason to be careless or unobservant. Someone was using an electromagnet on me to fizz my skin while the silver-haired woman eyed me. They turned it off when she left the room. Nice technique. Not my problem.

We'd inched slowly forward to the check-in desk, where Bob and Marcia Koenig greeted returning guests and met the new ones, both with equal amounts of down-home hospitality.

Our joint task force partner at the Secret Service, Enrique Martinez, was already undercover at the dude ranch as a trail hand. The assumption was it wasn't Bob and Marcia Koenig who were printing out fake bills somewhere. It was probably their son, Wolf, who ran the ranch while his parents ran the inn. Both Enrique and Rose were junior agents where I was a senior agent with long years of experience, and I'd draw my own conclusions based on the kind of evidence that would stand up in court.

Those long years of experience weighed on me now. And they weighed exactly as much as the small case in my hip pocket, where a shameful folding pair of reading glasses now resided. Permanently.

A millstone around my neck.

I knew what they meant. They meant youth was now and

forever lost to me. I was a field agent. I belonged in the field. At least, I used to. Now I was washed-up and useless. Probably going gray. Nothing left in my future but old age, isolated and alone in a perpetually weakening body.

As I'd been doing for the four days since the optometrist gave me the news, I shook out of my blue funk and focused on the case.

"Next? Yes, sir?"

We'd made it to the front of the line, and Marcia Koenig exuded a cheerful welcome. Caucasian, short, plump. Early- to mid-sixties. No distinguishing marks. Short hair, bottle-blonde to cover the gray. Brown eyes. Air of happy innocence. Mother of our primary suspect.

"Dash and Rose Williamson," I said, holding out my ID and a credit card.

"Oh, the Williamsons!" Marcia Koenig cooed. "Our last-minute guests! How remarkable you called for a reservation moments after the Robinsons had to cancel!"

I had it on good authority that Bitsy Robinson had a small crystal meth lab in the basement of her summer home at Tahoe. She and her husband had gotten a provident knock on the door from the DEA as soon as we knew Rose and I needed a room at the Triangle-K, but I let none of that show.

"Well, their loss is definitely our gain!" I gave Marcia a big smile, which she returned.

"Oh, you're going to have such a good time! Here's the Prophecy Week agreement you need to sign. Every year, the mystics have us make all the guests sign it. Silly, isn't it? But each year the ranch sells out, so we love those prophets!" Marcia put the agreement on the desk before us, and Rose suddenly betrayed me by stepping away and gesturing to the paper with a grin.

And suddenly the small weight in my hip pocket threatened to drag me six feet under the ground.

"Damn it," I ground out.

Marcia was startled and looked at me.

"Sorry," I said and grumpily fished out the reading glasses. It was like holding a scorpion in my hand, or a vial of curare. This was death. Unwilling, I unfolded the glasses and put them on.

Rose laughed out loud and explained to Marcia, "First pair of reading glasses. He thinks he's dying of old age."

She and Marcia laughed merrily. Heartlessly. Marcia's hand reached out to pat mine. The Grim Reaper in an embroidered cardigan. "I remember when I got my first bifocals. It's a bad day. You poor sweetie. I promise—aging isn't all bad!"

I feigned a smile, and this time her husband, Bob, joined in the hysteria. "Don't worry, son. There's life after presbyopia!"

Funny. They were all charming. Like sledgehammers were charming. I scanned the agreement as Marcia told Rose about Prophecy Week private readings and group events. Buried in tiny, vision-defying legalese near the bottom of the contract was the reason why no law enforcement agency would intrude on the con artists' week-long scam: the all-important phrase "For entertainment purposes only." Of course. Now we were all legal and aboveboard.

I signed my name. Marcia beamed at me. "On behalf of those prophets, we thank you. Now, can I sign you two up for any of the ranch activities?" We leaned our heads together as she went over them. "We've got campfire cookouts and roping lessons—not on a living bull," she confided, "and trail rides. You'll love our trail rides."

"I don't much like horses."

"You'll like our horses! How about I sign you up for the beginner ride tomorrow? Short and easy. Everyone gets a personal guide. Get your fears all taken care of?" I opened my mouth to rationalize away my fears, but she was having none of it. "Your wife would like it, wouldn't she?"

Beside me, Rose was wreathed in eager smiles. "I used to ride as a girl! Let's go, Dash!"

"All right." My dislike of riding had to be overcome. Rose and I needed to spend time with Wolf and his ranch hands, our most likely suspects.

"And glamping—glamorous camping. Oh, it's wonderful. You take an all-day trail ride. Or," she amended, seeing my face, "you can go up the jeep trail with the staff. We have luxurious tents set up in Smuggler's Basin, and there's a gourmet meal, and you can sleep under the stars and sometimes see the northern lights! It's the most beautiful part of the world. Like a fairy tale. I know you want me to put you down for that?"

"I'd be a fool to miss it."

She beamed. "And skeet shooting. And what about fly-fishing in our rushing river?"

"Marcia, why don't you sign me and the missus up for everything and let us know where we're supposed to be?"

"Oh, you are going to have such a good time! And don't forget the square dancing in town on Thursday night. It's a Triangle-K tradition!"

Time for me to insert the first probe. "Say, Marcia, what accounting software are you running on that thing?" I nodded to the laptop visible behind the registration desk.

"Accounting software?" she said, surprised.

Rose nudged me. "Dash! You said we'd take a real vacation. No more accounting, please!" She turned to Marcia. "He's such a nerd!"

Marcia smiled in commiseration, but the hook had been set. Bob turned away from the family he was checking in to verify what he'd heard.

"Accounting software? Are you into accounting, Mr. Williamson?"

Rose laughed, the long-suffering wife, and pushed me away to talk to Bob while she and Marcia completed the registration.

"Call me Dash. I'm curious—what are you running there? Don't tell me it's QuickBooks, please."

He laughed and leaned in, interested. "NetSuite, actually. You're in the business?"

"I'm a CPA. If you're running NetSuite, do you have the macro for the new tax laws?"

"What's that now?"

Rose put a determined hand on my shoulder. "Dash, really. Leave it alone. Could you back off for once?"

I shrugged and smiled apologetically at Bob. "Have you looked into Patriot? They've got some great features."

"Well, I love the name. And God knows I hate paying those taxes!" Bob grinned.

Rose wheeled and glared at me through her smile. She was perfect. "Dash. Stop."

She mouthed "sorry" to Marcia, and I mouthed "talk later" to Bob, making a me-and-you gesture between us with my finger. He grinned and gave me a thumbs-up. Bait taken. Hook set.

"We'll have your luggage delivered to your cabin. It won't be a moment before the prophets do their welcome. You can wait right here in the lobby," Marcia finished with a smile, and Rose and I turned to mingle with the other guests.

"Well?" Rose asked me when we had a quiet space to ourselves. "How'd I do?"

"You were perfect. I'll have full access to their computers in no time. There's no hiding from us now."

And then the double doors were thrown open, and the Sun God stepped out.

ACKNOWLEDGMENTS

I thought writing was supposed to be solitary. Hah!

Mindy Klasky suffered through endless questions and allowed me to mainline romance information directly from her vast, experienced, and generous brain. I gasp like someone drinking straight whiskey. *Smooooooth!*

Meredith Bond was my book coach, guide, and patient answer lady.

Angela James taught me huge amounts as my extraordinary editor. Isabel Ngo was the copy editor, and Larissa Pienkowski was the proofreader.

Wait—I'm not done yet! Heather Roberts at Elle Woods Promotions taught me about marketing. Kim Killion herself at The Killion Group created my delicious covers. My sister Twig designed my glorious website.

And Anna Dulik, Elizabeth Salo, and Meg Napier (all authors themselves) were my generous beta readers.

That's eleven people. Add me and it took an even dozen to write one frolic of a book. Dang; not so solitary an experience after all!

THANK YOU, SWEET POTATO!

My little plum blossom, I'm all giddy and happy that you bought and read my book; it's a buzz like you can't believe!

Since my goal is nothing less than a GLOBAL PUBLISHING EMPIRE (ma-hah-hah-hah-hah, evil laugh), it would tickle me like going over the top of a roller coaster if you'd leave a review on the website where you bought my book. Wilya, huh?? (Winking at you in a coy fashion.) Every review makes Amazon rank me just a little higher in the "If you liked this, you'll also like this" algorithm. So is it any wonder I'm longing for your feedback?!

And let's keep this going! Sign up for my newsletter, Bliss & Giggles. It's supposed to be the author's IDEAL MARKETING TOOL, but mostly I use it to rant and snort and amuse myself. I think it might amuse you, too! You can sign up on my website at https://www.pruwarren.com/

CONTENTS

ALSO BY PRU WARREN

The Ampersand Series

Cyn & the Peanut Butter Cup

Dash & the Moonglow Mystic

Ellyn & the Would-Be Gigolo

Farrah & the Court-Appointed Boss

The Surprise Heiress Series:

Breath of Fresh Heiress

Full of Hot Heiress

Vanished Into Thin Heiress

You Decide Books:

Emma's Mission

A Spirit Guide for Anna Maria

Joan's Journal (Love Gone Viral) (out of print, alas)

ABOUT THE AUTHOR

Pru Warren (who is writing this in the third person as if simply too modest to toot her own horn) bores easily and thus has been a daydreamer since roughly the Bronze Age.

She is addicted to writing because in a novel, you can make things come out the RIGHT way. Life and karma really ought to take note; there are BETTER SOLUTIONS to these pesky daily annoyances!

Beside her in-the-laptop God Complex, Pru laughs often and easily, loathes cooking, and plays way too much solitaire. She's plotting world domination even as you read this, as long as she doesn't have to wake up too early to accomplish it.

Sign up for my newsletter, sweetpea! Here's the link (or click the frog, if you're in an ebook):

https://www.pruwarren.com/

My newsletter philosophy? Never take yourself too seriously. Skip the boring stuff. Amuse yourself; maybe others will be amused, too.

There's generally a smoochy gift to thank you for signing up. Maybe a free epilogue, maybe a peek at the next book, maybe something that gave me the giggles. C'mon and check it out; we'll have much delight together!

Made in United States
North Haven, CT
31 March 2023

34784001R00180